The DarkLand Portal Series Book I

The Hero of Aridhold

Damien D. Kenworthy

SkyGoat Publishing House
www.skygoatpublishing.com

This paperback edition 2020

978-0-6489213-0-1

CONTENTS

ACKNOWLEDGMENTS

I have to dedicate this acknowledgement to my beautiful wife. She is an endless source of support and never ceases to amaze me with her talents and resourcefulness.

The final product of this saga would look nothing like it does if it wasn't for her.

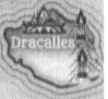

The Plateau

Bambara
Conorbatia

The Great
Desolation

Demon's Landing

Ancient Submerged land bridge

Karathalle

...elago

The Darkland Portal

1 THE WEST YIELD ADVENTURERS

Jaeger winced at the snap of dead branches beneath his friend's foot. He had always been banned from venturing west into the forest as a child, and as teenagers they were both old enough now to know why. Unfortunately, the pair didn't tend to let much get in the way of their adventures and this was no exception. Again, Jaeger cringed as Grum broke the eerie silence with his heavy feet, while leading them deeper down the slope of the woods.

"Watch where you're stepping" Jaeger whispered fervently. "We should have stopped at the woodcutter's cabins if you can't tread quietly."

"There are either scaleskins nearby or there's not," Grum replied in his most matter-of-fact tone. "And if there are, we will hear them long before they hear us." Jaeger's friend made only the slightest attempt at keeping his voice down, while Jaeger simply gritted his teeth and stared at Grum's platted brown hair as he tramped ahead. Arguing would only make it worse.

Grum remained just a little shorter than Jaeger while they were youths, and this was only because dwarves developed earlier than humans. His jaw was already much thicker and his shoulders much broader, however Grum had likely reached his full height already. Jaeger on the other hand, would almost certainly keep growing. The unusual pair went everywhere together in West-Yield, continually challenging each other to test their bravery in a game of dares that they allocated back and forth. This, along with their natural desire for adventure, had always been a recipe for disaster.

Eventually the slope began to steepen, and they were now treading terrain where no woodcutter would dare to venture. The Plateau was a relatively developed and civilised nation. Within its clear borders, mankind had managed to establish a thin veil of safety. But once the edges of The Plateau started to slope, there was no doubt that you were beyond those borders. As a town on the far western fringe of The Plateau, Jaeger's parents argued that the borders of West-Yield were actually more clearly defined by the tree-line. That tree-line was where all scaleskin raids emerged from, and as far as they were concerned, once you crossed into it you were quite literally in no-man's land.

The slope was now steep, steep enough that Jaeger would have to cling from the bases of one tree to the next to continue. He wasn't so sure that Grum had the same reach.

"How are you planning on climbing down that?" Jaeger asked his friend.

"Team effort?" Grum suggested with a cheeky grin.

"Might as well," Jaeger stepped down first. He

wedged his foot into some exposed roots, while grasping a flexible branch behind him with his right hand. He offered the left hand freely in front of him for Grum to climb past and take.

They pushed down the unchartered terrain for the better part of an hour as the sun climbed towards the middle of the day. Neither of them had any reliable idea of how far the descent was to the bottom. From all accounts, The Plateau was a geographical wonder, standing quite tall against the jungle plains below. All that Jaeger and Grum knew, was that they had agreed to reach the lowlands as part of their latest challenge. They would just have to keep going until they found it.

Grum was the first to detect a distinctive odour waiting for them further down.

"Are you smelling that too?" he asked with disgust.

"Yeah, it's just starting to grow on me now," Jaeger agreed.

"Grow on you!?" Grum exclaimed. "It smells like a colony of dead rats! Remind me to never come round to your house for dinner."

"Not grow on me, the smell is growing. It's getting stronger," Jaeger clarified.

"Yeah right, not sure I believe that."

"Oh shut up, and sharpen up while you're at it. Whatever it is, that smell isn't natural. That could be a camp of scaleskins below that we are discussing at the top of our voices."

"Fair enough," Grum muttered quietly. Jaeger nearly let go of the small tree he was bracing against in his surprise.

They both sharpened up as they continued on now. The truth was that there was really no innocent explanation for such a foul smell this far beyond their borders. They were quite possibly in the vicinity of mortal danger as they moved closer to the source of the stench.

Eventually the slope began to level out. The smell was nearly unbearable at this stage, but Jaeger was suddenly too excited to care. They really had made it. They had reached the lowland jungles below The Plateau.

A rough trail passed through the heavy foliage that tangled the even surface at the bottom of the slope. On the opposite side of the trail, a viciously maimed human body was on display, nailed to a tree by several crude spears. They both froze in their tracks when it came into view.

"That's not good," Jaeger mumbled mildly in shock.

"Not good for him or for us?" Grum asked incredulously.

"Well for him obviously, but not exactly good for us either Grum. I didn't even know somebody from West-Yield had gone missing."

"Woodcutters mate, they keep to themselves for long enough out here that none of us would know."

"We need to leave," Jaeger pointed out. "And we need to take this poor guy with us."

Grum turned back to Jaeger and nodded with a distinct look of respect. Jaeger had observed that all dwarves shared a strong sense of bravery and honor, two traits that weren't necessarily attributed to all humans. Jaeger's statement clearly had his friend's approval. They were in a dangerous place, and climbing back up the slopes would be challenging enough already. Carrying a rotting human body on their return journey seemed to have finally surpassed their insatiable desire for adventure.

Despite this they both knew they had no other choice in the matter. This man had been a member of their community, and he was going to be laid to rest where he belonged. Admitting where they had discovered the body was going to be yet another problem. Jaeger decided that at least they could deal with that problem once they had made it home. With very little further discussion, they unpinned the body from the tree and began their return journey.

"Where do you think the paths up this slope are?" Grum asked during a particularly difficult section of climbing. He was near the end of his turn carrying the dead man.

"Not sure Grum. But even if we knew, we couldn't use them." Jaeger pulled roughly on the dead man's remaining arm to help Grum reach the stump ahead of him.

"I didn't say I wanted to use them. I was just wondering where they are. The scaleskin raiders lead small armies up these slopes, sometimes on the backs of wolves. I doubt they make their way up from the lowlands by hiking from tree to tree like we are."

"There will definitely be paths and trails," Jaeger agreed.

"We should find them and defend them," Grum grunted fiercely. "Sit at the top waiting for them, instead of letting them burst out of the tree-line like they always do."

"And if they have more than a few trails? then what?" Jaeger countered. "They'd circle around and surprise us in the woods. At least they have to cross open fields to get to West-Yield. The jungles have always belonged to the scaleskins. There are too many of them to go in there and do anything about it."

Grum just grunted unpleasantly and continued hauling the heavy body one step at a time. Jaeger marveled at the strength of dwarves. The pair were born at opposite ends of the year, making Jaeger almost a full year older than his stocky friend.

Despite this, the young dwarf was able to carry a body of equal weight to his own, up a hill, and for twice as long as Jaeger. Jaeger sighed; it was nearly his turn to take over again. The afternoon was wearing away and the return journey from their little adventure was becoming very long and unpleasant.

The fallout from their discovery was no small event in West-Yield. It was one of the larger towns on the western fringe of The Plateau, but not so large that the horrific death of one of its people didn't rattle the tight community.

While West-Yield did have a physician, it fell to Margie, the town healer, to examine what remained of the body that had been recovered. She had kept her thoughts to herself when the boys delivered it to her, but had promptly requested later that day for them to return to her immediately.

"His name was Bretane," she explained without looking up as Jaeger entered the room alone.

"A woodcutter?" Jaeger guessed.

"Yes, he spent more of his time in the forest cabins than in West-Yield. All year-round mind you, not just in winter. For an unmarried man of his middling age, solitude must have been a preference. Nevertheless, he was well known and well liked. Come closer Jaeger."

Seeing the man's dead body entirely naked was even more disturbing than finding him in the jungles. There were savage wounds all over him, while his left arm and both feet had been hacked off.

"When you found him, did you notice anything unusual?" Margie asked at length.

"What do you mean?"

"I mean where you found him, did anything about the place look symbolic to you?"

"Not particularly, he was nailed to a normal-looking tree with spears. I can't say it stood out as symbolic to me, unless you tell me something specifically that I should be trying to recall."

"Perhaps the spears? Did they seem to have a pattern to them?"

"Nothing that stands out in my memory I'm sorry Margie. Why are you asking about patterns and symbols?"

"Because of this" she said, turning Bretane's body so that Jaeger could see a tattoo that had been roughly engraved onto his back just below the neck. The brutality of his death was clear, but there was something else about that tattoo that made Jaeger feel a chill of dread throughout his entire body.

"What does it mean?" he asked eventually.

"I don't know, but I know it is something far older than the scaleskins' primitive society."

"How can you know that?" Jaeger asked

suddenly.

"We healers do study, Jaeger. We don't just mix different herbs together until we find something that works. I may not be a scholar of iconography, but this symbol is ancient. And evil."

The conversations about the incident at home were only marginally less serious. Jaeger's parents were furious. Initially, Tevin had been calm to the point of seeming unsurprised. Mendel on the other hand, was not so calm to hear that her son had descended the slopes of The Plateau deep into hostile territory.

Jaeger was nearly finished with his final year of school, and Mendel practically demanded that Tevin give him work on the farm to cover any spare time that could be spent on more adventures.

The prospect of completing his studies and then moving into a strict lockdown didn't appeal to Jaeger at all. Studies typically finished after sixteen on The Plateau, which was when a transition into working life began. Promising students were occasionally invited to continue their education beyond this age in The Plateau's capital city, Conorbatia.

In the capital they could learn higher arts such as; medicine, world physics, and even magic, all of which were taught by colleges there that specialized in these disciplines. Jaeger had always enjoyed tales of the powerful mages who defended The Plateau, and often toyed with the idea of learning at their college.

Right now however, a career in spellcasting couldn't have felt further from his reach. He didn't have much of a reputation as a student, and his duties as a farmer's son seemed to have already been decided.

The only person in their class who seemed likely to do any differently was Faline. She was quite a smart girl who always seemed to have an answer to everything. Surprisingly, she often turned quietly to Jaeger of all people if she didn't know something. Jaeger quite liked Faline.

"Weren't you worried that they would find you when you saw Bretane's body?" Faline asked. She sat with Jaeger out by his father's bullpen as he explained their tragic discovery.

"Yeah, at that point I was. We knew it was time to get away from there as soon as we saw what they had done to him." Jaeger pondered the scene again thoughtfully, for some reason he felt a strong compulsion not to mention his conversation with Margie. "We actually hadn't reached the bottom of the slopes until we found him. Up until then we had pretty much just been climbing."

"What was it like?" Faline's tone changed almost excitedly. "The lands below The Plateau that is."

"Pretty much just thick jungle," Jaeger explained. "The woods at the top are just trees mostly, but at the bottom it's thick with vegetation. There was a scaleskin trail where we found Bretane, but if you weren't using a trail down there it would be very difficult to move."

"Even finding one of their trails would give me the creeps," she shivered. "Just walking somewhere that was made for those creatures is a scary thought."

"You know humans used to live down there before the Great Invasion of Evil." Jaeger pointed out philosophically.

"Yeah, but the Great Invasion of Evil was centuries ago. That trail you found wasn't made by humans."

"No, you're right," he agreed. "It was quite disturbing when we found their trail. It's hard to say what it made me feel though, because we pretty much found Bretane's body at the same time. I think that if it wasn't for that, it would have been exciting too. That's why we went down there, to explore into enemy territory."

"You two are both crazy," Faline pointed out, "I feel sorry for Mendel."

"Oh, she wasn't impressed at all," Jaeger laughed.

"She shouldn't be. I'm not either, don't go down there again," she chided.

"You're not impressed? You know you sound impressed," Jaeger teased.

"Shut up you!" she laughed. "I'll be more impressed if you make it to the end of the year and graduate the way you're going. Don't go adventuring down from The Plateau again. You need to stay alive long enough to help me pass cartography, then I'll tell you just how impressed with you I am," she flirted.

"Oh please, you're halfway there and you've already passed. Besides, you never needed my help in the first place," Jaeger added.

It was only recently that Jaeger had begun spending time with Faline. Now that they were in their last year of school, she often began asking him for help with schoolwork that she already seemed to be good at. Faline had a reserved nature that complimented her quiet confidence neatly. Her hair was silky black and slightly wavy, and she had smooth skin which was naturally a few shades darker than most of her classmates.

She also seemed to take pleasure in constantly flattering Jaeger, before sitting back to observe his reactions. Their private study sessions seemed to be the perfect setting for this little game of hers.

"You're taking this very seriously Jae," she laughed during one such evening. She had just been pulling sarcastically enthusiastic faces at Jaeger while he attempted to explain night time navigation.

"You literally asked me to explain this to you, and then started acting like a smartarse the moment I did!" Jaeger complained.

"I know, you're just taking it very seriously. I find it cute," she added with a wicked grin.

"Alright then, I take it Faline has reached her attention-span for the day" Jaeger complained.

"Aww you're blushing' she laughed. "You know you blush a lot Jae."

Jaeger had decided that it wasn't that she was always smiling that made Faline, Faline. It was that she was always laughing. In fact, he tried to think if he had ever seen her just smile, but she never did. Anything that would make a normal person smile she laughed at, which was ironic, because despite this she was actually quite mature. Jaeger had made up his mind that Faline was quite perfect.

They also both enjoyed wandering down to the old rope-bridge at the western end of the river together. From here they would walk alongside the river until they were far beyond the borders of West-Yield. It was usually the subconscious target of their walks to reach the vacant woodcutter's cabins in summer.

Even above the slope of The Plateau, the forest was still relatively wild this far west. As they walked together, they often startled the wary animals as well as the occasional predators that hunted them.

Jaeger's fascination with the forest appeared to have rubbed off on Faline, and they both enjoyed the added element of adventure to straying out this far. Beyond the hard borders of West-Yield and its watchtowers, they both knew that they were beyond the safety of their community.

2 ALARM BELLS

As the end of their year finally came around, so did Grum's day of second naming. On this particularly significant birthday, Grum's name was to be permanently extended to Grummason, thus sealing his vocation in life as a stonemason and builder by profession. Jaeger arrived relatively early along with Faline, allowing their little trio to enjoy some more personal time together before the crowds arrived.

As the night settled in, Grummason was soon forced to abandon their private corner to greet and thank everyone for coming. This left Jaeger and Faline to themselves for some time, while the cluster of dwarves at the table broke into raucous singing. They were joined intermittently by others at the party, but were often left alone to enjoy extended periods of quiet conversation together.

The pair were conveniently seated next to a large barrel of ale and could rarely finish a drink without it miraculously filling up again. Soon Jaeger found that everything he said was coming out easily, while sounding wittier than he had ever remembered being before. Only a couple of hours past sunset, and just before the speeches began, Jaeger realised that he was decidedly drunk.

The speeches were fairly standard for a dwarven coming-of-age party, and began with his grandfather officially addressing his grandson as Grummason, before reciting some old lore. It was very strictly explained, and indicated a determination among the dwarven expatriates to maintain the traditions of their heritage. Tradition seemed to be increasingly important knowing that only the very eldest among them had been alive before they were cut off from the distant kingdom of their own people.

As the speeches wrapped up, Jaeger looked into his empty tankard, noting for the first time that there was no tap within reach. He turned to Faline who was watching him with amusement.

"Do you want to wander outside? I feel like I should really put down my beer for a while, but this crowd will probably kick me out if they see me do it." It was probably true, but not entirely why he suggested it.

"I think you've done pretty well, but you're probably right" she agreed. "Let's walk." Faline held her arm outwards to Jaeger which he pleasantly linked into his own. Although once he had staggered a few steps forward, it was clear that her gesture had been for the sake of his balance.

They wandered clear of the family's living quarters and past the smithy, where numerous dwarves as well as a few humans were settled into small crowds drinking together happily. It became darker once they had walked some distance from the lanterns that lit up the party, and they both now looked up to see impossibly dense concentrations of stars in the sky.

"Look at them all," Jaeger admired. "It's amazing how many there are when the moon is gone." He tried to lower himself to the ground to sit, plonking himself down once he had gotten close enough.

"It's beautiful" Faline agreed. "I love stopping to enjoy things like this." She had lowered her voice to an awed whisper as she sat down beside him with far more grace. They both leant back until they were lying beside each other.

"You know Faline, the entire time I have known you I have liked you." Jaeger had decided to plunge straight into blurting exactly how he felt about Faline, propping himself onto his elbows so that he could face her. "I think you are the most perfect person I have ever met," he said with complete conviction.

Faline giggled a little and then also sat up to face him. "What a lovely compliment" she said, and leant forward giving him a light kiss on the cheek. Her kiss was so close to his lips that he almost mistook where she had placed it.

Jaeger's heart began to race, he found himself leaning forward towards her without thinking, kissing her fully on the lips. It lasted for a few moments as Faline returned the kiss, before they both rolled back onto their backs again, looking up at the dotted night sky.

"Beautiful stars" Jaeger murmured, as they lay silently for an unknown period of time. They returned to the party in the early hours of the morning.

Jaeger rose late the next day, feeling like death but entirely pleased and unrepentant for the night he had just had. He doubted he would be able to stomach any food so early, so as soon as he was washed and dressed, he left the house. He had contributed chairs and other items to help with the party at Grummason's last night, and thought it would be a good idea to use this as an excuse to pop by early for a party debrief.

He hadn't normally noticed the distance between his house and the Mason's, which wasn't far, but today Jaeger was counting every yard that passed by. Realizing how much further distances felt when he was counting them, Jaeger decided to concentrate hard on drifting off into his thoughts.

After that, it felt like it took no time to get there. He had walked right up to the front door and knocked, before consciously realising where he was, managing to process this just in time to see Faline open it.

"Good morning" he chirped brightly, "I'm on my way to Grummason's to pick up some stuff that I left there, do you want to come with me?"

Jaeger wasn't the least bit bothered that he had found his way to Faline's by accident. He must have subconsciously ignored the turn off to Grummason's a short way back.

"Hi Jae, yeah I have a few things I have to do first, give me an hour and I can join you."

Jaeger was a little caught off guard by how complacently Faline had said this. She was missing the enthusiasm he had expected, and even more surprisingly, she hadn't teased him about being in such a cheery mood himself this morning.

"Sure, why don't we head down to the

woodcutter's cabins when I get back."

Faline paused for a moment, "Ah, sure we can do that."

"Excellent," Jaeger forced some enthusiasm into his response. "I'll see you later" he waved.

"See you then" she called back.

Jaeger decided to head home and deal with the loaned furniture later. After considering the short talk with Faline, he figured he should go home to clean himself up. The effects of the night before were starting to set in, and he couldn't shake the deflated feeling he had now.

He hoped a wash and a light nap might help things. At home, Tevin and Mendel were sitting down to some lunch and were not surprised to see their son looking a little worse-for-wear after the big night at the Mason's.

"I see you didn't escape Grondmason's quest to out-drink his own cellar." Tevin looked amused.

"They said that they wouldn't sleep until they finished every barrel!" Jaeger exclaimed, "Grummason was passed out when I left."

"You've caught onto his new name quickly" Mendel noted, "I think it's a shame how early they have to grow up. He probably won't get to spend much time with you anymore." She seemed to have already perceived that Jaeger was feeling a little empty.

"Yeah, he'll be more than up to it though" Jaeger replied trying to brush off her insight. He turned down most of the lunch and tried to tackle a small piece of bread for his first bit of food. After finishing the bread with the assistance of a cup of water, he washed himself vigorously and changed clothes. He felt a lot fresher and a little less sick now, as he left for Faline's house again just after noon.

When he got to the door, Faline opened it before he could knock. "Don't you look a sight better than you did this morning" she noted cheerily.

"I can't say I'm feeling better on the inside but thanks, you don't really look like you even took part in the celebrations last night. I mean in a good way" Jaeger clarified, and she really did for some reason.

"Oh, you're just saying that. I feel terrible" she laughed, while Jaeger wondered if she was lying. Nothing would have surprised him with Faline.

"So, do you want to go walking today? I feel like heading towards the river so I can dunk my head in every time I start to feel wretched" he mused.

"Sounds good to me, let me just pack a bit of food if we're going for long, come inside."

Jaeger came in and helped her pack, insisting that he carry it when they were ready to leave. By the time they reached the river, the heat of the day had fully set in and the first thing they both did was wash their faces and drink the cool water. They both then sat down on some shaded rocks where they could dangle their feet in the running water.

Here Faline opened the bag of bread, fruit, and dried meat she had packed. Once he had eaten all that he could with his weak stomach, Jaeger began to think about the night before. Without properly thinking it through, he put his arm around Faline and leant across to kiss her.

She looked directly at him without changing expression and moved her head back just the slightest distance. Jaeger froze in his movement then sat back in complete silence and confusion. He knew what he wanted to say but couldn't for the life of him find the words.

"So last night…" was all he could muster up after some time. He at least hoped she would pick up the general meaning of the statement.

"I know Jae. It seemed right and I wouldn't take it back, but don't you think that it would be better to just leave it as something between friends? I think it's something we both wanted to happen, I just didn't mean for it to be any more beyond that," she explained. Somehow, she had made the most unfair thing in the world seem logical.

Jaeger was crushed, he couldn't just let it go like that, not without getting his own feelings off his chest. "I was actually hoping it was more than just that. Faline you must be aware that I'm interested in you more than just some one-off night? You're a smart girl."

"I did kind of know I guess" she admitted with her trademark giggle, "but that's okay. We both love to spend time around each other which is all that matters." She was making it seem so simple.

"So, you don't have any feelings for me beyond our friendship then?" It was a blunt question.

"I don't know. If I do, it's not something I'm ready to take further yet, but yes I have felt about you in that way."

"When?" it sounded a little petty, but his immediate thought was that the answer to this question would pinpoint what he had done to make her feel that way.

"I can't say, I don't want to say."

"There's no reason why you shouldn't, I'm

being fairly honest with you."

Faline had a troubled look on her face which was rare for her, "I just can't, it wouldn't help things if I did" she murmured.

They went on in this way for a bit more and by the end of it, Jaeger didn't feel like he had gotten anywhere, except for divulging a number of things in a few short minutes that he had kept to himself for months. Strangely though, he wasn't embarrassed while they spoke. He did know however, that now it was out there he would never be able to take it back.

In the end it was all pointless anyway. Faline just wanted to be friends with Jaeger and he realized that he was going to have to reach some compromise from what he really wanted.

"I guess I'll have to be fine with this then," he conceded. "You know how I feel about you, but I value our friendship just as much. So, if you just want to be friends then that's that." Faline's eyes lit up, she leant forward to Jaeger this time and hugged him before sitting back and taking his hand in hers.

Jaeger swallowed, feeling miserable inside. Today hadn't gone at all how he had planned and all the excitement from last night had completely left him. Their discussion had left a sick feeling in the pit of his stomach, although it was hard to know if that wasn't just his hangover.

They finished the food they had brought then sat back and relaxed beside the river in the heat of the day. Once they began chatting comfortably again, hours went by without either of them mentioning how long they had been there. Neither felt like they had other things they should be getting back to, although every now and then the time crossed Jaeger's mind.

It was far later than they had ever stayed out in the woods when they finally began walking home. Dusk was beginning to set in as West-Yield came into view from the tree-line. The sun was setting faster now and they both fell silently into their own thoughts as they continued to walk.

Jaeger was contemplating to himself how late it would be before he got home. He would have to walk Faline to her doorstep first, before tracking back across town to his own home.

"We both just went completely quiet a few minutes ago for no reason," Faline noted with a little curiosity in her voice.

"Yeah, not an awkward silence though. I've noticed we go quiet a lot from time to time when we're talking, but it's kind of like... a comfortable silence" Jaeger concluded.

"I agree, that's the perfect word for it. I'm always so comfortable around you," she giggled, looking pleased at their new discovery. Jaeger tried to ignore the tense feeling growing in his gut.

They both continued walking in silence for a few more moments after hearing the bells, without thinking anything of them. It hadn't immediately registered to either of them what the noise actually meant.

"Oh no!" Jaeger realized as a look of pure dread spread across his face. Turning back, they both saw smoke rising from the forest where the woodcutters' lodges were located. Faline now fully comprehended what this meant too. She froze, looking desperately at

Jaeger for reassurance, while he let out a string of curses. He grabbed her hand roughly and yanked her to start running with him.

They were still no more than a hundred yards from the forest, and had no idea if an entire army of scaleskins was going to burst out of it at any moment. These fears were soon justified when an arrow dropped out of the sky just a few yards ahead of them. A handful of goblin scouts had stepped out from the trees and were just on their range to hit Jaeger and Faline.

A few more seconds passed and the baying of wolves could now be heard. A quick glance over his shoulder showed Jaeger that they were at least beyond the range of the enemy's archers now. The town was still just under a mile away, but the shouting and clamor of its population preparing to defend themselves could already be heard.

Jaeger let go of Faline's hand, realizing that his pulling to make her go faster wasn't helping. Instead, he ran alongside her, continually glancing back to check if any wolf-riders had emerged from the woods yet. He was calculating in his head how much further Faline and himself had to run to get to safety, and how much the wolves would need to gain if they emerged out of the trees at that moment. Every glance that didn't reveal wolf riders, gave him more hope that they would not be able to close the distance in time.

Jaeger was starting to gain hope, as he reckoned that they were nearly halfway between the forest edge and the village borders. At this same point a row of riders suddenly emerged in hot pursuit. The wolves they rode were enormous, yet somehow their colouring and features were off. They were far taller than normal wolves, but this abnormal growth seemed to have come with unwholesome side-effects.

Jaeger guessed that the riders would have to travel twice as fast as Faline and himself in order to catch them, which was encouraging. Faline was sobbing alongside him as she ran. Glancing back again, Jaeger could also now see the reason to panic. His reckoning had been optimistic at best and the riders were clearly gaining enough ground to catch them. Faline's distress only slowed her down even more.

They were only two hundred yards from the town's western entrance when the barking of the wolves turned into snarls of aggression. They were within reach. Jaeger saw a few armed militia-men now gathering in the distance, before he felt an overwhelming compulsion to turn. He twisted just in time to see the first of the five closest riders bearing down on him. In an action born out of pure reflex, his left hand whipped around a spear that was leveled at his back, catching it just behind the tip and pushing it aside from impaling him, while gripping it at the same time.

The wolf was so committed to riding through its prey that it ran right over Jaeger as he fell, pulling the spear away and yanking the mounted goblin from its saddle. Regaining his feet, Jaeger hurled the spear directly into the wolf's neck. It had paused as its attention shifted to Faline, and fell in a violent frenzy of spasms. He then leapt upon its dazed rider, wrestling its scimitar away before it could get to its feet.

Once in possession of a weapon, Jaeger cleaved straight through the top of the goblin's head then turned to face the four other riders. They hadn't slowed their charge despite having just witnessed a blindingly quick turn of events. Jaeger resolutely braced himself, ready to defend Faline with his life to save hers.

The next two riders then converged on Jaeger, who slashed at the face of the left wolf before impact, felling the beast and sending the rider hurtling into the air. Luckily this wolf fell across the path of the other, interrupting its attack. The right wolf hit him at such pace that it didn't manage to bite or do anything but collide with Jaeger, driving him into the ground. It then wheeled around, preparing to pounce on his sprawled form. A spear emerged from the back of its head before it could lunge.

It was Faline, she had retrieved the first rider's spear from the neck of its steed and acted immediately when Jaeger fell. She pulled the spear from the wolf as it tumbled to the ground twitching. Jaeger rolled to his feet all in the same motion as being bowled over, looking up just in time to see her drive the spear down into the goblin who had been flung from his saddle. Both Jaeger and Faline then braced themselves for an attack from the two remaining riders. They held back. It seemed an unlikely reprieve while they were at their most vulnerable.

Suddenly a roar went up behind them, and they both looked back to see that a small portion of the village militia had run to their aid. They had now nearly reached the pair and raced hard towards the remaining riders. The mounted scaleskins retreated a few metres at first, before fleeing altogether.

Everybody stopped when they drew level with Faline and Jaeger. Merve the butcher moved first.

"We'd better get back to the buildings before the main force of those murdering devils arrive."

Too out of breath to verbalize a response, Jaeger nodded. He looked down at the three dead bodies strewn around him. The goblins were smaller and lighter than he was. These were the lesser breed of scaleskins known as slags. Their stringy arms were scaled like the skin of a young snake, and green with a yellowish hue. Observing them sprawled across the field they looked like vicious malformed parodies of human children, with sharpened teeth.

Jaeger pushed against his exhaustion towards the town entrance again. Faline was also breathing heavily as Kurt and his father Karnsmith escorted her to keep her moving. Once they crossed the town entrance, everybody began racing around back into positions.

"They'll have to contend with the archers we posted in those buildings if they want to challenge us from here!" Karnsmith declared, pointing at the guard houses on either side of the town entrance.

As they passed the houses, a handful of supply carts drew up and were lined sideways in a row to block the road. A portion of the militia then climbed the carts, standing on them with spears in hand, ready to defend their town from the higher ground. Tevin was part of this unit. He was efficient in both setting up and taking his place, having practiced this role many times during the town drills.

After a short wait, the main force of the scaleskins came into view just past where the little skirmish had occurred minutes earlier. The sun had completely disappeared and visibility was too poor to accurately tell how many there were. The noise they made as they drew closer indicated that this was a small army, almost equal to the entire town population.

They were jeering and hooting and a few howling voices rose above the rest, as a handful of the larger more savage scaleskins began to work themselves into a frenzy. Jaeger stood over Faline, massaging her shoulder gently as she sat and watched the crowd of militia form up behind the wagons. Karnsmith stood on her other side, the young dwarf hefted his well-crafted battle-axe confidently.

"The good thing about these primitive beasts is how predictable they are" he observed calmly. "They have always attacked villages from just one direction and the outcome of the battle is usually hinged upon whether they strike with the element of surprise or not. Don't worry, with our barricading and archers, this will be a short melee."

Even as he finished his sentence, howls of pain broke out from the scaleskins, as a volley of arrows was released from various vantage points. It was hard to see in the dim light, but their noise more than confirmed that many of the arrows had landed accurately amongst their front ranks. Without another word, Karnsmith took up his weapon and ran to join the fight.

"You're going to be fine Faline, I just think you're in shock. Now get to the town hall where your mother will be waiting," Jaeger said protectively.

"I'm ok, will you walk me there? I don't want you to go back and get hurt. You got hit really hard back there." Faline's words weren't patronizing and Jaeger felt warmed by her concern, however this matter was beyond discussion.

"No Faline, I'm sorry. I want you to run there as fast as you can, but I can't join you. I have to go now. Run!" He urged.

He didn't wait to see if she had listened because he knew that she would stay there as long as he was watching. So, with those words Jaeger turned and ran to the barricade, picking out a strong metal pole from a pile of leftover weapons that had been hastily gathered. He leapt onto the middle wagon at the barricade in search of his father.

Tevin was at the front edge of the wagon just north of Jaeger, jabbing at the scaleskins below alongside the tightly formed line of defenders around him. Jaeger could see that this front was well protected and picked out a wagon on the south edge of the barricade. A gap between the last wagon and the guard-house had allowed a number of scaleskins to force their way into the town.

Fierce hand-to-hand combat now raged around them, and Jaeger had to leap over three wolf carcasses atop the wagon as he raced in. The bodies served as clear evidence of the ferocity of that first wave of attackers. They had leapt blindly into certain death in their desperation to get at the defenders atop the barricade. Jaeger made sure not to step on, or come into contact with the handful of dead neighbours that had also fallen, and was adamant not to look down at them too closely.

In front of him, the guard house on the main highway was ablaze. Flaming torches had been thrown in the windows, forcing the archers to abandon their posts to escape the building. From the vantage point he was standing on, Jaeger could clearly see the scene below him in the added light from the flames. Emotion took over.

As he reached the last wagon he leapt off in rage, hurtling into the backs of three scaleskins facing away from him. They had been in the middle of a dense unit that was trading blows with a crowd of desperate defenders. The hasty defensive formation barely hemmed them in to stop the breach from spreading.

Jaeger's knees made the first contact, and all three scaleskins buckled under his momentum and weight. He landed more or less on his feet, striking a smaller goblin to his right full in the face as it turned towards him. Morne and his father had been standing toe-to-toe with the tight unit and leapt forward now while their enemies were vulnerable.

Jaeger was immediately set upon from many different directions, as he had leapt directly into the middle of the raiders. He was now relying on reflexes he didn't know he had just to stay alive. The numerous blows directed at him didn't even leave him time to be surprised at this startling ability.

His fighting instincts didn't involve blocking, but instead catching every blow directed at him at a slight angle and redirecting the stroke past his body, allowing for a small window to strike back at his opponent while their guard was down. Each attack seemed to send a jolt of fear through his body, even before he saw them coming. It was like listening to some kind of instinctual warning system. One, two, three, he systematically used the technique to eliminate every enemy near him, while more scaleskins fell to the counter-charge from the militia.

The raiding party continued to take heavy casualties for a few short moments before they panicked and fled, surrendering their biggest breakthrough in the attack. Seeing their comrades defeated and fleeing, the rest of the scaleskin force being held at bay also broke, leaving the town defenders spent but nevertheless victorious.

Arrows continued to fall amongst the disorganized retreat as the last of the scaleskin raiders escaped beyond range. The bodies of townspeople lay strewn intermittently amongst the piles of dead scaleskins at the barricade. The assault had been short but savage.

3 THE EMPEROR'S MEN

Jaeger woke much earlier than normal the morning, or maybe it was just that he chose to get out of bed the first time he woke up. He had been a mixture of exhaustion and worry before he had fallen asleep and that anxious energy was still there when he opened his eyes.

He had slain five scaleskins the night before, and reckoned that at least two of them were the larger warrior breed they called mucks. Great hulking cousins to the goblin; mucks stood taller than all but the tallest humans, although their physical proportions were more like a dwarf's, with short powerful arms and enormous chests.

Physiological studies of muck cadavers had revealed that their spine actually connected to their massive heads at the back, rather than at the base like in humans. This finding meant their true size was even greater than what their height represented.

Jaeger's body ached and his right eyelid had

swollen almost completely over his eye overnight. One of his enemies had resorted to throwing a vicious punch into this region after Jaeger had diverted its sword stroke to the ground. When he moved to get up, he also felt the full effect of the pain in his body.

Everything last night had happened so fast that he had felt little pain at the time. He hadn't anticipated this crippling tenderness in the morning. With a surge of determination, he gritted his teeth and stood up, forcing his back to straighten against the pain and hoping that most of it would go away once he started moving around.

As the sun rose, Jaeger went out to see the devastation that had been caused by the attack. If he felt that his body felt bad, the town looked even worse. For a number of hours after the scaleskins had retreated, the townspeople busied themselves with their dead and wounded, as well as the fire that had enveloped the southern guard-house. The bodies of the attackers could wait until morning, while the wounded needed the most urgent attention.

West-Yield eventually recovered from the losses on the night of the raid, and over time everything went back to normal, perhaps not better than before, but at least they had learned something. A number of new buildings and roads were implemented during the rebuilding process, with the town fixing several vulnerabilities facing west into the forest.

The main road leading in from that direction was hemmed in by brick walls, narrowing towards the town creating a funnel. Both walls were over ten feet tall and were wide enough to accommodate a sunken path through their centre, allowing archers to walk along them behind partial cover.

Somewhere in all of this, Jaeger's eighteenth birthday came and went, and so did Faline. The two events were closely tied together as she decided to choose the night of his party to tell him.

"I love that we can still have these comfortable silences after all these years," Faline said just above a whisper, reminding Jaeger that he had once coined their own private phrase a long time ago.

"It is good out here beyond the noise," he agreed. They had walked together out beyond his father's bullpen. Jaeger could still hear his friends and family drinking and celebrating back inside.

Faline shifted a little and turned, facing Jaeger as though she wanted to say or do something, but didn't know how. His mind was telling him that she may have been waiting for him to kiss her, but his instinct disagreed. He gave her a quizzical look.

"Jaeger, I wanted to talk to you about something and I thought that tonight would be the right time to do it. Now that we are here, I think it might not be" she explained, making little or no sense.

"I have no idea what you're trying to say, is something wrong?"

"No, it's just that I have decided to leave West-Yield and I wanted to tell you first, I haven't mentioned it to my parents yet but I will in the next few days." The announcement came crushing down on Jaeger.

"Where are you going?" he asked eventually.

"To the capital, I have been thinking about moving there for a while now and made up my mind a week ago."

"What's there? Do you want to go to the school of medicine?"

"I'm not sure what I am going to do there yet" she admitted, as if this was completely normal. "The idea of living there just appeals to me, so I am going to go and see where it takes me."

Jaeger considered this for a little while again in 'comfortable silence'. The fact that Faline was leaving with little money, possessions, or plans, seemed to sum her up quite accurately.

For a moment Jaeger wished he could be like that and began to consider doing the same thing. But the truth was that he didn't share these traits. He was a planner, he worried about everything around him and was prone to burdening himself with the problems of others and the world.

"You haven't said anything for a while now" Faline commented, dragging him from his thoughts.

"I don't know if there is anything to say, I'm going to hate not having you around" he confessed.

"I know and I'm sorry. I think I was wrong now to think that telling you at your party would be the right time and place," she admitted.

"I guess not. Come on let's go back and forget about it. We'll talk it over another time."

Faline and Jaeger walked back to his party beside each other, for the first time in uncomfortable silence. Both wanted to get back inside and move on from the brief yet depressing discussion. Jaeger didn't feel like laughing and celebrating anymore and Faline decided to give him some space.

He found Grummason who handed him a welcome tankard of ale. With his best friend and many other happy revelers around him, Jaeger decided to take his mind off Faline and try to get back to enjoying his party. The rest of his night remained a blurred memory in his mind ever after, and looking back he couldn't have said if he had enjoyed himself or not.

Only three weeks later, and a week after Faline had left, a troop of soldiers arrived at the town's eastern entrance at around midday. They were dressed in the blue and orange livery of the emperor's army, and were led by a tall, straight-backed man, draped in a green cape that indicated the rank of elite guard.

The leader's flaxen hair was tied back in a tail beneath his beret, and he moved his horse through the streets at walking pace, acknowledging the farmers and townsfolk as he passed them. Jaeger noted the man's piercing gaze as he spoke to them and for some reason, he immediately felt a desire to be noticed.

"Would I be right in guessing that that building at the end of the street is the town thane's?" the troop leader pointed. As he leant down from his horse, he raised his left eyebrow almost comically and Jaeger noted numerous battle scars on his face. "We are here on behalf of the emperor."

"That's right" Jaeger confirmed. "The thane of West-Yield is Thelonius, he's a helpful man and will be able to assist you with whatever you need."

"Then I look forward to meeting him, it says a lot about a man when his townsfolk speak highly of him. Especially when he is not listening" the man winked.

"You're welcome. My name is Jaeger," Jaeger offered boldly, as he stepped forward with his hand outstretched.

The troop leader took his hand with a firm but measured grip and looked him directly in the eye, "Darroch of the emperor's guard." He sat back up and casually turned to the tall young soldier riding to his left, "what a wonderful town, our fortune has clearly been blessed to lead us through here, wouldn't you say Marrick?"

"It hasn't been cursed," Marrick replied with a sly grin. He had short, neatly trimmed dark hair and Jaeger reckoned he could not have been more than a couple of years older than he was. They both continued past Jaeger through the street.

News spread the next day that a town meeting was to be held, in order to address the tidings that Darroch had brought Thelonius on the evening of his arrival. Jaeger was informed of the news quite early. He knew that the emperor's platoon would be put up at the new guard-house lodgings, and wandered around that way to nosey information out of Nashaw. The captain-of-the-guard in West-Yield, or town sheriff as the position was casually referred to, greeted Jaeger warily.

"Good morning, Jaeger, I see you've wasted no time in sussing out the whereabouts of our newest guests."

"True, I spoke to them yesterday and didn't get the opportunity to find out what the purpose of their visit was." Jaeger had already considered finding an innocent excuse for being here, but concluded that there was nothing wrong with admitting he was curious.

"Well, you needn't worry about being kept in the dark for much longer. They met with Thelonius yesterday evening and whatever they told him must have been important, because he's called a town meeting for tomorrow."

"Town meeting tomorrow, I suppose it was well timed to land on a Sunday. Do you know what it is all about?"

"As a matter of fact, I do. I dined with Thelonius and Commander Darroch last night. They are going on a mission beyond our western borders and are undermanned." Jaeger felt a shot of excitement go through him, but before he could speak Nashaw continued. "You will learn all you want to know tomorrow at the meeting. For now, you can put your enthusiasm to use and help me spread the word."

"What's the mission?" Jaeger thought pressing one last question was worth a try.

"If I told you a little, I'd have to tell you a lot, and today I don't have time for that"

"How far?" Jaeger persisted.

"Far" Nashaw confirmed. "Just take responsibility for ensuring that your dwarf friends hear the news and pass it on. The town meeting will begin at noon as usual and will be held below the thane's steps."

Jaeger decided to quit while he was ahead, "I'll make sure the dwarves and our neighbours are informed, you can cross that off your to-do list."

"Thank you Jaeger, that will be very helpful." Nashaw then turned and saluted Darroch who had just been tending to his horses around the side of the building.

Darroch cheerfully saluted back. "Looks like a marvelous day Nashaw. Good morning Jaeger," he waved.

"Good morning Darroch," Jaeger waved back as he made off.

Jaeger headed straight back towards home after that and passed the word on to Tevin who he found near the stables.

"I'll be visiting Karnsmith for some horseshoes later today, and if he hasn't already heard I can pass the news onto him then." Tevin promised. He sounded far less interested than Jaeger had expected and Jaeger wondered if it was just himself who was excited by the arrival of the emperor's soldiers and talk of missions to the west.

"Well, the earlier I tell the Masons the more people they are likely to bump into and pass the news onto throughout the day, so I'm going to pay them a visit now and get back to my work later if that's okay?"

"It shouldn't be any trouble. Just remember that those cows in the north paddock need moving today and I can't do it by myself," Tevin insisted, deliberately pointing out Jaeger's priorities.

"That's the first thing we can do when I get back" Jaeger played along.

"Good, well I'll have the gates ready for when you return then."

It didn't take Jaeger long to reach the Mason's and spread the news, but he didn't stay for long either as Tevin's plans for the cattle made him feel like he was in a rush. Grondmason promised to ensure that all the dwarf families would be informed by sundown, and after having done his part in spreading the news, Jaeger got back to work.

All of Jaeger's farm duties seemed to be moving

at an excruciatingly slow pace today, but eventually all the cattle were moved into a fallow paddock, and the sun went down signaling dinner time. Bellan at least seemed to find the current affairs to be interesting and pressed Jaeger for information on where the soldiers would be going.

"Nashaw said that they were traveling well beyond our borders. If they have come all the way to West-Yield though, my guess would be that they're spying on the scaleskins in the jungles, or even passing through to the stronghold ranges," Jaeger speculated. He was pleased that she had given him an excuse to discuss the news.

This managed to get Tevin and Mendel's attention now too, and Tevin was already making shrewd guesses. "So *that's* what has gotten you so excited, they want to visit the dwarfs. What exactly is the town meeting going to address then?"

"Word is that they haven't been given enough troops for the mission, I don't think the emperor is finding it easy to hold our southern borders anymore. If they need anyone from West-Yield to join them, I think I would be one of the most suitable for the mission don't you think?"

"And why would that be?" Mendel interrupted. "Your father needs you here on the farm. Also, we didn't go to all the trouble of keeping you from drowning in the river all of your childhood, just to let you run off into the jungles and get killed" she protested. Mendel was leaving no doubt about her opposition to Jaeger's plans very early.

"Fair enough the jungles are dangerous, bu-"

"Dangerous!? You were nearly killed last year

not even halfway to their borders. If it wasn't suicide, the emperor would have already sent an army in there long ago!"

"I agree the jungles are dangerous, but I spoke to Darroch their captain who is part of the elite guard, and the emperor wouldn't risk his elite soldiers if it was a suicide mission. What I was trying to say was that if any humans should be on a mission to visit the dwarves, I would be most suited."

"No-one has said yet that that is where the mission is being sent," Tevin reminded him.

"Your right, but if it is the case, I am just trying to give you both some notice that this is how I feel about the idea."

Mendel pursed her lips. "Well now we know, so let's just wait until the town meeting before we go making any more plans, okay?"

"Don't expect me to do your chores while you're gone Jaeger," Bellan teased.

The next day at noon, most of the town had gathered before the thane's steps. The clamour of everyone gathered and talking in one place rose, while Thelonius stood before them with Nashaw and Darroch on one side. Grummason-Greybeard and a few other greybeards stood on the other side of the town thane. A few more minutes passed while the last few people arrived, before Thelonius signaled a hush so that he could address the crowd.

"Thank you for turning out on such short notice. As I'm sure many of you are already aware, the man to my left is Commander Darroch of the emperor's guard. He has traveled to West-Yield on an important mission and if he would share this now, you may all listen to what he has to say."

Darroch smiled and shook Thelonius' hand, then stepped forward to the crowd with three measured and rigid steps. He had shrugged off his casual demeanor and was now a man of the emperor.

"Thank you Thelonius, and again thank you everyone for gathering to hear me today. I am passing through here on a mission to investigate scaleskin activity beyond our western borders, before navigating their jungles to reach the Stronghold Ranges. Many of you may also know of this mountain range as the Dwarven Ranges." This immediately gathered a few murmurs from the crowd.

"The emperor's resources are currently stretched to capacity. We have already begun increasing recruitment amongst the central towns throughout The Plateau, but our situation has become increasingly more vulnerable. The scaleskin hordes of the wild are pressing harder against our southern borders and in greater numbers than ever before. This mission was not given priority resources and I had to petition our emperor to allow me to abandon my customary posting to lead it."

At this more murmurs went through the crowd. "Your argument for elite guards not taking on suicide missions just lost its edge." Mendel whispered leaning forward to Jaeger, he tried to shrug off her comment and continued listening.

"If the assault on our southern front continues at this rate, then conscription will be inevitable, and my personal view is that conscription is unsustainable. Therefore, one of our alternatives must include renewing old alliances so that we do not fight alone. It is with this purpose that I am leading this expedition to make contact with the dwarves in their strongholds and coordinate a new war upon our enemies.

"The reason I have gathered you all here is to recruit men from our western provinces to join our mission. I ask this of West-Yield because those from our central cities who would fight, have already joined the forces on the frontline." He paused for a moment to assess the town reaction to this. Many people were thinking that the town was already too exposed to raids to be losing more able-bodied fighters. Some were quite vocal in expressing these concerns.

Old Hector could be clearly heard above the other voices. "Attacks on The Plateau have not just increased on the southern front. We already lost a number of good men a year ago to the largest raid I can remember, we can't afford to lose any more."

"I have not come to rob this town of its defenders, nor am I unaware of the recent series of attacks along our western borders. All I ask is that you spare what you can. Nobody has to decide immediately, we depart in five days and anyone who is interested will find me at your guard-house until then." Darroch left it at that, and retired from the front of the crowd so that everyone could discuss his request.

As they made for home, Tevin and Mendel continued to discuss the audacity of the capital to assume that border-towns were an untapped resource for recruitment. Jaeger walked behind, quietly contemplating the mission and trying not to let his family interrupt his thoughts. From what he had gathered, the mission didn't appear to be a very hopeful one. The emperor had not provided any of his elite guard readily.

However, Darroch had volunteered for the mission. Clearly, he had reason to place more faith in it than others did, tasking himself with its success. Despite knowing very little about the man, Jaeger felt that somehow that gave the mission a lot of credibility.

When they got home, Mendel involved Jaeger in her discussion. "I see that you have had a chance to quietly consider the folly of joining this quest, how do you feel about it now?" She seemed to be seeking closure for her fears that he may still be entertaining the idea of leaving.

"I'm glad that I know more, but I honestly believe there is something in this mission." Jaeger didn't expect to receive a warm reaction to this.

"I knew that commander would get into your head with his speech!" she erupted. "You have always been easily influenced by exciting ideas. He undervalues the need for this town to remain standing, we are on the frontline too you know."

"Yes, but couldn't you feel that there was something to what he said. We can't keep holding The Plateau the way we are now. It made sense to me."

"That's because it's his job to make radical ideas like this one sound sensible. He's a sharp speaker I'll give him that, and he would probably be quite a likeable fellow if he wasn't trying to lead our men to death. But he is, so you have to listen without becoming emotionally involved Jaeger."

"She's right Jaeger" Tevin joined in. "You and your mother both have a biased perspective on this idea, and it would probably do well to sit and consider this before making any decisions." Mendel's stern glare at Tevin indicated that she did not feel his attempt to support her had been very supportive. "I know you don't want Jaeger to leave and risk his life, but he is taking this decision seriously and if we don't provide him all the facts without bias then he probably won't want to listen."

"Okay" Jaeger agreed, he felt that Tevin's line of thought at least left a little bit of room for his opinion on the matter, as long as it wasn't a hasty decision. "I at least still want to think about it, so I will speak to you tomorrow or the next day about this."

"Yes dear, but please think about everything. Not just the glorified adventures you and Grum have always tried to create," Mendel persisted.

"I will, I promise."

The next two days, Tevin and Mendel left Jaeger alone and gave him space to consider his decision. Mendel looked like she wanted to say something on a number of occasions, but managed to show restraint each time with Tevin's help. Jaeger spent this time going through the motions of all his tasks, while keeping his mind on what it would mean to leave, as well as what he would be leaving behind. He tried to imagine what he would encounter at every stage of the journey, and realized that he had little idea of what lay beyond The Plateau, or even West-Yield for that matter.

Jaeger could piece together a little from the stories he had heard, as well as his brief excursion to the foothills of The Plateau with Grummason. Travel beyond the western borders would involve thick jungles full of scaleskins, minimal ways to gather supplies, dark nights sleeping under the stars, and a number of other things that didn't sound overly unpleasant. Reaching the dwarves in the mountains didn't seem to have any obstacles once the jungle was out the way either and the return journey would probably be far easier once they had completed their mission.

He didn't consider the many realities that any experienced traveler could have told him of, although there were few left in these times. The glamour of most adventures normally faded a few days in. This was when blisters, insects and sickness began to emerge, and the thickness of the jungles slowed movement to a labored crawl. Blissfully ignorant to all these obstacles, Jaeger had decided that he had made up his mind. He was determined to join Darroch on his mission to the Stronghold Ranges and meet the dwarves.

Convincing his parents to agree to this was difficult, especially Mendel. But once they could see that his mind was made up, they accepted that they could not change it and tried to do as much as they could to prepare him for the trip. Mendel insisted on Jaeger taking numerous versions of the same items, and Jaeger had to continually explain that it would only make traveling harder, since he would be carrying it all on his back. By the fourth day since the town meeting, Jaeger had mentally prepared himself and his family for the change. The only thing left was to approach Darroch and register his intentions to join his expedition.

"I was wondering if we would see you down here for the intake," Darroch welcomed Jaeger when he entered the guard house. "We have eighteen dwarves from West-Yield now, but I wasn't counting on luring many men into joining us, you're the second so far."

"It wasn't an easy decision to make" Jaeger conceded, "this appears to be a very dangerous mission and my parents believe that deciding to leave on a few short-day's notice is a little reckless."

"Less than most, as far as I understand you're a little more accustomed to dwarves than the majority of humans in this town. And something tells me that there is little keeping you here."

Jaeger was startled by Darroch's insights and decided to ignore his second one. "I do have a lot to do with the dwarven population of this town, I'm surprised you were aware of that fact."

"It pays to keep one's eyes and ears open whenever one is new to an area," Darroch responded with a faint smile. "We will be departing in the morning of the day after tomorrow. If you want my advice on preparations, you should pack lightly on all items other than food, water, and socks. And make sure your shoes are comfortable and in good condition."

"Thank you I will do my best with that" Jaeger replied, chuckling to himself on the inside about Mendel's packing. "Is there anything else I should bring or prepare for?"

"Just don't forget your sword or any other gear you would need to fight with. And remember what I said about the socks!"

4 SCALESKINS & SPIDERS

The sun had just risen when they set off in six files behind Darroch. The company was just over forty strong and all traveling on foot, as Darroch had informed them that bringing horses through the thick jungles would cause more hindrance than help. His own platoon numbered twenty, while the dwarves who had agreed to come along nearly doubled that number. Then there was Jaeger and Barley. Jaeger wasn't sure what had made Barley decide to come along, he wasn't married but still ran a fairly successful farm for someone in his late twenties.

Jaeger surprised himself to find that he spent little time with the dwarves while the party traveled. For some reason, the humans and dwarves separated into two groups every time they marched, and most of his time marching Jaeger spent talking to the soldier from Darroch's platoon named Marrick. Marrick was a quiet yet satirical man at the same time, he had the knack of a comedian to make subtle humour with an entirely straight face, but Jaeger was fairly certain that he could tell when he was serious.

"Darroch says that the forest and jungle will just blend together until it changes completely over the next two days. I think it should be an obvious transition though, don't you?" Jaeger wasn't overly curious, but felt like breaking up the boring silence that set in after lunch every day.

"It shouldn't be subtle," replied Marrick with a straight face.

"Have you traveled this way before?"

"No, but I have traveled similar conditions moving south before towards the jungles there," Marrick replied seriously. "It was with Darroch after I first met him a few years ago. He was leading the elite forces close to a large scaleskin tribe at the time to attack their camp. I was part of a large group of soldiers who had to wait at a checkpoint to protect their retreat. He led a tidy mission that night."

They both continued like this as they walked through the gradually changing terrain. Even though Jaeger couldn't quite put his finger on what the difference was, he found that his mind was often only half committed to their discussions, as everyone's voices gradually dimmed and a sense of wariness permeated through the group.

The dwarves that brought up the rear had gone completely silent and all trudged along with grim faces that bordered on anger now. Evidently the march through enemy territory dug up old memories and grudges. It was centuries ago now when the last dwarf settlements had been forced out of the lowlands, and ultimately the reason that none of them had ever seen their homeland.

Like Darroch had told Jaeger, the terrain slowly digressed over the following couple of days until it was predominantly jungle. By the end of the company's third night of marching, they had well and truly left the foothills of The Plateau. They were now buried in thick vegetation, which reduced the distance they could cover each day to a fraction of what they were achieving when they first began.

"This is becoming unbearable!" Jaeger exclaimed without stopping to consider that the comment probably incriminated how new to this he was.

"It's not easy to bear," Marrick agreed, turning to Jaeger with a grin that showed he knew exactly what Jaeger had been thinking.

"I don't think the width of this jungle is that long from east to west, it's just that we have to move much more slowly through it," Jaeger continued.

Marrick sighed as he let Jaeger's words in, then relaxed himself for a moment before renewing his efforts to push through the vines and large-leafed plants. "That will be just one of our problems soon. The humidity in here causes you to sweat and rash, and this place is habitat to all sorts of nasty little creatures… spiders ugh" he shuddered.

"We should be more concerned about encountering scaleskins shouldn't we?" Jaeger hadn't considered that any other creatures in here could cause him harm.

"They're all in league against us once you enter the jungle." Marrick hadn't changed his disgusted expression, and for once Jaeger wasn't sure if this was a joke.

Once again Marrick seemed to have read his thoughts. "Oh, don't get me wrong. the small spiders will just bite anything that moves in here, same with the mosquitoes, and they both make you sick. But those pests don't affect the scaleskins like they do us, I think they've become more or less immune to it. Probably taste like shit to bite too. The scaleskins also make use of the larger spiders and other evil beasts to ride, especially in battle."

"Big spiders..." Jaeger shuddered, beginning to empathize more with Marrick's disgust.

"Oh, they're big all right!" Marrick agreed passionately, then shook off this current spell of frustration and went back to chopping and moving forwards in silence.

As the sun pushed lower towards dusk that night, Jaeger began to understand why Marrick had so passionately declared his disgust for the smaller inhabitants of the jungle. Mosquitoes began to appear in clouds around the company, settling in to bite any exposed skin they could find. They couldn't even take the satisfaction of slapping the pests, their hands were preoccupied clearing vines and branches as they walked. Jaeger was also aware of the discomfort his feet were in, the humid conditions had resulted in his shoes retaining more and more moisture from random puddles. He now felt the build-up aggravating a couple of points on his feet that he wasn't sure he wanted to look at when he stopped.

As the sun approached the horizon outside, the

jungle began to dim and Darroch raised his hand at the front of the group. Everyone stopped, relieved that the halt had been called while it was still light.

"This is an adequate area, but we're going to need to clear some of this ground to set up camp for the night," the captain announced.

"That's a pleasant companion to share our sleeping space with," Marrick exclaimed in a sarcastically cheery tone. He pointed towards a bulbous spider sitting at head height in the middle of its thick web between two plants.

Unable to take his eyes off the spider, Marrick picked up a clump of wet dirt and squeezed it into a ball, before throwing it at the menacing spider sitting patiently in its web. The clump of dirt was a direct hit and the spider was now no-where to be seen.

"Now he's going to come after you while you sleep Marrick, you would have been safer to just leave him in that web," Darroch commented smugly. The taunt was directed at Marrick who clearly had a phobia, but Jaeger felt just as uncomfortable at the thought.

"He's right there!" yelled Darroch dramatically, pointing towards the ground a few yards from Marrick's feet. Marrick jumped and tried to locate his attacker.

"Where!? If you can see it then kill it!"

"I can't believe you can't see him," Darroch goaded. "He's as big as your head, he'll probably chew your whole foot off when he reaches you. Look he's coming for it right now!" Darroch continued to provoke, relishing the entertainment.

Jaeger spotted the now angry-looking spider as it raced toward its attacker. "He's right, look!"

Marrick now saw it too and picked up more

clumps of dirt to throw as the spider continued its unrelenting advance. Jaeger ran forwards and leapt, coming down with both feet pressed together, squashing it deep into the soft mud. The action exacerbated the pain in those tender-spots under his feet.

"Brave soldier," Darroch noted.

"Agreed," Marrick nodded a little more seriously.

By the time they had cleared enough ground around them to accommodate the whole company, the sun had gone down. "It is not advisable to light a large fire even when the jungle is this thick. The light shouldn't be a problem, but the smell of the smoke will attract any scaleskins nearby, either tonight or tomorrow when they smell the ashes. They have a keen sense of smell and can tell the difference between humans and other creatures by it. Even if there weren't other obvious differences."

"Should we not light one at all then?" It didn't seem like the right course of action to Jaeger considering Darroch's warning, despite how depressing the prospect of not having a fire felt.

"If you can find dry fuel then it won't cause us any immediate danger, and we can be far enough away from here by the time any scaleskins find it."

"Good enough for me" Marrick said quickly before Darroch could change his mind, "I think we could all use a bit of fire tonight."

"I'll help find some dry fuel then" Jaeger offered, and set about gathering any dead branches he could.

Nothing that was lying on the ground could be used because the moisture of the soil had waterlogged everything, so they didn't have much to work with when he was done. The fire was comforting nonetheless and Jaeger used the light from it to examine his feet. Pulling his shoes and socks off was difficult, and as he peeled the sock off the tip of his left foot, he had to move so slowly that it felt like he was deliberately torturing himself.

The firelight revealed a thick flap of skin that was hanging from the joint beneath his left big toe. His feet were also white and wrinkled from the extended period of time they had spent soaking in wet shoes.

"That's going to give me some trouble," he commented to Marrick who had gotten comfortable in his blanket beside him.

Marrick sat up and looked at the revolting flap of skin. "Certainly won't help. You'll need to bandage that now and put your socks on over it in the morning. Here I'll get you some salve to put on before you wrap it." He rummaged through his pack and pulled out a brown jar of ointment. As he applied the thick cream, Jaeger wondered how many other things he would need on this journey that he hadn't thought to bring.

Jaeger woke up to the morning light stabbing through the jungle canopy, with a few rays falling directly into his eyes as he opened them. The sight filled his entire eye and had a piercing effect that he felt sure was stabbing directly into his brain. His body immediately lost all tiredness and lethargy, but it had nothing to do with the light. There was an incredible amount of tension in the air all around him that sent a shot of adrenaline through his body and made him leap straight to his feet.

"I would get packed quickly this morning if I were you," Darroch said without looking up as he packed his own belongings away. He looked tired and Jaeger remembered that he had been on guard duty for the second half of the night. "Something out there is aware of our presence in the jungle, I'd imagine it was the smoke from our fire that has given us away after all."

"I can feel it, I didn't know that you can sense this sort of thing but I could feel the tension the moment I woke up," Jaeger agreed.

Darroch gave him a sharp look, his hands had stopped packing. "That's a strange thing to say Jaeger, explain this tension."

"I-I just felt very wary when I woke up." He paused and gave Darroch a questioning look, but Darroch appeared to be all ears, as if whatever Jaeger had to say was incredibly important. "It just feels like there is something or someone very angry standing right behind me, the kind of feeling I think you'd get when you're about to be hit in the back of the head. I just sense anger." Now he knew he had gone too far and sounded like a raving lunatic.

Darroch however seemed unsurprised. "I believe you have some magical aptitude Jaeger. Our mages sometimes say the same thing when they accompany us. From what I understand, what you're sensing is some sort of black energy that all scaleskins emit. I think it has to do with the link between them and the Great Invasion of Evil."

"So, it means that there are scaleskins nearby?"

"Yes, it may even mean they have a shaman with

them in the vicinity also, if an untrained civilian like yourself can sense it. We had better be off soon and we will need to be wary today."

The company set off promptly after this and were all instructed to avoid cutting their way through the thick vegetation if they could. Instead, everyone spread out, and slipped in-between the spaces between plants when they came to thicker sections. They managed to continue this way without incident until noon, and although Jaeger never felt the sense of impending anger wane, Darroch had decided to keep to a track they had found so that they could move faster. It seemed less important to maintain their stealth now and more important to set a faster pace and not stay in one place too long.

Jaeger wore new socks today and could feel some discomfort as he trod on the wrapped section of his left foot. He concluded that with the bandage supporting it, he wasn't doing any further damage by walking, but was still glad to take some weight off it when lunch came around and he was able to sit. Lunch was short, and once they had recommenced their march, Jaeger tried to force some quiet conversation out to break the weight of the silence.

"What are our chances of getting through today without bumping into trouble? Every step I feel like there are enemies just around the corner," he whispered.

Marrick replied in the same hushed tone "I couldn't say, everyone is doing a good job of moving silently and we have managed to cover a fair bit of distance between us and last night's camp since we started. That's the main thing enemies will use to locate us."

"Because of the smoke?"

"The smoke at first will draw them in from a distance, but they will be able to follow our trail easily enough once they reach that."

"So, they are going to be tracking us from now on until we leave this place? All because of that fire!" Jaeger felt like protesting that they shouldn't have lit it if they were all aware of this last night.

"It was inevitable that they would come across our trail in this jungle," Marrick replied philosophically. "At least now we aren't being slowed down by traveling off-road."

Jaeger gave a half-hearted grin, "off-road, that's very fitting."

Marrick grinned back at him "I pioneered that term myself, so you can remember that if you hea-"

Jaeger heard it too, it was the sound they were all straining their ears not to hear. A harsh yell reached them from ahead on their left, to the south west. The general sound of the yell strongly suggested that there were Scaleskins nearby, but it wasn't the noise they would expect to hear if they were being followed. Whatever it was, it seemed unaware of the company's presence in its territory.

Everyone went quiet and continued to advance in almost complete silence. They went on for another minute or so almost tiptoeing with their breath held, until the noise was loud enough that they could all easily hear the approach of a number of harsh voices getting closer. The sound was of trampling, mixed with the exchange of savage threats.

"It's definitely scaleskins all-right," Marrick whispered to Jaeger after Darroch had hushed the group and signaled for them all to hunch lower in the bushes. "What's more these ones sound like mucks, the larger scaleskins, always threatening and fighting each other to reassert their position within their hierarchy. I couldn't imagine living life like that but they do. They have no loyalty to each other, but they hate us and can pick up on your fear and hesitation like an anim-" Darroch snapped his fingers to get the entire group's attention, then signaled everyone to gather in closely to listen.

"It sounds like a small group of mucks are wandering through the area," Darroch whispered to everybody. "They wouldn't be scouts, not this deep in their own territory, but they can still read the ground like it speaks their language and they will know we've been here as soon as they cross our tracks. We'll need to surprise them. They won't be expecting us and we should easily outnumber them too, so I want everyone to spread out twenty yards in every direction and hide yourself as best you can. Wait for them to get as far into our trap without noticing us before you attack."

The company spread out in every direction, and without discussion; Marrick and Jaeger both moved in the same direction to find a hiding spot near each other. Marrick crouched below a large fallen tree that didn't touch the ground across the middle, while Jaeger moved towards the middle of a group of bushes that would hide him well enough as long as the mucks weren't deliberately searching for him in them. He looked around and found that he could only just see half a dozen of the soldiers from behind the cover of their respective positions.

The mucks were becoming increasingly louder as they drew closer, eventually coming into view to reveal around ten scaleskins in a disorganized mob, moving forward along the worn track. Ahead of the group, a single tree sapling had managed to sprout in the sun-starved environment below the canopy, and was aspiring towards the sky with single-minded purpose. As they passed the young tree, a bored looking slag at the front of the mob slashed the thin sapling, severing its fragile trunk. It appeared the action was no more than an expression of its hateful malice and the creature returned to its disinterested gait forwards without looking back.

A roar came from the back of the mob and Jaeger saw another larger muck run into view, scimitar drawn as it raced toward the smaller scaleskin in apparent rage.

"You'll payfa that you little hero!" the larger one bellowed as he charged and struck the cringing beast in the back of the head with the hilt of his weapon.

The smaller slag cowered down submissively as it was forced to accept a number of savage blows to the back of the head without retaliating. Once the larger brute seemed satisfied, the smaller one was then allowed to slink away, cowering as it moved towards the back of the procession. As it passed the others, it was subjected to a number of wanton kicks and punches from the rest of the group, who seemed only too eager to take advantage of its current vulnerability.

To Jaeger's complete surprise, he then saw the

larger beast turn and slash the same sapling several inches lower down its trunk, destroying what was left of the defenceless tree. For a few moments Jaeger stood confused at this new twist in his observations, then it became clear and he realized the true cause for the leader's anger. It was not angry with the senseless destruction of the defenseless sapling, but at the little one trying to mark its territory.

By now the mob had passed beyond the first couple of concealed soldiers and had still shown no signs that they were aware of the trap around them. Suddenly a wiry muck at the front froze, staring intently at the ground ahead.

"AYE! that's human tracks!" he alarmed, "only those *partjens* would-"

But before the group had time to respond to his discovery, Darroch had leapt from his concealment and beheaded the pack leader with one powerful stroke. The rest of the mob reacted with lightning-fast reflexes and the two mucks directly behind swung their blades at Darroch, almost before his first blow had finished decapitating their leader. Most of the others responded by fleeing after realizing they were in the middle of an ambush, as concealed soldiers appeared from all around them.

Jaeger drew the sword that Kurtsmith had presented to him as a gift on the night of his eighteenth birthday. It wasn't light but it had good balance, and responded quickly to any movements he made with it. Before he knew it, he was face-to-face with a frantic muck, swinging its scimitar down from above its head in a cleaving action. Jaeger's style of swordsmanship was again fluent and instinctive, as he continued to listen to the pre-emptive spasms of terror he felt before each blow came his way.

Rather than blocking the blow, he caught it with a graceful movement that redirected the scimitar a little off course, using his enemy's momentum to fling it to the ground. His second movement flowed forwards from the first, as he leveled the sword at the snarling creature's chest and drove the point through its heart.

Another slag came racing past Jaeger fleeing for its life. Despite this, it still couldn't resist the urge to strike him even in its desire to escape. Jaeger ducked the horizontal blow and swung around just as the scaleskin skipped beyond his reach. It didn't matter though. Marrick, who had already caught one scaleskin attempting to escape, blocked the goblin's path and landed a cutting blow to its thigh as it sidestepped him, bringing it to ground.

He didn't waste any time, cleaving the back of its head open even as it frantically crawled away, then watched the desperate creature fall to the ground dead. Jaeger felt a lump of pity well up in his throat. It was the same slag he had watched earlier being beaten by its peers.

With this execution the jungle fell silent, Marrick had slain the last of the scaleskins in their ambush, and the group of assorted soldiers stood looking around scanning for any other threats. Jaeger wiped the blood off his sword with a large leaf he had pulled off a plant. Marrick looked down at his tunic to observe some splatter from the skull-splitting blow he had just dealt.

"Even their blood is filthy," he noted with

disgust.

"I think out of the two of you he got the rough edge of the bargain," Jaeger responded in a neutral voice, still sick with the image he had stuck in his head.

"He didn't get the smooth edge," grinned Marrick.

Darroch was efficient in assessing every member of the company for injuries. Not a single human or dwarf had sustained worse than scratches from the skirmish. The scaleskins had been sprung so quickly, that they didn't have a chance to identify where every attacker was hiding, and most of them had been killed while they drew their weapons. Within ten minutes of the violent encounter, everybody was back on track and marching. The company was now buzzing with conversations, creating a stark contrast to the somber procession they had been just an hour earlier.

"You seem unusually quiet all things considered," Marrick observed, referring to the scene they had just left behind.

Jaeger paused while he tried to determine why he didn't feel like talking. "I guess I never expected to feel guilt or pity for scaleskins, but butchering them in that ambush seems to have left me feeling something like that."

"People who aren't accustomed to battles are likely to feel a little shook up from an encounter like that, it'll pass."

"Clearly," Jaeger muttered without thinking, immediately regretting his own self-righteousness. Marrick had heard him.

"What would you have us do then Jaeger? Ask

them to be good if we let them go? These creatures don't deserve our sympathy. They are evil."

Jaeger knew that what Marrick said was true and felt bad for his outburst, but still couldn't shake the guilt. "I'm sorry and you're right. I just can't help but think that they're more primitive than evil."

Darroch who had been walking a few paces ahead of them in silence, slowed his pace and drew alongside them.

"Jaeger, what you say is open minded and compassionate, which does illustrate the difference between our people and theirs. But do not confuse their vicious behaviour with ignorance. Their raids, wars, and torture of others, have nothing to do with necessity. Some of it has to do with being territorial creatures which is mildly excusable, but the foundation of their lives is based around innate cruelty. This is evident in everything they do, from their tendency to destroy any living plants and animals they see, to the torture of any captives they bring back from their raids."

Like a man woken from an unrealistic dream, Jaeger snapped out of his doubt-filled thoughts and remembered the bodies of all his townspeople during the mass burial a year ago. That was the work of his enemies. Anger welled up inside him as he realized he would never be able to speak to these people again, despite still having vivid memories of times they had shared together.

Darroch nodded to Jaeger and Marrick, then stopped walking and allowed them to continue their conversation alone. Their leader drifted further down the line of men and dwarves to see how others were traveling.

The next day, Darroch stayed to the same path they had begun following the day before. They were covering great distances in a short amount of time and Darroch now pushed everyone to take fewer breaks and sleep less. They all knew that somewhere behind them scaleskins would be following their tracks, which kept them from complaining about being pushed so hard. Jaeger could feel his body beginning to show signs that the physical stress was taking its toll. His lower back ached under the weight of his pack, forcing him to lean forwards to use different muscles for relief. This in turn caused other tensions around his body to build and he knew it was something that would only deteriorate further with time if he kept it up.

Around him, he observed that other members of the company had also added strange abnormalities to their walk, indicating similar problems with aches and pains. The only ones who weren't fazed by the perpetual trekking were the dwarves. Most of them were carrying burdens equal to or heavier than those carried by their human companions, despite the proportionate difference in their body-to-burden ratio. They carried their luggage on their backs as if it were an extension of their body. Darroch was the only human still faring well, he was more hardened than anyone else and also carried the most minimalist backpack.

By midday, Jaeger began to wonder if Darroch was going to skip the lunchtime break entirely and continue through until evening. Shortly afterwards Darroch addressed the company while they marched.

"Sorry to push you all so hard but my instincts

tell me that we couldn't afford to stop before," he shouted back down the line. "We will take a short break at the next good clearing we can find."

Marrick let out one heavy sigh as he walked, before mentally regrouping. "Since you're so receptive to the world at the moment, what else do your instincts tell you?"

"That we had better not sit around too long when we do stop," Darroch replied. "By now any Scaleskins that have crossed our trail will have had time to report it to their tribe and gather a hunting party. They will also have a number of advantages in the jungle that will help them to travel faster than we can."

"What advantages do they have?" Jaeger asked, hoping that it would be something minor.

"The biggest one is that some of them won't be on foot, but even those who are won't be carrying their homes on their backs like us. *This* is their home so they will travel light and only carry weapons. Also, if we're really unlucky they might even send scouts ahead to a nearby tribe so they can cut us off," Darroch added as an afterthought.

Marrick laughed. "Now that would be poor luck indeed. I've never known neighboring tribes to be that good at communicating verbally with each other, let alone sharing their sport and giving someone else all the fun. When have you heard of them doing that before?"

"I haven't, but the scaleskins along all borders have been doing a lot of things differently lately." For the first time since Jaeger had taken up with Darroch his reasoning sounded illogical, but for some reason Jaeger knew that it would still be foolish to doubt him.

"Well, I did ask for a report on your instincts so

I guess I had that coming, let's just hope you're getting ahead of yourself in your old age," Marrick tried to laugh, but it lacked conviction. He too seemed bothered by Darroch's outrageous predictions.

Darroch laughed. "Just ahead looks like there is a clearing to rest in," he inclined his head down the track, where a hundred yards away the path seemed to open from beneath the trees like the end of a tunnel.

A wave of relief passed through the group, as those who heard Darroch relayed the information back. Their long-awaited lunch break was just up ahead. Jaeger had been blocking out heavy physical exhaustion for hours now and he finally allowed it all to come flooding back in. His endurance immediately disappeared once he mentally surrendered to the fatigue, and he wondered if he could have walked further anyway.

As the clearing became closer, they realized that there were no trees at all beyond the opening. For a few short moments, Jaeger actually wondered if they had come to the end of the forest, before noticing trees and jungle as thick as ever in the distance.

"The land must dip immediately beyond our little clearing into a valley, but I don't see why the trees should stop just because the slope dips." Marrick was working through his thoughts out loud as he loosened the straps on his shoulder.

"Keep your pack on soldier!" barked Darroch suddenly. "This valley may be about to make a liar out of me."

The outburst took Marrick by surprise and he jumped a little. "What lies?" His voice drifted off as he said it, scanning the terrain that was coming into view.

"We won't be taking any break here," Darroch said bluntly.

Twenty yards ahead where the tree-line ceased, the bright afternoon sun showed a barren landscape leading into the enormous valley. It was like the opposite of an oasis in the desert, here in the middle of a jungle teeming with life, sat a vast bowl of sick and lifeless land.

As they reached the edge of the desolate valley, they could all see the landscape below was crawling with scaleskins. The territory was filled with shelters made of scrap metal and roughly hewn timber, which would not be fit for humans to reside in for any period of time. How they had come this far along an open path unnoticed was nothing short of a miracle, but that appeared to be the extent of their luck. The entire time, Darroch had been pushing them to march hard and fast, hoping to avoid the large tribes that lived in the jungle. Now they had walked directly into the lap of a crowded hive of enemies.

A strong river ran through the middle of the valley, exiting it on the western border, but nothing grew next to it, which was uncommon for any water source especially one in the middle of a thick jungle. The ground below was covered with Scaleskins that looked like tiny specks in the distance, and across this ghetto Jaeger could occasionally spot enormous black creatures walking amongst the ant-like figures. Marrick shuddered with revulsion.

"Those spiders look enormous even from here. In all this jungle you had to lead us here Darroch!"

Jaeger could now make sense of the large black monsters walking amongst the scaleskins, and walked to the edge of the path to where a steep drop-off gave him a better view of the valley closest to him. From the cover of a patch of remaining dead trees, he saw that the enormous arachnids were free to scurry through the village at will, trampling and eating any scaleskins that they crossed paths with.

He even saw one spider pick out and chase a slightly obese little goblin, as it frantically tried to run away. Gaining on its prey with astonishing speed, the spider ran the terrified scaleskin down, using the momentum behind its heavy body to knock its victim to the ground. It then used its two front two legs to pin the goblin down, before proceeding to nip and bite at the struggling bundle with its pincers.

The goblin kicked and screamed as its last few moments of life were spent being eaten alive, while the rest of the population continued moving past with no compassion for a dying fellow tribesman. A small crowd of scaleskins even gathered around the horrific scene to watch, apparently incapable of comprehending that any one of them could fall victim to this same fate next.

"This place looks worse than the hell beyond the DarkLand gates themselves!" Jaeger could find no stronger description for the vile pit that stood before him.

Darroch too looked on with an expression of pure disgust. "These tribes are a terrifying insight into the evil that may threaten all of us one day. But never draw that comparison again, unless you can say that you have seen what lies beyond the gates to the demon-world."

"My imagination can think of nothing worse than what I can see right now" Jaeger maintained, feeling physically sick.

"Neither can mine. I have slain many scaleskins in battle, but never would I subject them to the torture that is a part of their own daily existence."

One of the dwarves that had crowded around the vantage point with them spat, "nor would I, but it would be the same day that I renounced beer that I would feel an ounce of pity for these reptiles."

"Well, I'm sure we can all agree that right now would be the perfect time to turn and leave this place. Not far beyond the other side of this valley I think we will reach the end of the jungle. But we will have to go around, giving this place a wide berth before we get there."

The body language of the entire company dropped and grunts of exhaustion came from some as they mentally prepared themselves to push through severe fatigue. Darroch looked around the company, assessing their energy and morale.

"A man can say very little of himself with confidence, until he has been tested to within an inch of what he can take. You should all continue in the knowledge that we will soon be able say this of ourselves if we manage to escape with our lives from this place."

5 ESCAPE FROM THE JUNGLE

There was no monotony in the company's march now. They had pushed off the track and into the jungle just south of it, fighting the fatigue they had all let in as they went. Luckily though, the constant movement of scaleskins through the area had resulted in the destruction of almost all the vines and vegetation that would slow the company down. Darroch's plan was to circle the perimeter of the valley until they stood beyond its western border, before the race to escape the jungle began.

A couple of hundred yards into their 'off-road' march, Darroch raised a hand and stopped them, ordering everyone to remove any items from their packs that were not immediately essential to them.

"Any clothes that you are not currently wearing should be discarded, even blankets and other items for sleeping. I doubt we will have time to change attire or sleep comfortably anyway before we reach the mountains."

He pressed everyone to be ruthless in their assessment of what they needed and even the dwarves who were barely affected by burdens, discarded most of the less-important items in their packs. They then sat down to a quick meal, which was as much to reduce the provisions they were carrying, as it was to satisfy the demand for a lunch break.

Jaeger no longer rationed the food he was taking out and ate twice as much as he normally would. He figured that Darroch was on the verge of ordering them to discard their food anyway and that it would be much better off in his stomach. Darroch did not join them and instead walked back thirty yards with his sword drawn to stand guard while his company ate.

Without the added weight bouncing on their backs, everyone traveled much faster. Jaeger had only kept socks and what remained of his provisions in his backpack. He kept pace with the march far more easily now, as they moved forward at a brisk walk that seemed to be perpetually on the brink of breaking into a run. They no longer traveled in any kind of order either, and each individual moved past trees to their left and right without the inhibition of having someone alongside them.

Darroch held this rate for almost an hour before pausing to look back into the valley. By then Jaeger could feel his lungs labouring, while the rest of his body seemed to have adapted to the physical strain to some degree. Everyone followed Darroch cautiously now, taking note of his body language and keeping behind their leader. He led them to the edge of the heavy jungle terrain again, and from their vantage point they were again able to look down on the super-tribe below. They were now on the southern edge of the valley and not far ahead they could see that the river leading out of it would soon cross their path.

"That river is going to be difficult to cross unnoticed," Darroch muttered to no one in particular, and no one responded. They were focused on the tiny figures below which were all now moving in one general direction, towards the path that they had been using earlier on the eastern edge.

There they could see another group of scaleskins in different attire coming from the opposite direction. The newcomers were far less in numbers than the mob that was congregating in front of them, and Jaeger guessed that there must have been no more than fifty of them as they came to a complete halt before the growing hundreds that had raced up to meet them. He then saw one of the newcomers walk forward from his group, it was difficult to tell from this distance but the leader appeared to have his hand raised in the air above him.

A few moments passed while little movement could be seen, apart from the growing numbers walking in to join the super tribe. Then without warning, three or four small figures ran out from the larger mob and set upon the leader of the visitors, who went to ground beneath a savage attack. The visitors stood before the angry crowd, watching motionlessly while their leader was beaten to death before their eyes, before a few more figures broke forth from the assembled mob starting a chain reaction.

The fifty or so newcomers scattered and

attempted to flee back along the path they had come from, but many of those closest to the angry mob were taken and dragged back into the crowd. Many more were trampled by their comrades who were grabbing each other as they ran, or pulling each other to the ground to save themselves. About one third of the group appeared to be clear of the immediate riot, which had paused now to take care of those they had caught. They disappeared over the top of the slope and back into the jungle.

Darroch laughed bitterly. "Well, that was a slight improvement in our fortunes! I'm happy to admit that my instincts were a bit exaggerated this time. That smaller group was probably tracking us until they stumbled upon the valley, I think they were trying to alert their neighbours of our presence here. Fortunately, they weren't given much of an opportunity to do that."

Marrick laughed too. "Communication never was a strong point of theirs. I tell you if scaleskins ever stopped fighting each other and learned to get along, then the future for us humans would be a lot bleaker."

"From what I can tell they have been working on it," Darroch replied grimly.

Jaeger felt a shot of nerves run through him when he realized the peril they had been in. "That group of newcomers were only an hour behind us, they would have caught us by the end of the day if we hadn't led them to that massacre."

"Now you see why I drove everyone to push on, it will be the same once we cross that river. These scaleskins will be constantly around it, and once they cross our tracks we will be followed until beyond the borders of this jungle. We should continue while we can."

The company drifted back from the trees for a few minutes, until they were well back from valley's edge. Again, they spread out so that everyone could move freely amongst the dense trees, but their pace was not so urgent anymore. They continued steadily, conserving energy in anticipation for the long dash they felt would begin any minute now. Small plants were growing again around the height of their ankles despite the constant destruction of the scaleskins moving through the area. The soil here was rich and moist and they were coming closer to the river.

Soon they could hear the river running along its bed, and once again Darroch led them with a stealthy caution that everybody emulated. On the brink of exhaustion now, Jaeger could feel the tension in the jungle build to the highest it had been since he had entered. He noticed that he was now taking shallow half-breaths in his desire to remain silent, and was beginning to feel a debt building up from the lack of oxygen this caused. He opened his mouth as wide as he could to maintain his silence while breathing deeply, and at that moment Marrick looked back at him, raising an eyebrow. Jaeger froze and looked sideways back at Marrick with his mouth still open, trying not to laugh.

It was dead quiet now, too quiet to try to explain to Marrick what he was doing, so Marrick just shook his head while suppressing his laughter. They were only a couple of trees back from the desolate stretch to the river, and Darroch was now slipping from one tree to the next, warily assessing if there were any scaleskins along it in either direction. No one dared move as far forward as him and instead just glanced through the gaps in the trees ahead while they waited for him to give the all clear.

"Looks clear enough to me" whispered Gregcobble-greybeard, it wasn't much of a whisper though and his deep throaty voice crept into the words; 'looks' and 'enough'.

No-one replied and all eyes fixed on Darroch who seemed to be taking a long time, considering he only had to look left then right. He was no longer slipping from tree-to-tree as he walked back to everyone, which was a good sign that he didn't think they were in any immediate danger.

"This looks like as good-a-chance as any to cross that river. We can only hope that that little incident back there will keep everybody's attention at the eastern end of the valley until we are long on our way."

"Where are we going to cross?" greybeard spoke up again, "I'm guessing you want us to swim by the look of things."

"Indeed I do, and here looks as good a place as any. The water doesn't appear to be deep, and with good fortune; even you should hopefully be able to wade the entire way my stout friend."

"Ha stout, very diplomatic commander!" the robust greybeard laughed, patting his large stomach.

"I thought so too," Marrick grinned slyly.

Gregcobble-greybeard seemed un-offended by this and continued to laugh. "You'll be proud to sport a waistline like this yourself one-day, you men are built so lightly it's a wonder you don't blow over in the breeze."

"I could only dream of living so long and growing so wide little-father," Marrick agreed extravagantly. His humour was received well enough, and Jaeger noted that Marrick treaded the fine line between offence and humour well.

"If you two are done flirting, I would like to lead everyone across as quickly as possible" Darroch interrupted. The entire group fell silent as they were drawn back to the tense task at hand.

They crept forward in pairs at first, reaching the cover of the sheer banks of the river then ducking below. Once the entire company was gathered below the dry banks of the river, the first of them began the crossing. Marrick who was tallest, went across with Gregcobble-greybeard, holding their removed tunics and empty packs high above their heads as they waded. This turned out to be unnecessary, as the slow-moving water line never reached above the greybeard's waist.

After a few more people had reached the other side, Gramcobble looked across the river at those who had already made it, "well that is another piece of luck. Between this and the little tribal altercation earlier, I'd say the roll of the dice seems to have fallen our way today."

"Yes it has, and if we were here a month later when the rains arrive, this slow trickle would be un-crossable without a bridge" Darroch added as he motioned that it was Jaeger's turn to cross with Bregan.

The water was not overly cold, but it made Jaeger feel unclean all over when he emerged from the other side. He dried his feet with his trousers, then reapplied the bandage on his foot that he had removed and held aloft while crossing. His foot was still raw and the exposure to the river water made it sting. He tried not to think about what the scaleskins must have done to that water to make a moving current so unwholesome. The rest of the company seemed to share Jaeger's distaste for the river, and the dwarves carefully held the tips of their beards out of the water as they crossed, cursing the scaleskins under their breath.

Once they had all accumulated on the other side and clothed themselves again under the cover of the western bank, the group again moved in pairs quickly from the bank to the dense trees forty yards away. After a few more painstakingly slow minutes, they were all hidden again and the tense crossing was behind them. For all of its other faults, the water had at least woken everyone up, and a look of freshness and excitement now buzzed through the company.

"Now the finish line is in sight people," Darroch cheered them on. "You must all still put on what speed you have, to reach the end of jungle. But if I am not too bold in saying, I think we have managed to navigate the most perilous stage of our journey without major incident."

And with that he set off, while everybody followed with the same sense of urgency they had felt when they left the path earlier in the day. The sun was nearing the horizon now, but the will to push on was accompanied by a general sensation of energy that hadn't been there before.

They kept up this pace until well after the sun went down, before taking a short spell to sit, rest, and close their eyes before midnight. Jaeger was just beginning to feel himself nod off as he sat against a tree, when he was woken by the faint winding of horns, combined with what could have even been the baying of wolves just on the edge of his hearing. He leapt to his feet and found everyone else already standing with weapons drawn.

Darroch's sword was still sheathed as he knelt to the ground, striking his flint and tinder. "The hunt has commenced" he said in an ominously calm voice. "We might as well light torches to guide us now, the wolves will know where to find us by scent anyway. Are there any objections to resuming our march again early?"

Nobody spoke. A few of the others went about lighting makeshift torches in the deafening silence. To Jaeger it seemed as though every scratch of flint ripped through the night like the screeching of birds, and he was loath to speak for fear of how loud that might also be.

"Forgive my questions Darroch, but the last time we lit fire in here it brought us nothing but trouble."

"You don't need to be forgiven for your opinion Jaeger. One mind, however sharp, can overlook faults in a plan, but an entire company of minds who are comfortable voicing their opinions, will usually think of everything. As for the fire, this time there is nothing more that it can attract, we have already been found, we just haven't been caught."

"What about any Scaleskins that may be in the vicinity or ahead, they too would have heard the horns and will probably be hunting for us too"

Darroch gave Jaeger a sly grin "Oh don't worry I already have planned for them," and he pulled a leaf from a nearby plant then let it drop. It blew towards Jaeger as it dropped to the ground.

"We have rounded the top of a hill tonight and there is a strong wind blowing east out there above the trees," he said pointing to the sky, before deliberately thrusting his lit torch into a faggot of wood he had piled against a tree. "We don't have much time to waste playing at this game so spread out and set light to as much as you can north and south of here."

Jaeger fought his natural instincts as a farmer to complain that fires should never be lit in a strong summer breeze, but the purpose of this fire *was* to let it burn out of control. He looked across at Marrick who had already set a healthy blaze twenty yards to the south.

"This feels a lot like vandalism," Jaeger called above the roaring of the fires.

"You have good instincts Jaeger" he mocked. "Remember, everything is in league against us in here." Jaeger laughed with him this time and drew a few long sticks from the fire Darroch had started, then walked in a perpendicular line to the direction they were marching, setting light to anything that would burn.

Everybody drew back from the arson they had just perpetrated as the fire began to gain momentum, blazing out in a large radius from its fuel source. Darroch shouldered his light pack and walked backwards assessing the fire.

"That should do it, and hopefully buy us more time if it moves in the right direction. Might even take a few scaleskins with it if we're lucky," he added almost as an afterthought.

Jaeger still felt uncomfortable about what they had just done, but another point occurred to him. "Our trail will be lost in that fire, won't it?"

Darroch grinned broadly, "and you were beginning to suspect that I just liked burning things Jaeger."

They moved steadily for a couple of hours after their last break, but now the march had reverted almost to a stagger. The rush of energy they had run on since they lit the jungle had worn off, and the iron determination to continue was not enough to ignore the physical strain that their sleepless march was causing. They were now in the early hours of the morning and nearly twenty-four hours had passed since they had properly slept. Jaeger thought back to how convinced he was at the clearing that he couldn't have taken another step, that was hours ago.

He was tripping on snags constantly now, and was covered in nasty scratches on his cheeks and neck from the fingers of branches that he wasn't spotting. He considered that he could easily catch one in the eye at this rate, before realizing that he didn't even care anymore and went back to walking without the use of his mind. Darroch gave no indication that he intended for them to halt soon.

The night was almost past and they were still marching when the sky began to subtly change colour from black to a navy blue. Jaeger knew from all his mornings of waking before sunrise on the farm, that the sky would turn lighter shades of blue swiftly now, before the sun itself soon coloured the horizon.

Not a single member of the company spoke or looked across at each other, as they continued stumbling forward with their heads down. Jaeger was just beginning to entertain the idea of sitting down where he was and telling everyone to go on, when the plants behind them began rustling aggressively. Adrenaline and fear ran through his body for a moment and he drew his sword. A few moments passed without further noise and he let his sword arm drop, almost forgetting why he had drawn it in the first place.

The sound of a blade scraping against something was now breaking the silence, and he realized he was limply holding his weapon as it dragged across the ground. It took a conscious effort to put it back into its sheath and just as he raised it to do this, he heard another rustle in the plants a few yards to his right this time.

Everyone heard it now and the sound of their weapons drawing woke Jaeger from his daze. He heard more movement in the heavy vegetation to his left, before the sound of creatures overtaking the company could then be heard all around them.

"Come together!" Darroch barked, and Marrick ran to the back of the circle they had formed to join the defense at the rear.

Jaeger found himself standing side-by-side next to Gregcobble-greybeard. Despite the excitement, he still felt exhausted and clenched the muscles throughout his body to wake himself up. The age-weathered dwarf grinned at him fiercely.

"Come boy, sleeping is for people who don't have better things to do, a young man of your age shouldn't want for such luxuries." As invalid as the statement was, Jaeger actually felt better, and again focused his will on the imminent battle that was encircling them.

For a moment all the movement around them stopped, before a number of wolves began baying on the other side of their circle behind Jaeger. He glanced back over his shoulder to see, just as the plants in front of him burst apart with goblins hooting war-cries from the backs of their wolves. The charge hit them with brutal impact, and their side of the circle collapsed under the weight of the mounted charge.

Jaeger had stabbed forwards blindly and his blade was now embedded in the chest of the wolf that had leapt at him. It rolled off him crushing the rider, and he took the opportunity to leap back to his feet while he could. Beside him, Gregcobble-greybeard was being mauled alive by a wolf as he thrashed about, pinned beneath another that he had just beheaded. Rage and desperation, controlled Jaeger's movements as he took two long running strides and tackled the scaleskin sitting atop the wolf. It had been stabbing wildly with its spear at the old dwarf, who was already wrestling desperately to protect his face from the wolf's jaws.

Jaeger landed on the other side of the giant wolf and heard the wind escape from the rider's lungs as it crunched to the ground and broke his fall. He struck while his foe was stunned, tearing its metal helmet off then planting the helmet heavily into its face. For a moment the scaleskin had tried to protect itself with its hands, but they fell back to the ground before they could help after two heavy blows had knocked it unconscious.

Jaeger saw his sword lying beside them both and snatched it up, desperate to kill the beast that was still mauling his companion before it was too late. A moment later he brought his sword down with every ounce of strength he had, striking the wolf on the neck and severing its head completely. As the enormous beast collapsed sideways away from Jaeger, he got a clear view of Gregcobble-greybead lying on the ground attempting to bring himself to his feet.

In the short moments it had taken Jaeger rescue him, Gregcobble-greybeard had sustained large gashes along the length of his forearms from where the wolf had chewed on them as he fended its jaws off. His face was also bleeding from a nasty bite mark, but it was his chest that inhibited him the most. Jaeger raced to his side.

"Don't try to get up or you will bleed to death" Jaeger instructed, pulling him free from the dead wolf, although the advice seemed foolish with all the fighting going on around them.

"I can't very well lie here in the middle of a warzone boy! Help me up."

Jaeger slipped his head under the greybeard's right arm on the opposite side from his wound and lifted. The stout dwarf let out a vicious grunt as he dragged himself to his feet, and ignoring the excruciating pain it was causing, Jaeger ran Gregcobble-greybeard to a tree outside the circle of combat and sat him down. He didn't have time for words and simply turned to charge back into the fray.

Marrick and Darroch had worked their way to the center of the heated fighting now and somehow had attracted the attention of the majority of their foes, while the rest of the company fought in one-on-one combat around them. There were three mounted goblins surrounding the pair trying to break past their weapons, and another three on foot trading rapid blows, leaving them with only enough time to block. Marrick spotted Jaeger running to help and leapt forwards in a spinning motion, tempting one of the scaleskins to charge in from the side. Marrick's pirouette ended with his sword striking the scaleskin from the opposite direction it was expecting, cutting obliquely into its collar-bone towards the sternum.

The rider in front of Marrick had also misjudged his movement and ended up running straight through the now mortally wounded scaleskin that had been flung into its path. Jaeger ran his sword through the only scaleskin that Marrick had left himself vulnerable to, and Marrick then slashed the final rider and wolf, slaying them both as they tried to untangle themselves from the collision. He then turned with Jaeger to even the fight on Darroch's side.

Darroch was still blocking a flurry of swords and spears, but seemed untouchable. He had managed to open a large cut on the nose of the wolf directly in front of him. His arms were moving so rapidly under the relentless onslaught that they could barely be seen. Marrick ran up next to Darroch and engaged the wolf and rider trying to take advantage of him from the flank, Jaeger however had found a great deal of efficiency in slaying his enemies from the side and quickly ran a wide arc from where he stood until he was behind the attackers. As he ran past, he casually lopped off the raised sword-arm of a random scaleskin, it howled in pain before being run-through by the fallen soldier it had been planning to execute.

Jaeger now stood behind the three scaleskins that fought with Marrick and Darroch. The two riders were still mounted on their wolves and the third scaleskin had worked its way to Darroch's flank. Darroch's situation had improved when Marrick had joined him, but they still didn't have the upper-hand against the numerous enemies before them, Jaeger intended to change that. He rushed forward slashing the upper back leg of the wolf in the center fighting Darroch, a couple more paces took Jaeger to the scaleskin that was exploiting his captain's flank.

The injured wolf flung its rider forwards from the saddle in agony and Darroch caught it with the point of his sword as it flew towards him. Jaeger continued raining heavy, unskilled blows on his opponent, knocking its sword to the ground before he stepped forward and brought his weapon down on its helmet as it tried to turn and run. The scaleskin fell twitching to the ground and Jaeger mercifully finished it off.

As he wheeled around, Darroch and Marrick already had the last rider between them. In one synchronized movement, Darroch ran the wolf through while Marrick lunged forward stabbing through the rider's defences. Both rider and wolf fell to the ground incapacitated.

The three of them then made quick work of what was left of the attack, overwhelming each enemy they encountered as they moved from one skirmish to the next. When there were no more live scaleskins or wolves in the vicinity, Darroch looked around at the bodies littered amongst the vegetation of the jungle floor. Over half of the company now lay dead and the dozen victorious warriors, sported vicious-looking wounds that threatened to claim more lives as time wore on. Gregcobble-greybeard looked the worst.

Those few who had escaped relatively unscathed, were still exhausted from the battle. The short melee had followed a march in uncomfortable conditions with little food, which had already pushed them to the point of nearly collapsing. Only the primal instincts to stay alive had sustained the men during the fight, but now their fatigue was complete and overwhelming. The will to live had run its course, and Jaeger now felt like a deer that had been run into the ground by its predator. He would happily accept death now if it meant he could at least sit and rest.

The last remaining reserve of everyone's energy came out of respect for their fellow companions who had fallen in battle. The company worked together and gathered the sixteen dead men and dozen dwarfs to a patch of ground they had cleared. Jaeger's neighbour Barley was amongst the dead, whilst the others were part of Darroch's platoon. The dwarves, who had immediately formed a tight pack once the fighting erupted, had suffered comparably few losses considering the abundance of dead scaleskins and wolves they left around them.

They laid the bodies out in two rows, covering them with large jungle leaves for now. Darroch finished laying a large leaf on the last soldier, looking sober and grim. He still resisted the fatigue that was showing more evidently of everyone else's faces.

"We may have bought the right to a rest. From what I can guess those wolf-riders rode ahead to stop our escape, any scaleskins still pursuing us should be on foot and will have the task of picking up our trail outside the fire. Sleep now and we will honour our companions properly when we wake."

Everybody moved to clear themselves a place to lie down, although Jaeger felt happy to just drop where he was standing and sleep there. He was so physically, mentally and emotionally drained, that he was numb to the fact that a number of the men and dwarves who he had spent every hour of the last two weeks traveling with, were now dead. As he sat down, Jaeger saw that Darroch was not moving to rest, even now he was watching over his men and continued to go without sleep. Feeling a little shameful that he was not prepared to offer to take the watch, Jaeger closed his eyes and allowed sleep to take him.

It felt like he had not been asleep for more than a few minutes when Marrick shook Jaeger's shoulder to wake him. Out here he didn't have the luxury of gradually rising from sleep, so he sat up immediately. Looking around he saw that no one else was up either, as Marrick went from person to person waking them. Jaeger figured Darroch must have let Marrick take over the watch-shift at some point, and again he felt a pang of guilt set in, as he admired Marrick for making a sacrifice that he was hoping someone else would make.

"How long have we been asleep?" Jaeger asked, looking up at the sun directly above his head through the trees.

"It is just after midday now so I'd say at least

seven hours." Marrick didn't turn his head, as he moved through the company shaking people to wake them.

"I think that if you gave me three times that amount, I would take it all."

"I don't doubt it, but this rest will do you more good than you think it has right now."

"And you have had half as much sleep?" Jaeger enquired.

"More, Darroch didn't wake me up when he was supposed to."

"What about the scaleskins? Are they far behind us?"

"I couldn't say, I heard a few noises around us in the night but it seems they haven't caught us yet. They can't be far behind now though."

Jaeger moved to stand and found that many of the muscles in his body were so bruised and overworked that they now utterly refused to let him push them in certain directions. "My body feels like it was in a violent battle last night" he grunted, trying again to stand unsuccessfully.

"Your body doesn't lie. Except for the 'last night' part, it was actually this morning" Marrick informed him.

With a great deal of effort Jaeger rolled so that his feet were below his body, and slowly drew himself up until he was standing upright again. "I hope they don't catch us. This time I doubt I could defend myself."

Darroch moved through the company now, he looked from side-to-side assessing his warriors. "None of us are in acceptable shape for fighting today. If they do catch us, it will not end well. I hope you're all content with the rest you had."

Before they could leave, everybody picked themselves up and went about digging a grave for their fellow soldiers. There was a sense of urgency as they dug and Jaeger couldn't help but feel guilty again for rushing the funeral of his fallen friends, even though he knew it was necessary. Old Gregcobble-greybeard could not do any more than stand with one hand on his chest, and had to have sticks and other makeshift tools taken from him to prevent him from trying to help with the manual labour. How he would be able to march when they began was going to be the next challenge.

The bodies were placed in the shallow grave alongside each other and after being covered and reburied, Darroch had the trees on either side felled across the grave to make it harder to dig up again.

"I would have the bodies burnt to ensure nothing here can desecrate them, but it would only give away our location after we went to all that trouble of burning off the trail last night."

"Well, we can't stand here worrying about it anymore" declared Gregcobble-greybeard, "let's get going." He began taking staggered steps with the assistance of a branch he was using for a walking stick.

Darroch's look of exhaustion from the day before had not improved with his minimal sleep, and the wrinkles on his forehead became even more defined as he watched. "You are another matter. We will need to find some way to assist you if you are to keep up."

"If I am a burden then go ahead without me, I can at least vow to slay a few more of those scaly devils when they catch me," the old greybeard declared defiantly.

"Sometimes the body reaches a point where it won't do what the will demands of it. If anybody can take the burden, we will make a mobile seat and carry you with us"

"I will not accept it, there is no way you could carry me on a chair through these paths, just g-"

"Your opinion has been heard and we do not want to hear any more of it!" Gramcobble, interrupted with a surprising amount of authority in his voice for his age, he was Gregcobble-greybeard's nephew. "I will bear you and so will my brothers, your whiskers are now your heaviest feature Greybeard, we will barely notice the burden."

"Boy don't think that just because I have a few scratches on me I won't thrash you for taking that tone with me."

The threat didn't appear to be too genuine but Darroch stepped in anyways, apparently impatient at the time this was wasting. "Master greybeard, my company doesn't leave injured members behind. Your nephew's suggestion is a good one, now please allow them to carry you and prevent this debating from hindering us any further."

That settled the argument and Gramcobble and his brothers immediately set about fashioning straight branches and vines, then lashing them together. Within ten minutes Gregcobble-greybeard was held aloft as he rested his right hand on the front bearer's shoulder to balance himself, while the left was still clutching a padded bandage that had been placed across his wound.

The company was now eager to make off and

began their march with enthusiasm. Jaeger still felt stiff and was unable to bend his body from above his centre of gravity at all. The option of fighting again didn't seem possible. The pace they set was reasonable and Darroch organized the company to travel three abreast along the same track, so that by the time Gregcobble-greybeard and his bearers passed at the rear, most of the jungle obstructions were cleared.

A number of hours passed without any break. Occasionally the sturdy dwarfs at the back swapped sides to relieve the strain on one shoulder, but other than that they appeared unaffected by their burden. Jaeger marveled to himself at their endurance. He had spent months struggling to keep up while he worked for the Masons, but was still amazed at the apparent lack of physical limitations that dwarves had.

In the middle of his thoughts, he realized that the density of the jungle had been slowly easing, he looked at Marrick to his left and Bregan to his right and also realized that he was no longer shoulder to shoulder alongside them. In fact, the need for them to chop and clear a path for the procession at the back had also eased, and they were only occasionally forcing the vegetation out of the path now.

"I think we might have escaped the jungle. We're moving fairly fast" Jaeger commented optimistically.

Marrick drew himself out of whatever thoughts he was buried in and flashed Jaeger a sly grin, "we're not moving slowly." Jaeger immediately felt more at ease. Marrick's tendency towards these useless responses, was a sign that he was not troubled.

"I'll be happy when there is more certainty that

we have escaped," one of the soldiers commented cynically.

"It won't be a moment too soon if we do make it out" Marrick noted, "I don't think our stalwart friend at the back is faring too well, I can hear him wheezing from here."

Jaeger was too stiff to turn his head and look back at Gregcobble-greybeard from the front, and was left to imagine the condition that the aged dwarf might be in after the horrific wounds he had sustained in the attack.

6 CONTACT

As Darroch hastened the speed of the company over the light terrain, the silence became deafening. There was no sign or even rumour of any pursuit, but everyone could still remember clearly what had happened the last time the jungle had gone this quiet, just before their first encounter with the scaleskins. The jungle was thinner than ever, if it could still be called a jungle, and even the number of trees had begun to dwindle. Soon Jaeger found himself walking for consistent periods at a time, with the sun shining directly onto them uninterrupted.

The soil became dry and red, and the vegetation was more arid than it had been in the jungle, consisting mostly of bush, shrubs, and the odd shady tree. The grass was stiff and sharp, like dry hollow needles, and when it pricked the skin, it itched painfully as though the ends held some kind of poison. After half an hour of walking the new landscape, Jaeger was tingling and irritated all over his calves and ankles, whilst a numbness began to spread up through his legs.

"What are these bushes?" he complained. "The plant life here feels just as evil as it did in the jungle, they must be related. Even the dirt looks stained with blood."

"This vegetation is not related at all to the plants in the jungle, nor is it evil" replied Darroch, seeming strangely defensive of the grass as Jaeger eyed it off suspiciously. "Spïrïntesa the dwarves call that grass, and it is a product of the climate here, which has made it as hardy and resilient as the dwarves themselves. The colour of that dirt is the reason the dwarves thrive, they say it is laced with the same metals they mine in their mountains, and it is that which makes it red. Our stout companions could tell you more accurately how this is possible." He looked encouragingly at Gramcobble who had assumed the leadership amongst the dwarves now.

Gramcobble nodded appreciatively towards Darroch. "Aye captain, we mine the metal fërrum which is red in its raw form. The dirt here is saturated with traces of this metal, and in the days of our ancestors it is what led them here."

"I see the appeal," Marrick commented dryly, as he rubbed his hands together vigorously to clean off the accumulated red dirt.

"Don't complain. Your skin will absorb that stuff, it's good for the blood," Gramcobble chided.

"Is there anything this magic dirt can't do?" Marrick said with feigned enthusiasm.

By the time the evening began to approach, they had managed to escape a few miles out onto the plain.

The visibility was far better than it had been in the jungle, and every now and then Darroch would deliberately lead them over a hill or raised height of land, so that he could look back and check for any pursuit. The jungle was about five miles behind them and most of the land between could be seen from these vantage points. No enemies had emerged yet.

Gregcobble-greybeard looked terrible now. The wounds on his arms were oozing disgusting yellow pus, and he also appeared to be developing a fever. The stab wound to his chest still incapacitated most movement, but appeared to be improving the most out of all his ailments. Darroch surveyed the lands behind them and then looked thoughtfully at the greybeard.

"We at least have a couple of hours on any pursuit still and have earned a brief respite. My only concern is that now is not the time to take it, and if we were to, then we may find ourselves chased down by early tomorrow. The scaleskins will travel without torches so we cannot watch for them, and so I say we keep going through the night until the sun rises, then we can look back and accurately judge the distance between us."

Nobody spoke, but it was generally accepted that Darroch was right. Jaeger still felt rigid and vulnerable from the fighting, but the muscles in his body were hardened from constant hiking and did not fatigue like they would have a few weeks earlier. The dwarves re-shouldered their burden and started off, before the rest of the company followed behind with purpose.

At first during the night Jaeger had talked with

Marrick while they marched, before letting his mind shut down while his body continued. Occasionally he stumbled when his subconscious awareness began to stray, and in the early hours before dawn he struck up conversation with Marrick again when the stumbling became more frequent. As the shades of black in the sky lightened for the arrival of dawn, his exhaustion began to get the better of him. He was not yet pressed to the point they had reached in the jungle, and was grateful that the terrain didn't resist them anymore. Nevertheless, the signs of physical and mental stress were building, reminding him that he could not continue this forever.

In the distance he could see a larger hill rising up from the land, and it appeared that Darroch had been leading them in that general direction since he had spotted it.

"Once this sun rises enough, I will call a halt." Darroch announced, and they all pushed on harder, no longer conserving their energy.

The transition from dawn happened quickly once the sky began to lighten. So quickly that Jaeger didn't notice any difference until he was underneath blue sky and could see the landscape around him clearly. Darroch had led them to the top of a small hill and looked forward at the mountain still miles ahead, before turning back to assess what they had left behind. There was nothing moving as far as the eye could see, apart from the strange bipedal animals that grazed lazily on the Spïrïntesa, before bounding off with surprising pace towards another area to continue grazing again. Darroch appeared to be satisfied.

"There is still no immediate danger of a close

pursuit. We can set up camp behind this hill and rest, while one scout is posted here to watch for any movement. Any scaleskins should be detectable from miles away, which gives us a reasonable buffer to work with if we see them."

Jaeger stepped forward and offered to take first guard, determined not to become a passenger for this leg of the journey. He climbed a white-limbed tree atop the hill and laid back in its comfortable frame, while the rest of the company found shade on the other side of the hill to sleep. The sun slowly rose taking the chill out of the air, and he fought to keep his eyes open as he sat on watch, pushing himself to maintain his post for just an hour longer before waking someone else.

The sun was not far off noon when he could no longer find any way to keep his eyes open, and he finally began to slide down from the branch to take his sleep. When he dropped to the ground, his feet ached with pain after being wedged in the tree. The pain shot a burst of energy through his body, and he looked forward more clearly now to see a large crowd of black specks within the range of his vision. His heart began to race with a temporary surge of panic that would probably keep him awake for another few minutes before he crashed again, and he raced back down the hill to wake the company.

"I can see them!" he announced urgently as he shook Darroch from sleep. Un-phased, Darroch looked up at the height of the sun in the sky, then at Jaeger. His eyes showing that he had not been clouded by the sleep he had been woken up from.

"I expected that they would be visible by now,"

he replied calmly, "but why are you still on watch? You're making some pretty tall demands of your body, asking it to continue marching after all the time you have been awake."

"I didn't expect to see them and was just about to take my break now," Jaeger explained.

They moved to the top of the hill and looked back at the small army that was following them. A large cloud of red dust was rising from it and Darroch began to show a little more concern.

"They are moving swiftly, very swiftly, I wonder how long they have been marching at this pace. They too will be tired if they catch us and I don't think they will stop to rest. Come, you will have to continue without your break I'm afraid Jaeger."

When they woke the company up, everyone seemed slightly dazed but rejuvenated, and Jaeger angrily berated himself for foolishly not taking a break. Darroch once again laid out the plans before the march began.

"We will make for that large mountain for now, if they continue their pace and try to catch us today it will be a defensible spot. We can rest at the top while they tire themselves chasing, then throw rocks down at them while they climb." All Jaeger plucked from his speech was that they would be given another chance to sleep once they reached the top of that mountain in the distance.

Before they began, Jaeger entertained the idea of sleeping for just a minute or two while everyone got up and stretched, but was forced to admit to himself that he knew sleeping didn't work that way. He tried closing his eyes while standing and surprised himself by nearly falling asleep in the process, just catching himself from dropping like a felled tree at the last moment.

"That was impressive, you almost pulled it off," Marrick commented as he watched with amusement. "If you're looking for pointers on sleeping on your feet, you should ask the cows how they do it."

Jaeger looked at Marrick blankly trying to process what he had said, before Darroch came to his defence. "Our friend here is a victim of his own enthusiasm, he let everyone else sleep through the entire break."

Marrick laughed, "Jaeger have you ever heard the term; 'many hands make light work'? I thought you farmers lived by that motto."

"I forgot," Jaeger replied simply.

"Never-mind that now, we're all here for each other and I'm sure we can get you to that mountain," Marrick said encouragingly. And without another word he set off, taking Jaeger by the shoulders and facing him in the direction they were headed.

The march to the mountains was a blur to Jaeger. Around him everybody was talking as they walked, but he didn't bother listening or joining in at all. He just looked down and watched, as he put one foot in front of the other over and over again. His body didn't seem to be too sore anymore, or maybe it was just that his mind wasn't interested in listening to the pain. The only sensation he felt was the discomfort it caused him to continually resist the urge to sleep.

Every now and then Jaeger felt little surges of energy reach his brain, and for a few moments he would think that he had shaken off the tiredness. But these lasted for no more than a minute at a time. He discovered that he was falling asleep for short three or four second bursts while he walked, and that it was always after one of these micro-sleeps that he felt better. With this new revelation in mind, he became hopeful that he could continue the cycle until they reached the mountain.

At first the time had seemed to stretch on for an eternity while they marched, and the mountain didn't get any closer. But then the next thing Jaeger remembered, was standing at the base of the mountain looking up. He must have stopped looking up to check the distance, and had covered the rest of the march looking down for what seemed like only the blink of an eye. He even felt better rested now and was capable of climbing the steep slope without nodding off again.

"Feeling better now?" Marrick asked

"Yes actually, how did you know?" Jaeger replied in surprise.

"Well, you did fall asleep on your feet while you were marching. After you fell face first into a large bush; Bregan here and myself had to carry you with your arms around our shoulders the rest of the way while you slept."

"Oh" Jaeger paused putting everything together, "I'm sorry."

"Nothing to apologize for my friend, it wasn't actually that difficult. Just made the march a little sweatier in this heat, wouldn't you say Bregan?"

Bregan was sturdy set, yet he stood at the same height as Marrick, Jaeger wondered if his feet had even dragged against the ground between these two. "Pretty accurate, you didn't weigh much or slow us down if that's what you're worried about," the hulking soldier replied.

Jaeger still felt a little shameful, but was relieved that he would at least have enough wits about him to make the ascent. Most of the way they weren't forced to climb, although the incline was steep and many times Jaeger found himself walking with his hands as well as his feet. He also occasionally had to climb sections of rock for a few metres at a time, navigating them by the slim gullies running through that acted as steps.

They reached the top in less than an hour and there was still a fair amount of daylight left before the sun was due to set. Jaeger was thirsty and had already drunk the entire capacity of his water skin, which he had filled earlier that day at a creek they stopped next to. Darroch stood near the edge of the mountain top surveying the plain they had just crossed. The scaleskins had gained significant ground on them now and were no longer specks on the edge their of vision.

"They will reach the feet of the mountain in less than an hour," Darroch commented without looking back at Jaeger. "Take your rest now, we will wake you if we come under attack."

As soon as Jaeger found a shaded and clear patch of ground, he laid down and covered his eyes. He was pleasantly surprised to have found a large smooth rock the size of a small stable protruding from the mountain top, which he hid behind from the light of the sun. The ground around it was strangely smooth and clear of vegetation which he was also grateful for, as he considered the discomfort that the Spïrïntesa grass would have caused. With the exception of Marrick, Bregan, and a couple more from Darroch's platoon who were preparing for battle, most of the company joined Jaeger for another rest to add to the break they had earlier in the day.

He wasn't even sure that he had slept when he was woken. Once they had armed themselves, Marrick gathered everyone together at the edge of the mountaintop, before pointing out the large army that had amassed a few hundred metres from the foot of the small mountain. Jaeger stared down with dread; there must have been at least three hundred scaleskins below him in dozens of disorganized yet distinctively separate packs. As they approached the foot of the small mountain the army spread out, encompassing a large perimeter as they began the climb.

There would be no way to defend the mountain top from such a wide spread against such numbers, and the high ground advantage was starting to look less useful now. Still Darroch did not lose his composure and instead set about spreading the company into four groups about 30 yards or so apart from each other. Jaeger stayed in one of the central groups, and looked around to find that the rocks Darroch had collected, had been spread along the edge of the mountain top for easy use at many different points.

Minutes went past and Jaeger's heart raced for small intervals at a time, as he played out the most likely scenarios in his head. Soon the fastest scaleskins in the army had climbed above a steep section of rock a hundred yards below, and came into view in no particular formation. Jaeger hefted a couple of small stones that fitted nicely in his hand to throw, waiting until they were close enough for him to roll the larger ones down.

He hurtled one stone hard, wincing from the lingering soreness he still felt from his last battle, scowling as the throw sailed beyond the approaching scaleskins and disappeared beyond the steep section of rock they had just emerged from. A loud squawk of pain came from beyond his view and Marrick began howling with laughter.

"If we ever survive this, I'll be telling that tale at the next pub we go to. The mountain slope must be crawling with them below the drop-off!" Jaeger suppressed his own mirth at his unsuspecting victim's poor luck.

Darroch calmly stood looking down at the impending attack with a grim smile. "I believe we can take that as our cue to commence the bombardment. The frontrunners will regret their enthusiasm when they find that everyone behind them is either dead or unconscious."

And with that he took two small stones in his hands, throwing one hard and high to follow Jaeger's stone beyond their sight. The second stone he drew back in his hand behind his head, before launching it forwards and down with deadly precision, striking the nearest scaleskin square in the face about fifty yards below. The force of the blow knocked it backwards off its feet and sent it tumbling down the slope, clutching at its shattered face and howling in agony before it dropped off the rock-ledge and disappeared from view.

Jaeger began collecting more small stones to

throw. He tried to hit a couple of the closer targets that were in view, but they were too few for his poor accuracy, so he left them to Darroch while he lobbed his high and far, using his shoulders as much as he could to reduce the strain on his stiff and bruised body.

Occasionally the bombardment was rewarded with a howl of pain, but slowly and surely the numbers ascending rock-ledge became thicker and the attack pressed closer to home. Darroch barked the order to roll the larger boulders down the hill, which had a devastating effect. The boulders gathered great momentum and split open many ranks of scaleskins approaching, before falling below sight to inevitably claim even more unseen enemies.

The attack remained relentless and soon Darroch had to call the outlying groups together for their final stand, before the hand-to-hand combat commenced. The company concentrated one final hail of stones and boulders on the closest scaleskins, before drawing their weapons. Jaeger felt for Gregcobble-greybeard, who would be found alone by that large smooth rock on the middle of the mountain-top, when the company was finally overcome. He kicked one last large rock before drawing his own weapon, when they were all caught by surprise.

"So, you're the trouble makers who were kind enough to lure that filthy army onto our lands!" boomed an enormously broad-shouldered dwarf behind them.

The whole company spun around with weapons drawn to meet this new threat that had snuck up on them from behind. Nobody seemed to be able to process what had just happened or what the new arrival meant to them, but it hardly seemed like an appropriate time to stop and chat. The dwarf who had spoken, stood confidently between two other heavily-armoured dwarves, who were possibly his personal body guards. He seemed to be unaware of how close the scaleskins had come now.

"We are indeed. Luring them here wasn't intentional, but 'that filthy army' is now too close for us to talk my friend!" Darroch shouted from the back of the group that was now facing the dwarf.

He signaled to his men to turn back to the advancing scaleskins and prepared himself for the first wave of the assault. A handful of foolhardy mucks ahead of the main force, charged him from below and Darroch began to chop at them as each one came within range. The entire company joined in and slew the small pack without sustaining a single scratch from the encounter.

The newcomer swore and muttered something under his breath. He then drew a steel wrought horn from his side and winded it, producing a deep and rumbling tone that echoed out from the mountain. His bodyguards followed him forward to join the defence, and for a brief moment Jaeger gained hope from their fresh reinforcements, before looking back down at the massed army climbing towards them. Many of the Scaleskins would soon scale the top of the mountain onto the flats at various points that were not defended, and the company would then be overwhelmed by foes on level ground as well as from below them.

The first major wave crashed around their feet and everyone began chopping and stabbing at the enemies below. The scaleskins seemed unbothered by their tactical disadvantage and pressed the attack despite taking massive casualties for little gain. Jaeger mused that if only all of them came to fight at this one point, they might have a hope of winning.

As his thoughts were interrupted by another scaleskin coming within striking range, Jaeger saw out of the corner of his eye to the right, that the first of them had reached the flat and would soon charge their company's flank. It wouldn't be long until it was all over now, and Jaeger would never know where this strange dwarf and his two body guards had come from, or what possessed them to join the company in this doomed hour. The scaleskins were now pouring over the mountain top on either side, but they didn't charge the company's flanks, and instead seemed to stop for the first time bracing themselves.

A moment later, the war-cries of dozens of dwarves came from all around them, and a large heavily-armoured force swept onto the first ranks of scaleskins that had scaled the mountaintop, driving them back down the slope. For a moment everybody around Jaeger paused to look. At a glance there were at least fourscore dwarves nearby. They appeared to be highly trained soldiers, fighting shoulder-to-shoulder and pacing forwards in unison as they drove the attackers off the mountaintop.

The charge of the scaleskin army slowed. The majority of their force had cleared the rock-ledge a hundred yards below, and was now accumulating behind the frontline, who seemed less enthusiastic to continue their reckless assault on the higher ground now. Already over a hundred scaleskins had been slain by rocks and fighting, and only two thirds of the army remained, still taking rapid casualties. The dwarves hewed away at the ranks below them, while Darroch led his men relentlessly, slaughtering the scaleskins before them who seemed to have no idea of what alternatives they had to standing and dying.

Eventually after the combined forces upon the mountaintop had reduced their enemies' numbers to nearly match their own, the front ranks of scaleskins lost their nerve and fled back down the mountain. This of course was another cause for heavy losses, as the fleeing mucks and smaller slags bowled their fellow soldiers over, causing a living snowball effect comprised of terrified soldiers tumbling down the mountain-side. Tangled in each other's grasp as each tried to save themselves from being battered to death, the last of the scaleskin force disappeared from view.

A cheer rose from the dwarf army as their foes fled and died, and the heavy-set leader made his way over to Darroch, immediately recognizing who the commander was.

"Well met friend, it would seem that now may be a more appropriate time for introductions." Jaeger felt more at ease hearing the dwarf's friendly tone. Despite having just fought alongside each other, he knew that dwarves had an interesting set of principles and could easily have perceived the luring of a scaleskin army into their lands as a personal grievance.

"Well met indeed friend. My name is Darroch of the emperor's elite guard and leader of this company, we are in your debt for your timely arrival," Darroch added formally.

"That you may be, but the debt is already returned for providing us with such an effortless victory, we don't usually get to kill scaleskins. I am Grokhammer, general of my king's eastern borders."

Jaeger walked back from the edge of the slope a few paces and rested on his sword hilt while the two leaders continued to exchange pleasantries. He wondered if it would be appropriate to sit and rest, now that they had finally fought their way to safety. Forcing himself to remain standing, Jaeger didn't have to wait long before Grokhammer led the company back towards the centre of the mountain-top. He led them back to the great boulder that Gregcobble-greybeard had been resting against, but the wounded greybeard was nowhere to be seen.

"I see you have already found our wounded companion," Darroch observed without any note of concern in his voice. Jaeger felt like he was missing something.

"Aye we spoke briefly before coming to your aid, he is in our care below" Grokhammer replied, walking deliberately over to the large boulder. He then stopped and stamped his foot heavily on what appeared to be an exceptionally sharp rock pointing upwards.

The rock sank mildly into the ground, as a quiet click sounded high above the dwarf's head. Jaeger had expected a rock that sharp to pierce the soles of any boot under such force, but was now more interested in the clearly visible door that had opened outwards from what had previously appeared to be perfectly smooth rock.

"I can now invite you into the halls of our

eastern watch-post to rest," Grokhammer announced. "I myself am going to join the hunt for any surviving scaleskins left in our territory, but I will leave my attendant Brinwarden at your service until I return."

Darroch and the rest of the company thanked Grokhammer wholeheartedly as they passed him through the watch-post door, and Jaeger began counting the minutes it would take him to reach the nearest bed to sleep.

"Our resting quarters are in the third room to your left once you reach the bottom of the stairs," announced the warden that was waiting for them inside, he was looking at Jaeger in particular while he spoke. Jaeger gave his thanks and continued with the majority of the company down the stairs to the resting quarters, while Gramcobble requested to see his uncle before joining them.

When he entered, Jaeger saw the resting quarters were lined with low-lying beds that looked a little small for a tall man to comfortably fit in, but to Jaeger they were better than his own bed back home right now. A large urn of water stood on a table next to the entrance and a number of clean mugs were placed around it for the use of any inhabitants. Jaeger had forgotten his thirst until now and refilled his mug multiple times before he stopped drinking. He then picked out a bed and lay down. They had made it. They had passed the jungles alive and were now within reach of their destination, under the protection of a fortified hold in dwarf occupied territory. Jaeger closed his eyes feeling the most relaxed he had been since leaving West-Yield, and fell asleep.

7 HOSPITALITY OF THE DWARVES

When Jaeger woke there was nobody else around. His body had taken advantage of the long sleep to heal, and was now as stiff and tender as it had been the morning he woke after their battle in the jungle. He looked around the room, which was still messy with a number of used and unmade beds. There was no way to tell the time in the underground accommodation, but his eyes felt puffy and his head was clouded with the sensation that one gets when they have slept for longer than they are used to. As he got out of bed, Grokhammer's attendant entered the room.

"Hello Brinwarden, good morning." Jaeger choose his greeting carefully. He was hoping to find some gauge of the time based on Brinwarden's response.

"Good morning lad, you and your company have all slept at great length. Do you have any immediate injury concerns that need to be addressed?"

"Nothing but a little stiffness, where is

everyone? And how long have we slept if you don't mind my asking?"

"Not at all, your companions are above ground on the mountain-top mostly. It is nearly noon now and you went to bed at dusk last night, so you have slept for nearly three quarters of an entire day. As you can see you are the last to wake, but not by much. I will show you to our food stores before you are free to wander if you would like?"

"Yes thank you, are we free to wander anywhere in this guard-post?" he was curious about how much their hosts trusted them.

"Anywhere above the third sublevel, Grokhammer does not have the authority to invite humans or any other outsiders into our underground highway. Come this way."

Brinwarden led Jaeger to the food stores, where he was provided with all the food he could eat and carry. They were well stocked with salted porks in their cool-room, as well as many cheeses, breads, nuts and berries, all farmed in their mountain ranges further to the west. After eating a small meal with Brinwarden who only took some salted pork and cheese, Jaeger packed the rest into a basket to take with him. Brinwarden then led him through the military post and showed him back up to the large boulder exit on top of the mountain.

Outside, half of the company was moving about atop the flat of the small mountain. Marrick was with them walking beside Darroch, investigating details of the battle yesterday.

"You look like you need more than one good-night's sleep," he noted as Jaeger limped his way over to them.

"True, although it does feel very good not to be sleep-deprived anymore."

"It can't feel bad," Marrick grinned.

They did very little that day. Jaeger washed himself for the first time in weeks and then checked up on Gregcobble-greybeard. The grim dwarf was receiving plenty of treatment for his injuries and was already looking much better after being cleaned up. Later on, he went outside again and ate a full lunch under some trees on the mountain, before returning underground to rest again and relax.

By the end of the day, the various dwarf hunting parties had returned with Grokhammer, reporting that many of the surviving scaleskins had been tracked and slain. Only a small few had tirelessly outrun the dwarves and managed to escape back to their jungles.

Grokhammer spoke at length with Darroch in the evening and appeared to be more open-minded to the emperor's proposal than anybody had expected.

"Things are not at all well in the mountains either," he informed Darroch at the dinner table. "We have noticed similar trends in the roachkin attacks. They show more persistence and organization now, which has concerned us all greatly. We have always been grossly outnumbered by them, but until now they have been no match for us tactically. The High King may have to consider some policy changes if we are to weather the rising tides."

"For this reason, we have passed through the scaleskin jungles to reach you, so that I could propose a coordinated alliance to the High King." Darroch pressed his intentions.

"That will have to be approved by the High King then, as much as I like the concept. I cannot even permit your use of the underground highway between here and our stronghold. We will escort you there above ground, where hopefully your plans will be received with enthusiasm."

The two leaders discussed many other things over the dinner table, and were still sharing news of their own realms when the company retired to the resting quarters for the night. With the exception of the exposed and infected flesh underneath his foot, it took Jaeger only a couple of days to recover from the journey. The entire company stayed on for a full week after their arrival, while Gregcobble-greybeard recovered from the worst of his wounds and infection.

During this time, the old dwarf suffered from a high fever and his arms were immobilized within their bandages. When the company did depart, he was advised not to leave his hospital bed to see them off, for the sake of the spear wound in his chest which had been stitched up nicely and was just beginning to heal.

Each of them saw him off one by one from his quarters, before assembling on top of the mountain with Grokhammer's entire regiment. He had sent word via the underground to his king requesting reinforcements, which allowed him to take his own men to escort Darroch and his now travel-hardened company. Jaeger was curious about how far the distance could be, if a message could pass one way and troops could return the other, all in less than a week underground. But he was informed that above ground it would take more than that just to make the trip one-way.

It actually took them seven days in full to complete the march above ground, moving slowly with approximately a hundred dwarfs and Darroch's men trailing behind the two leaders. This stage of the journey was far more pleasant without the threat of a violent death nipping at their heels, and Jaeger took more time to appreciate the surroundings. He had developed a knack for stepping in the spaces between the sharp Spïrïntesa grass plants now that he was traveling on a full night's sleep, and had decided that these harsh plains were definitely not the evil that he had made them out to be initially.

The plants, trees, and animals, all displayed a rugged defiance of the elements that Jaeger admired. He felt that their resilience epitomized the inner strength that all living things had within them when forced to adapt, and he now understood the appeal of the open road. There was a sense of mateship that developed from living out here beyond the borders of civilization. A man could trek these lands in silence for decades, with no other purpose than to merely spend time with himself and the world he lived in.

As the evening set at the end of the seventh day, the path they were following tapered and delved into the mountain side like a roofless tunnel. The dwarves had deliberately carved the approach to their gates out of the mountainside, so that any army foolish enough to assault the fortress gates would be hemmed in between impenetrable walls on either side. The path was still thirty yards wide, which easily accommodated the small force that was now walking it to arrive comfortably, and as they pushed deeper, the dwarf escort separated from Darroch's company allowing them to walk ahead. When they reached the colossal roller-gate, it was already open to welcome them in.

They walked through the gates and into the underground, past motionless dwarf soldiers wearing polished armour that shone in the reflected sunlight. The light was amplified from an unknown source deep in the roof above. Darroch lectured them while they walked like it was a tour.

"The dwarves are the most sophisticated race on the continent for craftsmanship. Their weapons and inventions led the world in both warfare and infrastructure before our peoples were separated, and many of our greatest feats in industry were based on their ancient designs. Even the dwarven citizens that live on The Plateau protect the secrets of their craft from us almost fanatically.

"It is said that the Elves have their physical arts, and perfect themselves in both body and mind until they can move like water around their enemies in battle. While dwarfs perfect their buildings and weapons, giving them an advantage over any enemy before they even take to the battlefield."

"What about humans? What defines us?" Jaeger already knew the factors that defined other races of the world, but couldn't place how humans fitted into the grand scheme of things.

"Us humans? I suppose we take after the dwarves mostly as a result of the closer ties we have with them. Some may say we are without any skill or feature, but I believe we are defined by our balance and adaptability. We have smoothed the edge off the extremes of other races, and have integrated them comfortably in the middle."

"Actually, I'm pretty sure we stole that trait from the halflings in our northern province" Marrick added. Darroch just laughed and continued to follow his way past the underground halls from the entrance and back under the open skies within the stronghold.

The main citadel of Aridhold had been carved into the top of the enormous mountain. Here, markets, taverns, industry and housing all sat underneath the open skies, but far above and unreachable to the lands below. The outer ring of the citadel was a circle of high walls that retained the external sheer cliffs of the mountain outside. Jaeger noted several enormous entrances to underground levels below, but it appeared that the majority of the population resided in the fortified heights of the stronghold.

At length, the company was greeted across the open circle of the fortress by a large bodyguard of dwarves. They marched in unison behind a wisened old greybeard, a king who bore his crown with the weight of all the responsibilities and burdens that came with it.

"Welcome to Aridhold, I am king Borgisliege but you can just call me Borgis. We received brief details of your travels and mission nearly two weeks ago now and are eager to hear your counsel."

"Thank you Borgis. I am Darroch, captain of this company and a commander of the emperor's elite guard," Darroch replied with perfect formality. "We too are eager to share counsel, we have survived a perilous journey to find you. Our meeting with Grokhammer near your outpost was timely."

"That I have also been told" Borgis grinned. "A wing of the palace has been prepared and is ready to receive your men before anything else."

"Much appreciated" Darroch bowed. "Our fortunes have improved greatly since we found your people."

"Then hopefully this meeting is a sign that all fortunes will now improve. I will show you to your quarters within the palace."

Jaeger already felt good about things. The king had conveyed his welcome personally and appeared to be comfortable speaking directly to Darroch and the company, a trait which didn't fit Jaeger's normal perception of dwarf customs. Clearly there was a lot going on in the Dwarven Ranges also, if their Kings were willing to forgo custom and take immediate counsel with uninvited guests.

The quarters allocated to the company were a marvel. Jaeger had heard that dwarf kings lived well, but until seeing the inside of the palace, he hadn't known that many of the luxuries in there had even existed. Each guest had their own room, which opened into a long hall many stories above the city grounds. These rooms must have been designed especially for large companies, because not only did each open out into the same long hallway on one side, but they also opened into a passage on the other which led to the visitor's private washrooms.

The washrooms consisted of a large pool in the centre which increased in heat as bathers swam to one end, until the water was near boiling. At this end, there was a row of tap-controlled showers, which could each be adjusted in temperature individually using a large lever that pulled left to cool, and right to heat the temperature of the water pouring in. Also attached to his room, Jaeger had access to a small privy, which could be rinsed with boiling water simply by loosening a tap that was within reach of anybody using the service. Running water was also supplied to a small basin for use afterwards.

After making full use of all these facilities, Jaeger dressed back into some plain, clean, clothes that had been made in preparation for Darroch and his company's arrival. The clothes had been waiting neatly folded on every bed when they were first shown to their rooms. Jaeger now felt the most comfortable and well-rested that he had in a long time, and was already looking forward to a relaxing night's sleep and all the healing it would bring. He lay down on the bed enjoying the soft mattress, and had to coax himself for many minutes into sitting back up to leave for dinner, which was getting closer.

After coming dangerously close to falling asleep in his new surroundings, Jaeger finally sat up and put a pair of sandals on. They had been provided especially for him, so as not to interfere with the new bandage that was wrapped around his infected foot. He left the room and made his way to the dining hall he had been shown earlier, to join anybody else who might be there now.

The hall was enormous and already full with dwarves and most of Darroch's men. A series of long hardwood tables were arranged along the centre of the hundred-yard-long rectangular hall, with two large fires burning opposite each other against the walls halfway down. Jaeger found a number of spare seats had been left for himself and other members of the company at a sturdy hardwood table at the end of the hall. The seats were quite near to the King and his household, where a roast buffet had been arranged to pick from. Jaeger tried to maintain his composure while he took chicken, mutton and a number of cooked vegetables for his plate and filled his tankard with a dark, rich-looking ale.

The beer was particularly strong and took some getting used to. With every sip Jaeger took, his appetite for both food and ale increased. The aroma it produced was equally strong, allowing him to savour the taste of everything he ate with a new appreciation that he had never felt before when dining. By the time the entire company had cleared their plates, they were all laughing merrily together and now felt at ease amongst the unfamiliar hosts they dined with.

Once he had cleared his plate and satisfied his hunger entirely, Jaeger leant back in his chair to allow the meal to settle. His head swam from the effects of the strong ale and he chatted away pleasantly with Bregan next to him who had also finished eating. At the head of the table, Darroch was next to King Borgisliege engaging in a similar tone of conversation, as the two shared tidings of the separate realms they spoke for that had been brought back together again tonight.

"It's beginning to quiet down a little now," Bregan noted as the dull roar of the hall decreased. Many of the dwarves at other tables were carrying their tankards away to continue drinking privately amongst their clans.

"I'd imagine that they have been told to give the king a certain degree of privacy, so that he can hold counsel with Darroch" Jaeger replied, looking at the two leaders shift from serious to merry and back again as their conversation changed.

"Is it always their custom to make counsel with ambassadors while heavily inebriated?" Bregan asked incredulously, he was relatively unfamiliar with dwarf culture and was still surprised by some of the stark contrasts to humans.

"That is precisely their customs. Rarely will a dwarf hold serious talks with someone sober, it is considered to be a sign of mistrust."

"But what if they make poor decisions because they were drunk at the time?"

"Then they will realize this when they are sober and get drunk again to discuss new plans," Jaeger laughed.

"Really?"

"Yes actually, to the best of my knowledge."

Bregan pondered the concept for a while. "That actually makes better sense than I thought it would," and they both laughed and drank and continued talking.

Eventually the hall emptied until there was only Darroch's company and the king's household left. Everybody remaining shifted their seats towards the head of the table so that they could all take part in the post-feast counsel. A few of the household dwarves excused themselves from the table temporarily and indicated to the guests that if they also needed to do so, now was the appropriate time to take a short break. Once everybody was back, a silence fell in the room and the king addressed the audience before him.

"I have spoken at length about the many goings-on of our two peoples with Commander Darroch, and both the details of your journey and situation on The Plateau are better known to me now for having done so. But we have left the main purpose of your travels until now, and so it is that I ask you what proposal the emperor makes, that can benefit both our peoples in worsening times?"

Darroch acknowledged each member of the king's household as he responded. "Times are indeed worsening and I believe the new wave of attacks we have repelled against the scaleskins on The Plateau, are somehow linked to your growing problems with the roachkin in these mountains."

"Aye" the dwarf king agreed. "The dwarves have little to worry about from the scaleskins of the jungles, no matter how hostile they become. Our defenses are too sophisticated for them to breach and we do not have many vulnerable settlements beyond our walls like you do. Our main trouble comes from the roachkin, who always find new ways to tunnel through our fortifications or ambush dwarven miners and farmers. The roach-peoples that assail us in our strongholds have also increased their attacks, both in frequency and tactics."

Darroch nodded as if this was a cue for his next point, "I believe that there is more similarity in these attacks than just that, although I have not had much information to support this theory until now. You say that the attacks have also been more cunning of late. The scaleskins on our borders have begun using tactics that they never understood before."

"Yes, I would agree that this is true with the roachkin also," Borgisliege acknowledged.

"This is what concerns the emperor. With further investigation, we believe a link between these attacks may reveal the source of our new threat, and therefore improving communications between our peoples is what the emperor proposes. I have come here to request on his behalf, that the underground highways which you have long kept secret, be made available to just a few of our most trustworthy agents. At your own discretion of course."

The entire hall sat silent. It did not seem like an unreasonable request or a bad idea to Jaeger, but he knew that dwarves were stubborn with their secrets. For centuries the magical blacksmiths, or 'runesmiths' of the dwarves, had not shared their secrets with anybody but their most dedicated apprentices and heirs. Even then many would still die before passing on the recipes to their magical runes.

"Regretfully I do not have the authority to grant this permission, and even though it may be long overdue, we do not lightly share such valuable assets with peoples outside our realm. I will refer this request on to the High King so that he may consider its value, but I would vouch that you will not be successful and I believe our only hope of steady communications, would be to clear the jungles between us."

Darroch nodded without surprise and did not look disappointed. He must have known that he was unlikely to receive any other response when he started out, but somehow Jaeger didn't think that Darroch would lead a mission through the jungles just to be

123

turned down. At length he spoke.

"We expected this to be the case when I began this quest. You say that you do not lightly share your assets and you are right in not doing so. Unfortunately, even if we could clear the jungles and deserts between The Plateau and your mountains, I do not believe that we could hold any lowlands to keep the way open. I made this journey to let your people know that even though the decision is yours to make, we feel that these times may be desperate enough to justify at least asking."

Borgis set his tankard down and looked directly at Darroch with a new level of respect. "I am honoured that you came this far just to tell us that. I will refer the request to the High King immediately, it will reach him by this time tomorrow and return shortly after. Until then you are all invited to stay here with us, and as long as you would afterwards also."

The day following King Borgisliege's banquet went by quietly. Jaeger ate breakfast and lunch with his company, but spent most of his time relaxing and recovering his body from its hurts and tiredness in his room. The raw wound on his foot already looked better now that it was cleaned and properly dressed and Jaeger sat around prodding at the different muscles in his body that were tight, massaging them casually if they were not too tender.

Looking in the mirror after bathing, he noticed for the first time how much the short period of traveling had changed him physically. Although his work had always kept him fairly fit, he was now leaner yet at the same time more muscular than ever before. He felt stronger both physically and mentally from the perilous journey he had just survived. He also considered how much he had learnt about himself not just from travel, but his intimate experiences with violence too. He had now fought four deadly skirmishes in his life time and three of these had taken place in the last fortnight.

Of these three, he isolated one as being the best example to learn from; the ambush they had sprung on the unsuspecting scaleskins after first entering the jungle. In every other fight he had fought out of instinct and desperation, recklessly throwing his body into his foes to save his own life and others. But in that first ambush when he had seen each attack coming, he had shown swordsmanship, working his enemies' swords past him as they swung, then striking back when they were vulnerable. Jaeger tried to retrieve his exact memories from the fight and went through the motions in his head.

If he was going to pursue a life of quests and battles, he would need to hone his skills with the sword. He decided that he would approach Marrick for training in the coming days.

By evening, everybody was well rested and eager to receive word at dinner from the king. Gramcobble and the rest of the dwarves had been out exploring the stronghold and becoming acquainted with the local populace. He had now received word from his uncle, who was recovering well from his injuries and was no longer bedridden back at the Eastern outpost where they left him.

King Borgisliege chose not to make them wait until after dinner for the response he had received from the High King that day, and once everyone was seated, he informed them immediately. He cleared his throat a little and looked for a moment across the table at his guests before he began.

"I am sorry to say his high majesty has informed us that the dwarf kingdom still cannot justify revealing our underground passages which has remained one of our greatest secrets for so long. It has been with great difficulty that we have managed to maintain our subterranean highways from being discovered and infiltrated by the roachkin, who primarily use tunneling to break into our strongholds. Opening them to outsiders, however trustworthy, would jeopardize our position."

Darroch once again did not display any outwards signs of disappointment and nodded respectfully at the king's decision. "I too am sorry to hear this news, but we understand your desire not to place this great asset at risk. I would however ask that you allow us to stay here for a week before we begin our return journey, there is still much that can be gained from being here with you and learning from each other."

Borgis grinned and lifted his tankard, becoming merry once again. "My friend you and your company are welcome here as long as you would stay." He raised his drink to clash heavily with Darroch's, and with that the matter seemed put behind them.

As the revelry began, Jaeger tried to take his mind off the thought of traveling back through the jungle on his way home. He suspected that the success of their first passage through the jungles was mainly due to the element of surprise, although even then they had lost over half their company. Darroch was a cunning and calculating leader, but much of his plan to pass through the jungles was based on moving quickly before being discovered. The densely vegetated terrain would now be teeming with scaleskins, wary of intrusion into their domain if the company wanted to return that way again.

Everybody else was focusing on the feast before them, becoming merry with food and ale, and Jaeger tried to put his gloomy thoughts aside while he remained in the comforts of the dwarven stronghold. He sat back quietly and listened, while the dwarves from his company discussed plans to document their visit, recording advancements that they had observed, since the time when all their expatriates were cutoff on The Plateau.

8 FOR YOUR CONSIDERATION

Situated along the western border of The Plateau in a small town called Varnak, Sharnard sweltered under the relentless midday sun. He felt the heat in summer more than he used to when he was forty years younger. Back then he was a strong teenager without an ounce of fat on his body, who could work through the full heat of the day after all the other men had either retired to the shade for a break or fainted.

As he sat down for a cold drink, his thoughts went back to the heatwave of 1464. One of his father's new farmhands had refused to stop working unless Sharnard did. He was a couple of years older than Sharnard had been, and had a hint of ego and stubbornness because of this. His name was Ferandis.

That day, Ferandis stood out in the summer sun pushing himself to keep up with Sharnard, until his words had begun to slur and he collapsed to the ground unconscious. When Sharnard had rushed to help him, he was surprised to find that the farmhand's skin had been clammy and dry, and he could not be woken to drink the water forced into his mouth.

They had been a couple of miles from the house, but Sharnard carried him the whole way without stopping, where his mother could treat the unconscious worker. When he arrived, she tried to re-hydrate him with water and a soaking cloth on Ferandis' lips, but it was not enough to save the young farmhand, and he died shortly after.

Sharnard recalled how his father had been devastated by the death of a worker on their farm. The town healer told them that the young man had worked for so long in the heat, that he had sweated away all of the water in his body. After that day Sharnard decided he would leave his own ego behind him if he was working in a team, he wasn't proud that his competitiveness had resulted in another man's death.

Now Sharnard was an old man. He had two daughters, one of whom had moved away to the capital city Conorbatia with her husband. The other had stayed to marry a polite young carpenter who Sharnard was now quite fond of. His own wife Maren had passed away nearly five winters ago. He still missed her every morning when he woke up without her beside him. His farm was now busy with many workers, but he still worked alongside them when he could. It kept him busy and helped to get to know them better.

These days he felt the heat just as much as the men who worked alongside him and understood what it must have felt like to work alongside his younger self.

There was no breeze about today even though it was well past noon. In Varnak if a breeze hadn't arrived by now it wasn't going to. The crop fields were on the eastern side of the town like all settlements on the western borders of The Plateau, although Varnak was far north of West-Yield and less prone to raids. He had just begun trotting back to the house when he heard the alarm bells of the city tolling. It had been many long years since he had last heard them, and never during the middle of the day.

Sharnard raced back to his house on horseback with many young farmhands running up behind him. He gathered them all together at the back door before allowing them to leave for the defense of the town. Only a couple refused to wait and listen.

"Before any of you go racing off with your eyes closed, make sure you are carrying a weapon you would feel confident with in battle," he lectured calmly to the anxious men before him. "Drink some water before you leave here, and remember that running off alone and unprepared will do this town no good when you're killed alone."

A few men rushed off muttering about him wasting time, but those who had worked on his farm for a long time and knew him well, heeded his advice and left together in a group. Sharnard himself let them go on ahead while he went inside and belted on his longsword. He then took a long drink from his water skin and poured the remainder over his head to cool off, before mounting his horse to join the militia that was arming itself in the middle of Varnak.

The entire town was a hive of panic. Everybody was rushing to prepare, while some men even ran off foolishly to the front to defend it alone. Sharnard found his daughter Elain in the crowd, as she watched her husband arm himself.

"I'm glad I found you," he said to her adoringly, it was still hard to see her as an adult. "What have you heard?"

Elain rolled her eyes and glared back, but all he could think was how much she looked like her mother. "Marthek's workers were attacked by a scaleskin raiding party and were all but wiped out, only one was allowed to escape and he raised the alarm."

"I've never heard of scaleskins attacking towns in the middle of the day, and how did anybody escape?" he queried suspiciously. "Marthek's fields are a long way from here, that doesn't make any sense."

"Now is probably not the time to be worrying about that father, we are about to be attacked!" she retorted impatiently and ran over to her husband to help him with his mail shirt.

The women, children, and elderly were escorted to the town hall on the eastern side of the village, away from the frontline. Sharnard was rounded up into this crowd without any discussion and was led away from the western front of the town. Despite feeling his age, Sharnard was in no-way incapable of fighting, he was still a tall man with enormous hands and broad shoulders. The heavy-looking longsword that he lifted confidently, would have been difficult for any man of even his size to wield in their youth. Once they were at the town hall, he fell to arguing with his daughter who had tried to stop him from complaining.

"Ah that's rot, protecting the ladies and little ones has always been a backdoor excuse so old gaffers don't have to lose face when they are told to hide and wait. Everyone knows that scaleskins won't reach us back here unless the fight is already over!" he growled.

"You know the rules father and you've been ordered to protect us. You still carry that old sword around like you haven't aged. You're an old man now. Just be glad that there are young men in this village too!"

"Pah!" he spat, "you never did have any respect for your elders girl. As long as I can walk, I'll carry this sword while there's fighting to be done." His face was just grim enough to disguise the hurt that his daughter's words had caused him.

They were all standing there, trying to hear the fight on the western entrance to the town, when there was a loud smash behind them. The sound of windows being broken erupted everywhere, followed by the savage war-cries of scaleskin raiders. The entire crowd froze in fear.

"Inside!" Sharnard boomed at them. "All of you inside now!" He scanned his townsfolk quickly and pointed a finger at one of the older children. "You! Run to the front of the town and tell them that we have been flanked at the town hall."

Everybody began moving obediently, grateful for orders. It was all too late though; a number of scaleskin riders had already reached them and rode past the defenceless villagers, slashing at those who were closest, unbothered by age or gender. One large muck riding an enormous wolf crashed directly through the centre of the crowd, causing terrible damage as they tried to hustle inside the town hall.

Near the centre of the terrified crowd, the wolf

was halted dead in its tracks, sending the muck tumbling off its back. Sharnard's longsword had entered at the beast's throat and was now protruding from the back of its neck. He withdrew the sword, allowing the wolf to collapse to the ground, then strode past it to meet the raiders head on. "Fighters to me!" he roared louder than anyone had heard his voice in years, or even decades.

At least a few of the old men had picked up swords or pitchforks when they heard the town bells tolling, and they followed Sharnard stiffly to form a human wall between the raiders and their families. The scaleskins seemed drawn to Sharnard, immediately identifying his challenge amongst the chaos.

Two wolf-riders tried to cut him down as they rode past, but he severed the outstretched arm of the first one with the long reach of his sword, then blocked the second rider's scimitar so firmly that it was flung from the saddle. It landed in the middle of the 'gaffer army' and was promptly set upon with pitch-forks, spears and various other makeshift weapons.

Another rider attempted to run Sharnard down, leaning back in the saddle and flinching as it anticipated the violent contact. But the wolf it was riding upon met the same fate as the one before it. Sharnard then stepped skillfully around the mortally wounded beast to chop its cringing rider from the saddle.

He now stood tall over the battlefield, already four wolves and their riders lay dead around him. Each of them had either fallen to his sword personally or as a result of his actions. The weariness of age had fallen from him and although he did not move with the speed he once had, he still compensated for this with the practiced skill of a once fearsome warrior.

Elain was the last of the women and children to enter the town hall. As she closed the large doors behind her, she looked out just in time to see the main force of raiders charging into the town square. The raiders charged in a tight group now towards the few remaining grey-haired defenders. Sharnard was also painfully aware that some of the first riders were still behind him, having wreaked havoc amongst the women and children. The enemy line drew closer increasing its pace to a charge. Sharnard raised his longsword far behind his right shoulder swinging it forwards in an oblique arc with all his might. Two wolves crashed to the ground side by side as his blade slashed across both their faces in the one powerful motion. On either side him, his brave yet elderly comrades fell under the charge of the mounted scaleskins.

He was left standing alone now and spun around trying to catch one of the wolves that had just ridden down his friends, but was too late and the rider and wolf continued out of range. He spun back around again to face any more enemies charging from the ambush in the east, as one rider veered left at the last moment to avoid confronting this ancient warrior and his colossal sword. Sharnard roared in fury and brandished the sword defiantly at the cowardly beast, before feeling the sharp piercing pain he had been expecting at any moment.

One of the raiders still charging had made directly for Sharnard while he was facing the other way. With all the momentum of its steed and the strength of a strong arm behind it, the large muck hurled a spear directly into his ribs, piercing his lungs and impaling him where he stood. He fell to his knees with a wheeze, looking back west at the massed carnage of his townspeople behind him. Beyond the bodies of women, children, and the occasional scaleskin littered across the ground, he saw the young warriors of his town racing in to rescue what was left.

As he fell to the ground, his daughter ran over to him. He closed his eyes and died only minutes later in her arms as she wept uncontrollably. She could barely contain her sobbing to speak. "I love you dad," was the last thing Sharnard heard, and then he passed away.

The casualties and damage caused by the raid was disastrous. "Nearly a hundred lie dead here sir, and that is just the women, children, and elderly alone," one of the soldiers of Varnak reported to the captain as they stood gathered near the town hall. The young soldier bowed his head in sorrow, feeling a little guilty that he was one of the only men not to have lost any immediate family members this day. "The survivors say that they would have all been killed had it not been for Sharnard. They said he slew many scaleskins before falling, while others were able to raise the alarm." Everybody in the vicinity fell completely silent at the mention of Sharnard's name.

"I heard of his reputation when I was a young boy," the captain replied somberly. "He was asked to join the emperor's elite guard as a youth, but refused so that he could raise a farm and marry his late wife, Maren. Not many people knew that, and he told even fewer."

Elain sat nearby, listening with her husband's arm around her shoulders comfortingly. She could hear clearly as the captain of the guard continued to discuss the devastating events that had wiped out nearly half their town in just one afternoon.

"Word will need to be sent to Conorbatia of this attack," the captain told his scribe, who was hastily writing everything he could down on a piece of parchment. "I don't know if Varnak can remain after this, but I hope that we are not forced to become refugees. More important to the emperor though is the nature of this attack. They released Rhine deliberately to lure us out to the western side of the town. I've never been manipulated by Scaleskins before."

His look became troubled as he processed this information and for a moment the town captain appeared to take his mind off the bloody massacre where both his sister and niece now lay amongst the dead.

9 THE KING'S BODYGUARD

The week spent as guests of King Borgisliege went quickly. After initially resting for the first couple of days, Jaeger began spending a significant portion of his time training with Marrick in sword-work. He noted with frustrated fascination that his reflexes were significantly worse in practice than they had been in the heat of battle. His body gave him no pre-emptive sense of where Marrick would strike next, and Jaeger was forced to begin with the most basic principles of swordsmanship. The stark contrast between the two did seem a little curious, but he didn't give it any more thought than that.

He also took to exploring the stronghold with the rest of his company, who also felt well enough rested to join their dwarven contingent. The housing and infrastructure in Aridhold was a marvel. Gramcobble spent an entire day explaining to Jaeger how the entire city had been designed to suit a system of plumbing that ran through it. The plumbing was driven by an ingenious compression system, powered by the strong river that ran through the depths of the mountain.

Jaeger enjoyed these little excursions during the day, and other than exploring the stronghold during the daytime, the company spent a lot of time socialising with the local dwarven populace in the taverns at night. Overall, the week was more like a holiday to the company, who all agreed that it was well-earned after the journey it took to get there.

Over the last couple of days, Borgis was unable to join them at dinner time. He had been dealing with matters of state that seemed to be troubling him. When Darroch had the chance to ask the king how his matters were faring, he was told they were "not well" and that relentless numbers of roachkin were being discovered and flushed out of colonies all around the mountain's tunnels. On the second last morning that they planned to stay in Aridhold, King Borgisliege burst into the dining hall while they were eating breakfast and strode over to the company urgently.

"Borgis" Darroch greeted, giving nothing away as he studied the dwarf king shrewdly.

"A large roachkin army has broken into the lower levels of our city's south-western quadrant. We are gathering our forces to face the army now. Will you fight with us?" the King asked bluntly.

Darroch's face hardened. "It would be an honour. How long do we have?"

"Our guards have sealed all the barriers and doors between the roachkin and our city, we expect they will have broken through and reached the surface in just over an hour."

"We will prepare immediately and meet you where you need us" Darroch declared, rising from the table.

"Ground level at the entrance to our stronghold," Borgis confirmed with a respectful nod, then turned and stomped out of the dining hall.

Everybody stood up, preparing to race to their rooms and arm themselves for battle. Darroch watched them calmly for a few moments.

"Wait!" he barked, and the entire company froze looking back at him, his eyes were stern and piercing. "We will all make for our quarters together. We have an hour to prepare and I don't want anybody in our small company getting lost in the confusion."

Everybody nodded and agreed, and he briskly led the company from the dining hall towards their quarters. The passages were now teeming with determined dwarves racing past each other, all on varying urgent business. Messengers, warriors and captains all navigated traffic efficiently through the ample passages, while the company marched in two files towards their quarters behind Marrick and Darroch at the front. Jaeger tried to count the minutes it took to reach their rooms from the dining hall but concluded that Darroch was right; if everybody remained calm, they would have more than enough time to be armed and at the gate within the hour.

Only ten minutes had passed since the dwarf monarch first burst into the hall, when they reached their rooms. Once again Darroch dictated the plan of attack for his company.

"Everybody will now arm and prepare themselves for battle in their rooms. I want you to then gather in this hallway once you are ready, so that we may then join the dwarf ranks together as a disciplined unit." He sounded like Mendel when she used to try to instruct Jaeger on manners, but for some reason Darroch's complete control over even the finest details in an emergency, had a calming effect on Jaeger.

Jaeger stepped into his room and belted his sword on, immediately getting the sense of forgetfulness one gets when they know they won't get a second chance to remember what they need. This was the first time he had stood ready and waiting for a battle to occur, and it was daunting to the point of anxiety.

If he had the choice; Jaeger would never have to fight another battle again and the world would simply continue to turn in peace. However, since this was not the case, he realized that it was much more preferable not to know that a fight was coming. Spontaneous battles didn't scatter his concentration and he acted on instinct. Knowing what was waiting outside eroded his nerves.

He found a small helm that had been provided for him, and after standing in his room for a minute unable to think of anything else to equip for battle, he gave up on trying to remember. Ultimately, he consoled himself that he at least had the most important item which was his sword.

As soon as he stepped into the hall and shut the door behind him, Jaeger realized that there weren't any other items left to worry about. He had already discarded all but his most essential belongings in the jungle. This reassured him as he reminded himself that he would be able to move more freely without armour, even though one of the major side effects to this was being softer to poke holes in and get killed.

It was one of the few times in his life that Jaeger had acknowledged to himself that he was doing something that was likely to get him killed. Almost all the noise around Jaeger seemed to disappear as anxiety kicked in, making his mind go blank. He was walking half in a trance in the midst of the company, as they made their way outside to the ground-level courtyard of the dwarven city.

The courtyard was still a hectic scene as masses of dwarves assembled in their clans on short notice. Many large units of dwarves were now gathered together in neatly shaped rectangles around the open spaces of the city markets. Within each unit, every dwarf bore similar weapons and armour, indicating the specific clan they belonged to. Jaeger hadn't considered until now, that in true dwarf culture the family a dwarf was born into actually dictated the weapon that they carried. Warhammers and then battleaxes were the most common weapons amongst the clans. Only one unit carried swords, and even these were still quite short and broad. They were probably the closest that a sword could come to resembling an axe, whilst at the same time imitating the stature of the dwarves who wielded them.

All told there were just under five thousand dwarves gathered so far, with a few latecomers still arriving. There were warhammer clans, battleaxe clans, and even several broadsword clans. Each was approximately fifty dwarves strong, or would be once the last of their warriors arrived. King Borgisliege stood at the head of a fierce battleaxe clan, holding an enormous battleaxe that would be impossible for anyone to carry if it weren't for the magical runes engraved on its blades to help lift it, amongst other things. Borgis motioned to Darroch and his company to join this unit, and Darroch acknowledged the offer with an inclination of his head, then turned to the company.

"I want you all to fall in along the left-hand side of the king's unit. Gramcobble, you and the dwarves are to sta-"

His orders were interrupted by a deafening crash. A two-storey building that stood with its back to the mountain wall west of the city, collapsed at the opposite end of the grounds. The roachkin attackers came pouring out from an enormous hole behind where it had stood. The defenders had all been assembled facing south, where the subterranean halls opened onto the streets.

Roachkin swarmed in towards the right flank of the assembled dwarf ranks, their brown bug-like wings pinned back as they ran on all six limbs. Their two bipedal rear legs looked awkwardly unsuited to this gait despite the extraordinary speed it gave them. The streets between the two armies were narrow and easily defensible, so the surprise route of attack didn't appear to be overly detrimental. Without hesitating, a great roar went up from king Borgisliege and spread across the army as he charged. His unit was now at the back of the attack, with only Darroch's company at a similar distance from the frontline, running parallel to the fierce battleaxes.

More and more roachkin poured out of the hole behind the collapsed building, as it smoldered with black and purple flames that distorted the surrounding air. Jaeger had heard of roachkin many times but had never seen them before; they were just like a human would look if he came to a fancy-dress party dressed up as a cockroach. They had evil black orbs for eyes and looked terrifyingly agile while running in their prone state. As their frontline rose upright on two feet, they seemed to become awkward and disadvantaged in armed hand-to-hand combat.

By the time the first of the dwarf clans reached them, only a hundred or so roachkin had managed to break into the streets without tightly assembling. The enraged dwarf army struck viciously into their disorderly ranks like a battering ram through soft wood, and immediately took the upper hand. Dwarf warhammers wreaked havoc on their foes, many crushing roachkin that had not yet risen onto their back legs. It would only take another minute before their thin vanguard in the streets were dead, and the dwarves would then be able to slaughter any more that tried to enter the city from the tunnel. Jaeger slowed his pace allowing his company to run ahead, the dwarves would not need their assistance in blocking attacks from such a small source.

By now the dwarves had cornered the roachkin in front of the breach. They were systematically splattering the roachkin that continued to emerge flat on all legs in a steady trickle, when another even more deafening explosion came from directly in front of

Jaeger this time. The buildings on either side of the street came down with an eruption of debris and dust. Darroch, Marrick, and a handful of other soldiers, appeared to have dived just clear of the falling rocks up the street, but Jaeger was now cut off from them. To his right, the king and his clan had been catching up and they too were now separated from the rest of the army by piles of broken rock and mortar. Plumes of dust mixed with the same black and purple flames of dark magic shrouded the wreckage.

On the other side of the rubble more explosions could be heard. It sounded like every building in the street was being leveled, pushing the large army on the other side further away from their king, if not crushing them altogether. Jaeger did not know where these supernatural attacks were coming from, but he had never seen any form of magical forces in action before and had never known they could be so powerful. His thoughts went to his company on the other side and he wondered if they had escaped. It was possible that few or no men and dwarves were killed in the explosions, and that the primary target of this hidden warlock was the king, who was still alive for now.

There was no time to ponder this, as the clash of steel on steel rang out from the king's unit. A larger force of roachkin had entered the grounds from the southern entrance, and silently crept up on the unsuspecting dwarves while they took the bait at the west end of the street. Now rows of the king's battleaxes had suddenly fallen without resistance as his unit was surrounded by roachkin.

Jaeger seemed to have slipped under the radar,

in the shadow of the western buildings which were still standing. He watched the royal unit slowly shrink, despite their vicious resolve to take as many enemies as they could with them while defending the King. He could see no way of running alone into the middle of what must have been at least three hundred roachkin, so instead Jaeger flitted through the streets, stabbing and beheading any individual roachkin that were not attached to the larger force, and remaining unnoticed in the mayhem.

King Borgisliege had now pushed his way to the front of his dwindling unit which was backed against the rubble, and was waving his enormous axe fluently in front of him. The figure-eight he drew in the air with its glowing blades, sliced through his enemies without resistance and the weapon itself was moving so fast that it was hard to keep track of.

Soon all the roachkin directly in front of him refused to approach the death-zone of his reach, and instead redoubled their attacks on the clansdwarves around him. They were no more than ten in number now and Jaeger saw as the warriors to his left fell down, leaving the king vulnerable to a larger radius of attacks. Borgis desperately leapt forwards in a reckless frenzy, slaying numerous roachkin and again forcing them to falter in their attack, before the dance of death that his magical battleaxe was weaving suddenly ceased, and he fell unconscious to the ground.

One daring roach had run around behind him and brought its sabre down heavily upon his helm, splitting it open before the creature itself was beheaded by the King's remaining bodyguard. The clansdwarves leapt forward over Borgis' unconscious body in a final display of unwavering loyalty, sparking a similar surge of passion and anger inside Jaeger. Berserk with rage, he charged forwards hacking wildly into the crowd of roachkin who had their backs turned to him. His blows made an awful snapping sound as he cut through wings and rigid sticklike body parts, carving a path towards the dwarf monarch.

The intensity of this new threat caught the roachkin off-guard and they recoiled before his wild strokes, leaving a small gap in their thinnest ranks. By now over two-thirds of the roachkin unit lay slain, bringing them to less than five score. Two of the king's clansdwarves had now dragged him back to the foot of the debris, while the remaining three desperately shielded his retreat before falling covered with slashes and stab wounds.

Jaeger scaled the mound of rock and leapt down alongside the remaining two dwarves standing over king Borgisliege. With their backs to the rubble, the three of them formed a semi-circle facing outwards, with Jaeger standing to the left of the middle. He remembered little of this brief skirmish, but if he had been able to recall the fight, he would have remembered standing alone above the dwarf King after the two axe-wielding clansdwarves beside him had fallen to the serrated sabres of the roachkin.

He killed many, while their swords managed to bite him several times, leaving many relatively small open wounds that he didn't feel on his arms and one deeper gash on his right thigh. A studded club then came down on his left forearm breaking the bone, and he snatched the sword into his right hand and tried to continue lashing out at his enemies with little success. Moments later the same club came down upon his helm and Jaeger fell unconscious, remembering no more.

10 A NEW ERA

When he woke, Jaeger was lying in a bed in the medical facility. Surrounding him were many other beds, filled with injured dwarves wrapped in bandages and slings. The room was dimly lit by a few lamps and it was dark outside. He tried to raise himself, immediately becoming dizzy. Despite this, he eventually managed to prop a couple of pillows behind his back after persisting to sit up. The dizziness then turned to nausea and he began to retch involuntarily onto the ground beside the bed, before rolling back limply and falling unconscious again.

The next time Jaeger woke it was still dark and he was lying flat again in his bed. He remembered vomiting and decided not to attempt sitting up this time, gently raising his head instead to carefully look around the room. The nausea and dizziness returned immediately, making him groan from the sickness.

"Try not to move your head too much," a voice told him from the direction of the foot of the bed, it was a female voice but rougher than most women he had heard. "You've had a blow to the head. It does not look that bad externally, but I have seen dwarves fall dead from less, only days after being released from treatment."

"I can believe that," Jaeger complained feeling worse than he had the morning after his birthday. "What happened? From the last thing I remember, it didn't look like we were winning the battle."

"Ah" she said coming to his bedside with a warm smile, she was an older dwarf lady with a rough but kind face. "From what they told me when they brought you in, that *would* be the last thing you remembered. Berninghammer and his clansdwarves saw you struck down standing over the king, just as they were able to come to his aid. I think you will find yourself quite popular when you are well enough to go out."

"I wasn't the only one standing over the King defending him, his clansdwarves were killed dragging his body away from roachkin surrounding them."

"Yes, they will be forever remembered for their sacrifice. If it wasn't for all of you, he would have died at the hands of the roachkin." Her voice lowered in disgust at the mention of roachkin.

"King Borgis is not dead!?" Jaeger exclaimed.

"No, he has similar injuries to your own. Visibly they are a worse than yours and he still has not woken up yet. But he is alive and breathing steadily." She smiled warmly again and Jaeger relaxed back into sleep.

The next time he woke it was daytime and a new dwarf nurse was on duty in the hospital room. Jaeger gingerly leant forward, his head still went dizzy and made him nauseous when he lifted it. A jolt of searing pain went through his left arm as he tried raising himself with it. Looking down he saw that it was in a sling and remembered the club that had struck him there. This was the first time he had been able to look around without blacking out, even though he felt dangerously close to it. To his left was King Borgisliege with a bandage around his head and a patch of blood on the right side of the wrappings. He was awake.

"King Borgisliege," he addressed the king formally. He had never spoken directly to him before. "They said you hadn't woken when I spoke to the nurse, how are you faring?"

"I'm well thanks to you, please call me Borgis."

"Yes Borgis."

The king looked directly at Jaeger, "I requested to be moved here when they told me what you did. I will be forever in your debt."

Jaeger couldn't think of how to respond, "I was glad when they told me you were alive," he said simply.

"As was I Jaeger," Borgis chuckled, and Jaeger began to laugh with him, remembering the same sense of surprise he had waking up and realising he was not dead.

Jaeger remained relatively bedridden for a full week under the hospital's strict orders. Borgis too was forced to remain under care, although he argued a lot more passionately than Jaeger about this. It reminded him of Kurt and his father Karnsmith back home in West-Yield when he was just a young boy.

Nevertheless, Jaeger's week in hospital went

quickly. He spent most of it flooded with visitors, mainly because he was being treated in the same room as the king. By the time Jaeger was released from the care of Aridhold hospital, the room he shared with the king had been transformed into a busy headquarters for advisors and generals moving through on different orders.

Borgis had decided that if the nurses would not allow him to leave to attend the duties of his people, then they could not stop him from bringing these duties to him. From the confines of this room, Borgis had declared a state of emergency upon the entire stronghold. Every dwarf was now required to fulfill any royal demands made at any time of any day, meaning any rest and leisure time had been suspended in the stronghold.

The citizens of Aridhold were spending every waking hour serving emergency orders. Any human populace would have rioted, but the dwarves were tireless. Within a week of the attack, Borgis and his generals had managed to inspect every tunnel and hole within ten leagues of the stronghold. Here they had flushed out pockets of hidden roachkin colonies and collapsed any new tunnels that opened into subterranean levels of the stronghold.

Jaeger was glad to vacate his hospital bed when he was finally released. Although the King had trusted him to be present for all counsels, he became exhausted by the relentless stream of information and demands passing through there. He now understood why Borgis had looked so burdened when they first met the King. Every aspect in the entire kingdom had some sort of inverse effect on everything else, and Borgis was responsible for the entire system.

In return, king Borgisliege was treated to all the luxuries and respect that the life of royalty was renowned for, but Jaeger realized a good king had very little time to enjoy such things. After seeing this first hand, Jaeger concluded that only a fool would wish for such a life.

Darroch and the rest of the company were gathered waiting for Jaeger when he returned to his quarters with them. They had visited the hospital briefly on a couple of occasions while he was recovering, but the crowds of dwarves passing through had made it impractical to spend too much time there. Now that he was allowed to leave his hospital bed, he finally had a chance to catch up on how they were all faring.

Gregcobble-greybeard had now also arrived in the city while Jaeger had been recovering. The vicious encounter in the jungle had left him with angry scars that made him look even fiercer and grimmer than before. Chatting to Jaeger, he seemed unconcerned about his maimed appearance.

"I hear you have made some big impressions on the locals while I was gone," the old dwarf grunted.

"A lot has happened while you were gone. How are you now?"

"I've been restored to full health, which is more than I can say for the rotting carcass that attacked me," he grunted with bitter satisfaction.

Darroch smiled with amusement and turned to Jaeger. "How are *you* now? Your brave stand has made our journey worthwhile. We have just been invited to another war counsel this evening."

"I still become quite faint when I move my head, but the nurses believe the risk of dropping dead has passed." Jaeger laughed holding his fingertips to his temples. "Do you mean they might reconsider our request now?"

"The counsel is to discuss a new course of action against our enemies, and it is likely they will reconsider, yes. Dwarves are an honour-driven people as you know. They are more likely to consider breaking policy for a debt than they are for any other reason."

"That's great news, but if you knew it would take something this significant for them to accept, why did you ever decide to take the quest on in the first place? It just seems very fortunate that things have turned out this way."

Darroch flashed his trademark grin. "It does appear to have been a gamble. But recent events have vindicated my decision, so it was a good one."

The counsel was held in the great hall, now that Borgis had been discharged from hospital and was free to walk his own streets again. He was wearing his crown again also, which sat precariously on his head above thick bandaging. The meal before them was not a feast like it was at their last meeting there, and the tables were emptier and significantly less merry than last time also. The atmosphere across the city had changed a great deal since declaring a state-of-emergency.

Borgis too was less merry. He had resumed the grim demeanor they had seen when he had first greeted the company, while the weight he appeared to carry seemed even heavier than it had been then.

"A lot has occurred in the past week since the

roachkin attack. This was their most successful attempt to overthrow one of the five major dwarf strongholds yet. Again, I thank you Jaeger for saving my life and Darroch for the aid of your entire company when we needed it most. I mean to offer something more substantial than just my thanks though. Jaeger, I have instructed for a fitting gift to be prepared for you that may take some time to complete. All good things take time and I understand that humans are hastier than dwarves, so I ask for your patience with this and offer you my gratitude until then."

Jaeger was surprised, he hadn't expected any personal reward from the king which now quietly excited him. "I wasn't expecting any reward so I thank you."

"The fact that you expected nothing in return only makes you more worthy. I look forward to presenting it to you," Borgis' face was still serious with stress, but also sincerity. "Darroch, I said at our last meeting that we could not place the fate of our most guarded secrets in the hands of another people. I apologise for any insult that may have implied."

"It wasn't taken that way," Darroch replied.

"Nevertheless, now it truly would be an insult not to trust you after the debt we have to you and your men." At this point he rose from his seat to address both his own advisors as well as Darroch's company, and cleared his throat for a speech he appeared to have rehearsed.

"I have considered long and hard the unknown powers that aided the roachkin attack last week. Both my generals and I agree that there have been no warlocks among them before, that could do what they recently did in our own streets. In light of this, we have decided that closer ties will be required with our allies on The Plateau."

"That is excellent news!" Darroch acknowledged gratefully. "What exactly do you have in mind?"

Borgis seemed slightly less grim for a moment as he prepared to answer Darroch. "After sending further requests to the High King, he has now agreed to open our hidden highways to the humans of The Plateau, provided that you personally are charged with the responsibility of maintaining the secret from your end Darroch."

Without hesitating, Darroch stood from his seat and took a knee to the dining hall floor, "I am honoured, and accept this responsibility."

The entire company sat there in shock. Despite having allowed the possibility of this to re-enter their minds, nobody had expected the King to announce so suddenly that he would grant access to the dwarf's famous underground highway. Borgis sat before them with a contented look upon his face.

"Well, that's that," he laughed and clapped the still-kneeling Darroch on the shoulder with his powerful hand. "Tomorrow I will make a public announcement of our new agreement. When would you like to return to The Plateau by subway?"

"We will depart as soon as we can tomorrow, I would have the company arrive at The Plateau before a month is up if that is possible"

"Oh, I believe we should be able to manage that" Borgis assured Darroch, sounding slightly amused.

The next morning, Borgis remained true to his word and arranged for a public announcement from a balcony on the first story of the palace. Once again Jaeger marveled at the thoughtful planning that had gone into the stronghold's infrastructure. The market square below the balcony had been designed like an amphitheatre, using the buildings and shape of the streets to enhance announcements made from the palace.

The company was now packed up and ready to begin the hopefully safer march home. The dwarves had provided tailor-made clothes for them all upon arrival, as well as a number of traveling provisions and items that would come in handy after having to abandon many possessions in the jungle. Borgis was richly dressed for the official public occasion. His bandages were temporarily removed for appearances sake, and the thick gold crown sat threateningly over a gash that was still healing above his ear.

He raised both hands in the air to signal quiet amongst the crowd, lifting a jewel encrusted scepter that he was holding in his left. From here he proceeded to address the progress they had achieved since their state-of-emergency had been declared just a week earlier. His final announcement however was the most significant, which he began by acknowledging the great service his visitors from The Plateau had rendered their people.

With a great deal of pomp and formality, King Borgisliege informed his people that their High King Fëadarliege had approved human access to one of their underground highways. The high king had gained the consent of every king in the dwarven union, and once again, Jaeger was left wondering how all these facts could add up. The four other strongholds were scattered hundreds of leagues apart in different directions, and it had only been one week since Borgis' most recent request could have been made.

King Borgisliege finally concluded by allowing Darroch to swear an oath before the crowd. Darroch was to swear to the safekeeping of the dwarves' greatest secret. As the commander stepped forward, he was handed a full tankard of dark strong dwarf ale by one of the dwarves in Borgis' entourage. Borgis too was handed a tankard, and they both clashed their drinks together before lifting the ale to their mouths, not lowering them until they had finished.

Gregcobble-greybeard was standing next to Jaeger as they drank and nudged him roughly. "They are drinking the famous Krikenbrewer's black ale, it is the most fast-acting and potent beer made. A tankard of that before swearing an oath satisfies custom of suitable drinking before oathtaking." Jaeger had not heard of the ale before, it looked foul.

11 A SAFE RETURN

The public announcement was well received by the majority of the crowd and the entire company was sworn in privately afterwards. Darroch wanted to begin the return journey as soon as he could after this, but Borgis insisted that the company stay and share one last feast with him and his household. Any hastiness Darroch showed seemed irrelevant to Borgis, who was unaffected by the urgency of their plight now to return as quickly as possible.

They now leant heavily on the backs of their chairs drinking slowly, having already pushed their plates away long before. The entire company was intent on becoming as relaxed and content as possible, knowing that this would be the last real opportunity to do so before leaving the stronghold on their long march home. At length, Borgis clapped a hand on Darroch's back and laughed.

"Now my friend, I can say that we have fare-welled our most welcome guests properly before they leave tonight."

Again, Jaeger thought he detected the same note of amusement in the king's voice that he had picked up on earlier. It seemed that he had been looking forward to surprising the company with something that he found funny, but Jaeger couldn't begin to guess what it was. Perhaps the thought of everybody attempting to start a long march, both full with food and slightly drunk, was humorous to the monarch.

Darroch also appeared a little surprised, "Borgis when you provided this kingly departing banquet, I assumed that you would want us to stay until the morning. Is it always customary for dwarves to begin long journeys after the setting of the sun?"

"We have no such customs for departing on journeys below ground because the hour is irrelevant when you are hidden from the sky. If you wish to depart in the morning, you are welcome to your quarters, however I have already arranged your travel tonight if you are happy to break your traditions for our subways."

A thought occurred to Darroch that made him grin. "When amongst dwarves, do as the dwarves would do," he recited an old saying from The Plateau, ironically appropriate this time. "We will depart tonight if you have gone to the trouble of preparing for us to."

Just over an hour after dining, the company shouldered their light packs and left the palace into the streets just as the sun was setting. Borgis was waiting with two rugged looking dwarf miners, who were supposedly the only escort the company would need in the tunnels. Jaeger still felt a little bloated from the filling banquet and let out a heavy sigh as they approached the king.

"I would like you to meet the guides who will convey you safely and swiftly to the eastern end of our great northern subway," Borgis announced. "These are the brothers Kevlarpick and Korganpick."

"Good meeting," Darroch stepped forward shaking their hands.

"Aye man, good meeting" said the one that Jaeger believed to be Kevlarpick. "Just Kevlar and Korgan will do. There's an awful lot of you to remember names in such a short space, I'll learn them better as we travel, eh?" An accommodating silence followed as nobody objected.

"Well, that gets the introductions out of the way," Borgis laughed, clearly unsurprised by the brief exchange. "I suppose that only leaves the opening ceremony," and he began to walk towards the end of the street where the second roachkin force had ambushed them just over a week ago.

"On to the opening ceremony then," Kevlar repeated grandly, Korgan grunted what may have been a deep throated chuckle that sounded more like a muffled drum.

As they crossed the town square, the large gates to the dwarven underground came into view. Jaeger felt a touch of nerves in his stomach that he hadn't expected. It suddenly dawned on him that he was about to place his name in history by passing those gates, no matter what happened after that.

Once they stood before the great gates, Kevlar rapped three times on them and drew back an enormous bolt, while at the same time a matching bolt was opened from the inside. The latch clicked open as the two bolts pushed it simultaneously. This latest ingenious dwarf contraption only made the roachkin ambush seem more remarkable. The doors opened inwards towards the lower levels and the brothers walked through immediately without noting any significance in the occasion. Jaeger now understood what the dwarf brothers had found amusing.

Beyond the gates, they descended down a long stretch of broad steps before reaching a platform which branched into four smaller staircases. Each staircase lead further down in a different direction. Everybody gathered and paused on the platform as Kevlar stepped forward to address the group.

"The stairs on your left will lead *to* The Plateau, the stairs to your right lead *from* The Plateau, so we won't be needing those just yet. Behind you are stairs to and from other destinations in our realm which you also won't be needing."

"I didn't realise the subways were so crowded that they need separate passages for each direction," Marrick observed, voicing Jaeger's thoughts.

Korgan gave another grunted chuckle and Borgis responded before Kevlar opened his mouth. "It isn't exactly crowding that we separate the tunnels for, as you will see in a minute."

"Off we go then," Kevlar clapped his hands together. "You'll need to separate into two groups, half of you come with me and the other half with Korgan." Another little piece of information that Jaeger didn't understand. The entire company was now engrossed in what surprise could be in store for them to make sense of everything.

Jaeger joined the dwarves in the second group

with Gregcobble-greybeard and a couple of Darroch's soldiers. Darroch and Marrick led the rest of their men down the stairs behind Kevlar to the next level, and as the staircase wound further towards the bottom it became brighter again. The end of the staircase opened onto a long platform, and once they reached the bottom, they looked across the underground hall in wonder.

Alongside the long platform, ran a large trench laced with neat metal retainers. The trench led off down immaculately maintained tunnels, and at the end of this trench was a line of metal carriages that were locked to the ground on metal rails. Just as they entered the underground hall, they saw a handful of dwarf miners boarding one of the carriages.

"It is remarkable!" Gregcobble-greybeard exclaimed.

The rest of the company was standing in silence as they took in the sight before them. To everybody's further amazement, the five dwarves who had just boarded the front carriage were then launched forwards down the tunnel, as an operator released a lever that was holding the carriage against some unseen force.

"Welcome to the underground highway!" announced Borgis grandly. "Our most extensive accomplishment in infrastructure. Now you can see why you needn't worry about arriving home late," he laughed.

"You were right to keep this a surprise my friend," Darroch marveled. "Although I still don't know how comfortable I will be in those things on a full stomach."

Kevlar shrugged. "Some dwarf lads have difficulty holding their food down in the wind-up carts, at least the first couple of times. You'll be the first humans we've tested it on," he added casually.

"Why do you call them wind-up carts?" Jaeger enquired.

"Because you wind-them-up. They are propelled by a system of wound-up tension. My brother will be only too happy to tell you all about it once you're traveling." As Kevlar spoke, Korgan gave Jaeger a friendly wink and nodded for him to board one. "Now if nobody has any objections, we can get underway." Nobody did and they moved over to the carts to examine them more closely.

After the entire company shook hands with Borgis and thanked him profusely, the separate groups loaded themselves into the front two carriages. Kevlar took Darroch and most of his soldiers in the leading 'wind-up cart', while Jaeger went with Korgan who took the dwarves and the extra soldiers. Bregan was seated opposite Korgan on either side of a large crossbar that was designed to see-saw up and down from a fulcrum in the middle. Ahead of them, a traffic controller shouted directions to Kevlar who listened intently, pumping the cross-bar up and down with Marrick opposite him, until it became too rigid to continue pumping. A few moments of silence passed, before the controller barked "clear!" and Kevlar released the lever on his wind-up cart, sending it shooting-off down the trench faster than a horse.

The first few minutes were the most difficult to adjust to. The constant lighting provided for the subways was flashing past in the corner of Jaeger's eye, and the wind-up cart would dip with enormous speed from time to time as it clung to its rail.

"This is very well lit!" Jaeger shouted to Korgan above the wind, trying to keep his mind off the churning of his stomach.

Korgan nodded, "that is relatively new. A few decades ago, one of our engineers claimed that the trips would be less nauseating if we could see what was around us, rather than bouncing around in the dark."

"It doesn't seem to be helping me too much," Jaeger noted.

"I guarantee it would be worse if you couldn't see," Korgan assured with a grunted laugh. He then pushed a lever forward, which seemed to have a slight breaking effect on the cart as it reached the top of a steep drop. "This is what we call the wind-up. When the lever is forward, the cart will collect energy and store it in a series of springs and stored tension. It's perfect for the descent from the mountain tunnels to underneath the desert plains. Then once we begin to lose momentum, I can release this tension to keep us moving."

"How far will that stored tension take us?"

"Not too far, when cross-bar becomes slack we are running out. That's when it needs pumping."

"That's incredible!" Jaeger marveled, "I see why you insisted on Bregan sitting opposite you on the cross-bar" he laughed.

Korgan grunted, laughing with him "No point wasting such a big man in the passenger seats." Bregan smiled looking eagerly at the cross bar.

Despite the lever resisting their descent, the cart

picked up enormous pace quickly and Jaeger gritted his teeth against his motion sickness. The wind-up made a distinctive noise that sounded just like something 'winding-up', and after a short time began clicking rapidly. Korgan leant forward and pulled the lever back into a central position and the clicking stopped.

"The middle is a neutral-lock" he explained. "Once the cart can no longer wind-up any tighter, the lever locks the tension in this position now ready for use. We have designed the tunnels to straighten out when we expect the carts to achieve full wind-up, that way we can use it up before all the potential energy in a slope goes to waste."

Jaeger didn't entirely understand what Korgan had meant, but sure enough the descent straightened out and the cart coasted for a little while losing pace. Once they had lost a significant amount of momentum, Korgan pulled the lever backwards, and with incredible force the cart accelerated again. This lasted for a few minutes and was released in separate bursts every time the last explosion of speed died off.

The trip was still a long one despite the speed they were traveling at. Jaeger had adjusted to the constant movement once the tunnels left the mountain slopes, but not before retching once over the side into the trench.

Bregan eventually became exhausted after a couple of hours and Jaeger had to take his place opposite Korgan, who was still pumping along tirelessly. Jaeger was glad for the exercise after sitting rigidly in his seat for so long, but began to tire very quickly behind the cross-bar. Opposite him, Korgan was reaching his hands high above his head at full stretch as Jaeger pushed his end to the ground, but on the return, it only came up to just above Jaeger's head at full tilt.

This caused his back to fatigue from reaching low and soon it began to ache, while his right arm screamed from the exertion of compensating for the injury in his left. He tried kneeling for a little while which he had seen Bregan do, but he was just a little too short to be able to fully reach the cross-bar at its tallest point from his knees.

His shift behind the cross-bar was only half as long as Bregan's had been because of this, while Korgan was still going strong across from him when he swapped back into his seat. Jaeger wondered if Korgan and his brother were capable of propelling themselves for an entire journey as tiredness took him. It was now well into the night and long past when he would normally be asleep. Despite the uncomfortable rattling of the cart, he let sleep take him.

When he woke, he felt disoriented and had a numb pain down his entire left leg, which felt like it had lost blood flow. Rubbing his legs and looking around to gather his wits, he watched the lights still flickering as they raced past. He saw that Gramcobble was now working opposite Korgan.

"How long have I been asleep for?" he turned to Gregcobble-greybeard.

"I couldn't say, Gramcobble is the second person to swap after your shift on the cross-bar, and Korgan says we are well past halfway now." The scarred veteran didn't even bother to look back at Jaeger while he spoke and continued to stare into the narrowing tunnel ahead.

"That's good. Although I am still honoured and grateful for an alternative to walking, it's not exactly designed for comfort."

Jaeger had no idea how Korgan could tell how far they had come. There were no markers that he could see, and no certain way of measuring time down here. He could only assume that the hardened miner had traveled the passages so many times that he knew them off-by-heart. Still, he felt the trip would be much easier to endure if there was some way to gauge their progress. Gramcobble had also swapped off the cross-bar shift now, while Korgan laboured on opposite his latest partner. Jaeger tried to push himself back into sleep, but couldn't now. He had only slept for a brief period, and despite the time of day pushing through the dark hours of the morning, he couldn't get comfortable enough to feel tired again.

Jaeger probably would have fallen asleep eventually if Korgan hadn't quietly announced that they were not far away in his deep voice. A number of questions came forward in Jaeger's mind, like 'how far is not far?' or 'where would we be if we were above ground?' But he resisted the urge to bother their guide further, having already asked similar questions earlier without properly understanding the answers.

Instead, he waited anxiously, sometimes staring ahead as if expecting at any moment to see a growing light at the end of the tunnel. Other times he sat back again and tried to occupy his mind with other thoughts. After all they had done and how far they had come, he only had what must be a few minutes more to go.

"That looks like a platform ahead in the distance," Bregan exclaimed looking past him.

Jaeger turned and saw the lights were brighter ahead. They soon revealed a platform with a cart stopped beside it, and he could just make out the figures of Kevlar's cart crew standing on the platform waiting. Korgan stopped working on the cross-bar, and as the platform came closer, he pushed the lever forward, collecting a small amount of wind-up from their remaining momentum while using it as a light brake at the same time.

"Glad you could join us," Kevlar greeted them brightly. "We must have been getting further ahead of you the whole time for you to be this late."

"No rush," Korgan replied simply as he stepped from the cross-bar deck to the platform.

Kevlar bowed energetically. "Aye I guess there wasn't brother, but traveling with these scallywags must have brought out the competitive streak in me. Next time I'll let you know we're racing."

"You wouldn't win if you did," Korgan assured his brother bluntly.

"You sound quite sure of that, perhaps I'll race you on the return trip" Kevlar continued, obviously trying to get a reaction out of his placid brother. "But I jest, Korgan here is a man of few words and great action. Come, if you follow me, I will lead you off this platform and onto the surface of your realm."

"Exactly what part of our realm have you managed to keep this secret entrance?" asked Marrick admiringly.

"It is not near any of your settlements and not

too far from the scaleskin-controlled jungles, which is why we have been loathe to draw too much attention to it through overuse. If you want to know exactly where you are, you'll remember that the tunnel never twisted or turned once, in direct trip to the northern borders of The Plateau nearest to your halfling province."

"You can't be serious!" Marrick gasped. Jaeger was shocked too, the northern halfling province was twice as far from Aridhold as West-Yield. The speeds in the underground must have been phenomenal.

And so it was, to everybody's shock and awe, that on the northern edge of The Plateau, Darroch's company stepped out through an outwards-opening door into the early light of a new day. The sun hadn't quite risen over the mountain slope yet, which climbed upwards to the south. Below them to the north, the slope was virtually sheer a few yards from where they stood, giving no man, halfling, or beast, any good reason to find the hidden entrance accidentally.

12 CONORBATIA

Jaeger sat in the military lodgings of Conorbatia with the rest of the company. Darroch had immediately led everybody here once they reached the capital, before sending word to the emperor that he had returned with messages from the dwarf high king. The emperor had immediately arranged for a welcoming feast to be held and his butler was now discussing these plans with Darroch outside.

After leaving the dwarf subway, they had trekked east on no clear path behind the brothers for half a day across the lands of The Plateau. Eventually they reached a rich-yielding apple farm on the border of the halfling provinces. The little people had been startled at first, when the company of men and dwarves appeared from a direction where there was known to be nothing for many leagues.

Jaeger would have almost found the reaction comical if he didn't feel so guilty at the fear they had caused. While proportionately similar to humans, the halflings stood about four feet tall on average, and looked particularly vulnerable when startled. Fortunately, the farmers quickly realized that the travelers were not scaleskins, nor any other enemy, and returned to greet them bashfully. In no time, the cheerful little group had mobilized a handful of mule-drawn wagons to escort them to the nearest town.

Darroch had not allowed his company to linger long in the town, which was buzzing with interest. The halflings were a generous people, offering the strangers food and other small gifts, while artfully asking endless questions at the same time. Rumours immediately circulated as to the reason for the group's arrival, some of which were alarmingly close to the truth. Instead Darroch had insisted on traveling further into the province to speak with their Lord, before making for the emperor's capital city, Conorbatia.

At length, Darroch now reentered their neat military hut. "We are to go to the palace and present ourselves to Emperor Hildebrante," he announced. "The emperor has arranged for a welcoming dinner tonight to greet the high king's representatives and discuss the news that you bring from your realm."

"I hope there aren't any misunderstandings that *we* are the high king's representatives!" Kevlar interrupted. "We are just your tunnel guides. Borgis gave us permission to visit The Plateau at this end of the trip with you, but as far as I know you are the representative to deliver his majesty's greetings Darroch."

"Lay your worries to rest friend, I will convey all

of your king's messages to the emperor and he will expect nothing official from you," Darroch reassured him. "However, you have traveled with us on this return mission, and your brother and yourself are the only ones amongst us from the mountain realm, so technically you will both be the representatives of your kingdom here."

"I can live with that" Korgan conceded.

"Aye when you put it that way, I suppose we can hold such rich titles for one day" Kevlar agreed, waving his arm extravagantly.

The streets of Conorbatia were busy nothing like Jaeger had ever seen before. There were many large and wide roads running through the centre of the enormous city, filled with stores matching the theme of the street they were in. The street Darroch led them through had a spice-oriented theme and on either side of him, stores were selling various spices and ingredients in large quantities. At the front of each store, were signs that indicated how much a buyer would pay for different amounts, and Jaeger realized that his numerical lessons from school would become very important if you lived here. At just a glance he could already tell that the more a buyer purchased, the cheaper commodities were per bag.

"That's a smart idea," Jaeger commented to Marrick pointing at the price signs. "They encourage customers to buy more of their goods by making it better value if they do".

"It works well for the storeowners yes, the further down the line you purchase your goods the worse the value gets. By the time these goods reach your family in West-Yield they will be far more expensive than they were here."

"That's outrageous! We're paying more because we don't know what they're worth!" Jaeger was furious.

"Hold your horses, it costs money to move the provisions. First, they have to manufacture items that you don't already make yourselves, then sell it to the storeowners in this marketplace. Most of the producers around here are smart enough to open their own stores in the marketplace and get a better price by selling it directly to the buyers," Marrick added pointedly. "Then residents here buy the goods for a small-stock price. Traveling merchants however will buy in bulk, and then travel to the towns around The Plateau, selling these goods for a higher price. You see these merchants need to make their transporting worthwhile, so it's most expensive to buy from them, especially if they have to travel very far with their goods."

"That makes fair sense" Jaeger agreed. "So why don't the producers who opened stores also deliver their own goods to the towns?"

Marrick laughed. "You've been here for less than a day and you already sound like a merchant. Controlling the supply of goods at every level is dangerous for the natural order of things, one landowner started this years ago. He is trying to monopolise the entire industry."

"What's wrong with that?" Jaeger asked, ignoring the fact that he hadn't heard the term 'monopolise' before and trying to keep track without asking.

"What's wrong with it is that once one man has that kind of control, he can run his competitors out of business then charge customers whatever he wants. But more importantly that kind of control creates a lot of power. The wrong person could intervene with a lot of sovereign matters, and believe me this person would be nursing aspirations to take over it one day!"

"If he ever tried that then the emperor would just have Darroch lead the army to arrest him. Besides I can't imagine that anyone would want to do that." Jaeger insisted on remaining in denial about the realities of the world.

"Oh, believe me the man that I'm talking about would want to, any items you see marked 'Silo' belong to him. You're right he probably couldn't overthrow an emperor, but you never know how far he could get to having his own army before anybody does anything."

"Who is he?" Jaeger was curious now.

"Donagarn his name is, and Darroch probably *would* offer to be the one to arrest him if it came to that. They have met a few times and don't get along. They're like chalk and cheese, both men epitomize the opposite forms that the human heart comes in. Darroch is a general in the emperor's elite guard, a devoted servant of the people. Donagarn is the wealthiest most successful businessman on The Plateau. He is totally driven by a desire to separate himself from the rest of us by any means necessary."

"I see," Jaeger commented with distaste, wondering if there was anybody that he knew who was like that.

They continued walking to the end of the spices street as Jaeger glowered at three wagons trundling past with the word Silo marked on their sides. Darroch continued to lead the company without stopping, as they accumulated a number of looks from the local populace. It might have been that they recognized Commander Darroch, or perhaps they were surprised to see an armed group passing through the streets without any uniforms, or possibly that the armed group consisted of both men and dwarves. Or most likely it was a combination of these factors. Whatever it was, the company had attracted the undivided attention of the crowds they passed through.

Jaeger had not paid attention to any people in particular amongst the large crowds, until they reached the end and he saw three young men and two women all around his age. They were dressed in robes that reminded him of stories he had heard about mages back home.

"Do you know who they are?" Jaeger asked Marrick quietly, trying not to point.

"Students" Marrick replied absently. The finely dressed group were obviously not an uncommon sight to him. "They are learning to become mages at Clouds College of Magic here. Looks like second years."

"Mages!" Jaeger whispered loudly in excitement. "I knew it! How do you qualify to learn there?"

"Firstly, most students register their interest before they turn sixteen and there is no shortage, believe me you're not the first person to find the idea of magic exciting. Then you have to pass a 'perceptiveness' test which I have no idea about, but apparently the master mages use it to determine if you have any skill in harnessing magic."

"So that's all?" Jaeger asked, ignoring the fact that he may be too old by now.

"That's all there is to it" Marrick confirmed.

"But I couldn't do that now because I am eighteen?" It wasn't really a question.

"Not necessarily." His hopes began to race again. "Most people from country towns who attend the college start later because they weren't around at sixteen, like you."

"I'd like to look into it," Jaeger concluded, content with the information he had gathered for now.

The many streets of the markets now funneled into two cobbled roads on either side of a large row of rich looking houses. The houses were far larger than those at the entrance to the city and Jaeger remembered Marrick telling him when they arrived, that the richest people in the city buy the most expensive houses closest to the palace. The cobbled roads ended with an enormous open space before the palace, marked by several stiff looking soldiers posted at many different points around it. Jaeger noted that there were quite a few posted in half-concealed vantage points and assumed there must be more that he couldn't see.

Each soldier promptly saluted Darroch as the company passed them, in what appeared to be more than formal courtesy as most seemed eager to acknowledge him. Jaeger reflected on his own eagerness when he had first met Darroch, the man had quite a presence about him.

"The last mansion in that street before the palace belongs to Donagarn," Marrick informed Jaeger quietly as they reached the steps to the palace.

On the inside, the butler led them to a series of rooms on the second level where they were to stay. Only a couple of months earlier, Jaeger had been celebrating his eighteenth birthday in his small home town, which he had never ventured further than a few leagues away from. Now he had been a guest in the palace of a dwarven king, and was standing inside the imperial palace of his emperor, as an honoured guest once again. The awe of this turn of events in his life finally hit Jaeger when he closed the door to his room behind him.

He wondered when he would get the chance to return home to tell his family all about it. The success of their mission and arrival safely back on The Plateau, reminded him that he would need to let them know he had survived as soon as he got the chance. Jaeger decided that he would waste no time sending a letter home to West-Yield at the first opportunity.

The guest room was nothing short of exquisite and Jaeger didn't want to touch any of its fine materials until he had cleaned and stripped off for a bath, which had been prepared earlier for him. Unlike the plumbing system in the dwarf kingdom, the baths here still needed hot water to be carried in, which made him a feel little defensive for his own people. This *was* after all the pinnacle of human civilization. Jaeger went out of his way to try and appreciate all the other extravagant luxuries that had been provided for the emperor's guests, before accepting that the dwarves had prided themselves on infrastructure for centuries.

Jaeger lay there relaxing in the company of his own thoughts for quite some time. The bath had gone cold by the time he heard a measured knock on the door of his room. Getting up, he covered himself with one towel and walked over to the door, drying himself with another. To his surprise, when he opened the door there was a young girl standing before him. She looked like she couldn't be more than a year or two younger than he was, and was wearing a plain but smart looking dress in the blue and orange colours of the emperor's household. She straightened herself before him professionally with her hands clasped in front of her, keeping her gaze firmly fixed on Jaeger's face.

"The emperor wishes to inform you that he will be holding dinner for you and your companions soon. Once you are ready, I will escort everybody there in half an hour from now."

"Thank you, I'll get ready and join you then" he replied sheepishly, feeling a little rude for answering the door in a towel to a girl he had never met before.

She relaxed visibly now that the formalities of her task were out the way and smiled girlishly. "You're Jaeger, aren't you?" she stated more than asked, as if this was significant.

"I'm sorry, yes," he apologized extending his hand.

"Pleased to meet you, I am Marigold," she took his hand gracefully, still smiling to the point of blushing. "General Darroch finished speaking to the emperor a short while earlier. The first thing I heard coming from his court afterwards was your name."

Jaeger was stunned by her comment for a moment, but gathered himself quickly. "I hope they are only saying good things," he replied casually, feeling his hand shaking a little by his side.

"Don't worry, they are," she assured as she turned to walk away, giving him a wry smile. "I'll be back when you're dressed for dinner." Jaeger blushed and closed the door.

As he shut the door behind him, Jaeger was still a little unsettled by the unexpected visit. He already felt caught off guard standing there in just a towel, but her comments about him afterwards had completely thrown him. He dried off, dressing himself quickly, and was still shaking with nerves when Marigold returned with the larger part of his company. Her demeanor was now entirely professional again when she came up to him, scrambling his nerves even further.

The company visited another four rooms and had to wait for Gregcobble-greybeard to catch up from one of the rooms they had already passed. The bluntly spoken dwarf had yelled through the door that he wasn't finished getting ready yet and would not be hurried. As Kevlar and Korgan walked alongside Gregcobble-greybeard and his nephew, Jaeger could now see that there were many distinct features which set the brothers apart from the other dwarves in the company.

They both had a slightly more hunched posture, which made them look even shorter and stockier than the already stocky build of dwarves from The Plateau. As a rule, dwarves were incredibly muscular, which complimented their broad frames. It was possibly their natural tendency towards physical professions, but even cobblers were notable by their enormous shoulders and biceps. The brothers however left the expatriates behind by a lot in this regard. Jaeger had first observed it on the wind-up carts. Korgan's arms were almost as wide as Jaeger's waist. Alongside the dwarves from West-Yield however, the difference was far clearer to observe.

The *most* distinguishable differences however,

were their hair and beards. The brothers had long beards that they had never trimmed, and a ring-tie separated each change in hair colour, marking different stages of their life. The clothes they wore in the mountain realm would also have been distinctly different, but they had been provided with clean clothes matching the rest of the company when they arrived in the palace.

The dining hall was on the first level of the palace and the company attracted a lot of intrigued looks as they made their way down. Marigold had risen to the occasion and walked at the front of the group with measured grace alongside Jaeger, having managed to draw him out of the middle by speaking to him. She seemed very proud of herself almost to the point of being smug, that *she* was guiding the company on such a momentous occasion, with an apparent trophy by her side.

Once she had escorted them to the dining hall, she stood at the door while they entered, making sure Jaeger didn't get through without a personal goodbye. This for some reason required her to grasp his arm continuously, leaving him with no further doubt that she was flirting.

Despite being a little young for Jaeger, he was forced to admit to himself that was she was quite a pretty young girl, even though he was more flattered than interested. Her blonde hair bounced on its curls as she walked, and she had prominent dimples when she smiled, which she used willfully. Her self-confidence and blatant flirting reminded him a little of Faline, making him think of her for the first time in weeks.

As he entered the room on that thought, Jaeger realized that he was actually standing in the same room as his emperor now. He was grateful that the emperor had been too busy talking to Darroch to notice that he had entered the room without even glancing up. Darroch was going through the company with the emperor introducing them, while each member tried hard to behave as regally as they could. Everybody seemed at least a little nervous in Emperor Hildebrante's presence, except for Darroch and the two roguish twins from the mountains.

When Darroch led Emperor Hildebrante to Jaeger, he extended his hand politely. The hand was taken with a firm grasp, and then to Jaeger's dismay, his emperor also clasped the handshake with his left hand, looking him directly in the eye.

"I believe I have a lot to thank you for personally Jaeger. Darroch and I spoke at length earlier and he has told me of the service you paid to his majesty King Borgisliege. Your heroic deeds have left me greatly indebted to the service you performed for myself personally, and to your people."

A chill of disbelief went down Jaeger's spine, "I am honoured your majesty. Thank you."

"And well spoken," the emperor smiled, before turning to his stand-in ambassadors, the twin brothers. "Welcome Kevlar and Korgan, we are truly honoured to have guests from the mountain realm here with us tonight, and doubly so given the recent developments with your people."

"Thanks your majesty, it's great to be here," Kevlar responded in the casual tone he had used when addressing both kings and colleagues for decades.

"Aye thanks," Korgan added.

Emperor Hildebrante gave no indication that he was the least bit offended by their response, nor surprised. Jaeger wondered if Darroch had already debriefed the emperor earlier on the two miners also. The emperor continued to engage the brothers without pausing.

"When you return, please tell your king that my first request to use your underground highways, will be to visit him and all the other kings of the mountain realm personally. If they will allow it."

"I'll pass that on for you. I'd say that will be fine though." Kevlar winked. Korgan grunted a chuckle.

"Thank you both, please let us all sit now and not delay our meal any further."

Jaeger was slower to move than the rest of the company, as he still stood in disbelief at where he was and what he had become a part of. Darroch winked at him, looking as though he could half-read his mind and Jaeger tried to shake his head clear as he sat down beside Marrick.

The dinner was as good as their first feast in Aridhold, but felt far more purposeful and serious. Emperor Hildebrante was straight down to business, discussing with Darroch and the brothers what their two peoples could achieve by opening communication and trade between them. Emperor Hildebrante had a scribe beside him while he ate, who noted anything that the emperor referred to as a 'good point to remember', so that he could bring his proposals to the mountain kings when he visited.

Darroch remained relatively silent while his emperor became acquainted with the miners. He patiently waited while they discussed communication and intelligence with the emperor at length, before contributing little ideas of his own for both parties to consider. He suggested the tactical advantages of having both men of The Plateau and dwarves of the mountain realm together in the same armies. There were weaknesses that both races had against their enemies, and Darroch described how many of these gaps could be filled by diversifying their forces.

"What it comes down to is that merging our armies together will not give us the advantage in numbers" he summarized. "We are only moving our forces around, not actually increasing them. However, what I hope to achieve is a notable improvement in our efficiency. Something closer to what we had before our enemies got smarter." Darroch's military genius was on display as he used his words to paint his ideas into everyone's minds.

"That makes sense, fight more battles and lose less dwarves," said Kevlar.

"Or men. You see on an open field, keeping the dwarf units central in the army, would protect them from the losses you normally take because of your poor mobility."

"I suppose there is no shame in admitting that dwarves are not the fastest on their feet" Kevlar acknowledged. "Our armour is strong and perfect for head on charges, but we struggle to regroup quickly when flanked by our enemies."

"Aye we have lost many open battles from being out maneuvered," Korgan agreed.

"If we provided our cavalry units and archers, your kings could begin marching out from your strongholds to permanently eradicate roachkin colonies on open battlefields, rather than having to wait within your fortifications to fight them," Darroch encouraged.

"Now that's an idea I think everyone can drink to!" Kevlar agreed. "But you haven't mentioned as yet how the alliance can help you."

"On our frontline, we are vastly outnumbered and have no choice but to defend. The dwarf citizens of our nation have done a lot to fortify our settlements to give them defensive advantage, but the centuries of perfecting this in your infrastructure would make your assistance invaluable. I also believe there are many areas where your renowned war-hammer units could turn the tide."

"I can't argue with any of that. I will relay these plans to old Borgis as soon as we return, so that he can prepare for your arrival emperor."

"That would be much appreciated Kevlar," Emperor Hildebrante thanked him, and they went on discussing other plans that could come from the alliance. Kevlar and Korgan also stressed the importance of keeping the entrance to the subway on The Plateau a secret, even to the wider human population. Both Darroch and Emperor Hildebrante offered measures that could be taken to ensure this, without drawing too much attention to the region.

By the time they had finished, Jaeger again was happy to leave the table and go to bed. It had been a busy day, even though he had seen far tougher ones. Being back in his own lands made him realize how spent he had felt for so long, and how much he wanted to forget about the troubles of his world from the comfort of a familiar room that reminded him of home. He was tired now and ready to push all the talk of war and struggles out of his mind, but couldn't relax until he found out the answer to something that had been troubling him for a long time.

"Why is it so important to maintain the subway as a secret?" Jaeger asked Gregcobble-greybeard on the way back to their rooms after dinner. "Surely if we can hold the frontline against the scaleskin hordes, we could hold the entrance in the north where there are few enemies." Jaeger knew that challenging the logic behind a dwarf's decisions was poor etiquette and hoped that his companion would not take offence.

"Because it is a direct route below ground," the greybeard replied. "If our enemies knew where the dwarf subways led to and from, then they could locate them at any point along the line without much difficulty. That would be a terrible loss for the people of the mountain realm."

"Of course, I should have figured that out by now," Jaeger chided himself.

"It is a simple enough concept, yes" Gregcobble-greybeard agreed, "but you do not have the mind of a dwarf. It is in our nature to consider everything that affects what we build and craft with our hands. I have grown up on The Plateau, but still I considered everything that went into building the tunnels while we traveled in them. When you think about it, it's not that different to how you would approach building a house, or a road, or even a shoe."

"Yes, you're probably right, I'm glad it all makes

sense now." And on that carefree note Jaeger retired to his bedroom for the most fulfilling sleep he had had in a long time.

13 CLOUDS COLLEGE OF MAGIC

The next day Jaeger woke late. He had not been disturbed from his sleep-in and it had done wonders. Propping his extra pillows behind him, he half sat up and dragged the curtain from the small window beside his bed open. It was a sunny day and although midday was still a couple of hours away, he could already feel it heating up. Jaeger sat back in his thoughts for half an hour, contemplating whether to leave his room and ask the company if they had anymore commitments today, or just stay here and hide from everyone until they came and got him.

In the end he got dressed and went looking for Marrick, if Marrick was still in his room then this would be a fair indication that the emperor did not expect anything from them today. Jaeger also figured that if he could find nothing else to do, he could at least continue his now-regular sword training with Marrick when he found him. Unfortunately, Jaeger didn't find him in his room, but bumped into Bregan who had seen Marrick earlier at breakfast.

"I will be visiting the army barracks today to see a few friends from my old platoon," Bregan informed Jaeger when asked if they were expected to stay in the palace. "You can come with me if you like? I hear that most of the others are also out exploring the city today and scouring the markets."

"Actually, I think I might do some exploring too, but thank you for the invite. I wouldn't want to intrude on you reacquainting yourself with old friends, and I have been meaning to visit the magical college they have here."

"Ah yes, Clouds. The college is a separate campus attached to the eastern fringe of the city. If you walk back the way we came through the markets when we arrived, you can turn east once you pass them. The path you will be on should lead you in the general direction of the college."

"Thanks Bregan," Jaeger replied, and went off to find some food before he left the palace.

They had passed through the market quite briefly when they first came through, and hadn't stopped at any of the stalls. This time Jaeger strolled slowly and stopped frequently to look at items for sale that he had never seen before, or to chat to the people walking past. Most of them were courteous when he introduced himself, but seemed quick to end the conversation and move on once they realized he had no specific reason to talk to them.

Jaeger figured it must have something to do with the size of Conorbatia, trying not to feel offended. In any of the towns around West-Yield it would seem rude not to get to know someone you had just met in the town. However, the populace in Conorbatia was so big that everyone must have given up on this custom a long time ago. Now they simply allowed strangers to walk by quietly without acknowledging them.

The majority of the people in the markets also wore a light fine material for their clothing. It looked particularly comfortable and gave the place a certain amount of culture that Jaeger had not seen before. Although he also concluded that the material would be hardly practical to wear back home, as it would be destroyed in no time once placed under the stresses of everyday labour. He had always assumed that differences in customs would only vary between races, but here in the same nation that he had grown up in, was a city that felt almost as alien to him as the stone cities of the dwarves in the mountains.

Once Jaeger reached the northern side of the markets where they had come from the day before, he double-checked with one of the local storekeepers on which road to follow to find the college of magic. The storekeeper was helpful enough to point Jaeger in the right direction, although he did seem a little puzzled as to what business he would have down there and Jaeger didn't care to elaborate for the vain-seeming man. He now had a lot of information to process as he followed the path down the road, leaving the noisy bustle of the markets behind him.

It didn't take long to reach the college district. It was a separate campus that consisted of a lot of neat gardens and open space, between numerous tall buildings that stood two or three stories high. Once Jaeger was there, he realized that he didn't know who to approach to talk to about the school. He had learnt quite quickly that people here were much less approachable than everywhere else. He also noticed that the students all walked together in groups through the many neat open spaces, doing lots of socializing and very little learning.

He eventually spotted an old man with a full beard who reminded him of Hector, his history teacher back home. The old man had just come out of one of the large buildings and was crossing the courtyard with his head down seriously, wrapped up in his own thoughts. He was of medium height like Jaeger and had remarkably clear and youthful skin despite his entirely grey beard.

"Hi there sir," he greeted the old man who had not looked up yet. "I hope I'm not disturbing you, my name is Jaeger" Jaeger continued, extending his hand to prevent this stranger from getting away.

"Well met Jaeger, I am Worley. Professor Worley round here when the students need something from me." The old man didn't express any irritation at being held up.

"Well then professor Worley it is," laughed Jaeger. "I have only been in Conorbatia for a day and am on a bit of a fact-finding mission about the college of magic here."

"You have come to the right place then. This is Clouds College of Magic and I am one of the professors here. A weary veteran, a retired mage, who has seen it all and wants to impart his knowledge on the ungrateful generation that has moved in to take our place as the future of this world," he announced extravagantly. Jaeger laughed a little uncomfortably, professor Worley spoke lightheartedly but seemed serious at the same time.

"But ask away young man, you have more manners than most your age and I'd imagine that's because you haven't grown up in this city. Don't let it change you!" he advised suddenly, pointing his finger seriously at Jaeger.

"Thank you, I have already noticed there are some slight differences in the culture here to most of the towns I have seen." Jaeger agreed delicately.

"Slight differences in culture!? Everyone in this city walks around as though their business is the most important in the world and they have no time to spare to help others unless it will benefit them."

"That is probably a more accurate description than mine if I had to describe it to someone back home," Jaeger conceded.

"I have spent a lot more time living here than you to put my finger on exactly what the problem is," Worley pointed out.

"True. Well, the reason I am here is that I would like to find out how to gain acceptance at this college and begin learning to become a mage."

Worley looked Jaeger up and down for a moment, like a tradesman giving an appraisal. "Well, there are a few permissions you would need, but the most important thing is that you pass the 'matter perceptions' test to prove that you have the ability to harness what's out there," he said, waving his hand at the air.

"I've heard of it before but don't know what it is, or even what it means exactly."

"Well, I can give you a quick crash course now

in the theory behind it. As mages we can feel the concentrations of magic that is all around us and harness it for our spells. In some places there is more of it to harness and in others there are none, at which point being a mage becomes quite futile. But the point is that when it *is* there, we can feel it. Most people can't. So, the 'matter perception' test is a spell we use, it acts all around you without affecting you. If you have the ability, you can feel this spell around you, if you don't then you won't know that anything is happening."

"That makes a lot more sense to me now, what are the other requirements?"

"They are more to do with satisfying the taxman and his clerks, mostly rubbish if you ask me. They test your academic knowledge, which anyone who went to school can pass, and they require for arrangements to be made for you to pay for the education. If you are really dedicated though, then these are unimportant and you can even gain a scholarship if you work hard enough. The one that really matters is the 'matter perception' testing."

"I really hope that I have the ability. It sounds like the only one that I have no control over," Jaeger admitted.

"I can do a quick test on you now to get a fair idea if you want?" Worley offered.

"Thank you, it would take a lot of nervous waiting away if I knew now."

"I believe it would," Worley agreed, placing all his paperwork on the ground. "Good luck son, I hope that I am not the one to ruin your dreams."

With that, Worley stepped back and lifted his

arms, reaching outwards on either side of his body with his palms facing Jaeger. He began to watch Jaeger intently without saying anything and then scrunched his face a little tighter, focusing heavily without taking his eyes off his target. Eventually Jaeger felt a tingling in his neck and arms that gave him goosebumps, his own palms felt as though they were being magnetically pushed apart to involuntarily raise his arms from his waist.

Jaeger grinned with joy. "I can feel it, it's all around me and it pushed on the palms of my hands!" he announced ecstatically, possibly a little too loud with the crowds of students still moving around him or sitting on the neat green lawns nearby.

Worley's expression did not mirror Jaeger's enthusiasm. "You definitely have some ability, but you would be just on the borderline to get in. I had to push the spell quite hard onto you before you were affected." The excitement drained from Jaeger immediately at professor Worley's sobering comments. "Don't let it dishearten you though, I just want to make sure that you are well-informed. You definitely have the ability there which is the most important thing, most people have nothing. If you were a wealthy nobleman's son, you could gain immediate acceptance with the perception you have" he added.

"Well, that's good enough for me," Jaeger declared, determined not to be discouraged by the thought that he did not have the natural ability that others had. "The rest I can achieve if I work hard enough and I can make sure that I excel in the other criteria to make up for a low perception."

"Precisely my boy!" Worley seemed surprised

by his conviction. "That is the kind of attitude we need more of around here. A man can achieve almost anything without a leg-up from others if he really has to, and if you ask me that's how it should be anyway. It has been good talking to you Jaeger and if you are serious about your application, you should find the college office of student administration and speak more with them."

"Thank you, professor Worley. If I get in, I will look forward to the classes I have with you."

"Good lad," the old professor approved, before picking up his papers and shuffling off across the lawns towards another large building.

Jaeger stood there with a mixture of emotions racing through him. He felt excited and positive that he had put in motion the first steps towards doing something that he had always fancied doing. He tried to let this excitement fill him, but at the same time he couldn't shrug off the nagging disappointment of finding that he was not more magically gifted. It was a difficult feeling to acknowledge that he had not been born as perfectly as he would like.

As he continued walking, he realized that professor Worley had not given him directions to the building he was looking for. He paused in the middle of the path, wondering if he was walking the wrong way and decided to approach someone for directions. A small group of students wearing richly decorated robes were passing him, and he decided not to sit and contemplate who he should pick to speak to.

"Excuse me, but I'm looking for the college office of student administration here," he stopped the young student closest to him. "Could I trouble you to point me in the right direction?"

"Do you have business there?" the student asked somewhat accusingly. "You're not dressed like you're from the city." He had short black hair that was so neatly arranged it appeared to have only been cut hours earlier. He was relatively pale compared to Jaeger and his hands were smooth like he had never used them for anything but combing that hair. His face was unblemished and his features could almost be described as pretty rather than handsome. Jaeger wasn't sure if he was being intentionally rude, but the tone of the young man had an offensive ring to it.

"No, I'm from West-Yield, it's on the western border of The Plateau. I have only been in Conorbatia for a couple of days so far." He had decided to uphold his manners until he was certain that this posh stranger was not just obnoxious. There was nothing wrong with obnoxious.

"Well, if you have the money, you should think about using it to buy some proper clothes so that you don't draw the wrong attention to yourself. That's only if you have the money though," he added smugly, his jibe was rewarded with snickers from the group standing around him.

"Which way is the office, smart-arse?" Jaeger demanded fiercely, he had just returned from a month of peril and fighting before arriving in the city, and had no patience to be insulted by a group of pampered brats.

The students behind the one he was talking to were caught off guard by his abrupt response, but their ring-leader scowled with disdain. "Move on and find out from somebody else, before I find out who you are and you regret ever meeting me," he warned ominously.

"My name is Jaeger, son of Tevin, in case you think I'm scared of a pretty-boy like you, what's yours?" he challenged. This time his words caught them all off guard including the ring-leader, but it was at the start of his sentence, when he mentioned his name that he noted the reaction.

A brief moment of curiosity passed across the young hostile's face, before he brushed off whatever thought he had. "I am Kostian, son of Donagarn," he declared arrogantly, then strode past Jaeger without glancing at him again.

Jaeger stood there for a moment fuming silently, until he realized that a number of other students moving through the area had stopped to watch the confrontation. Small crowds were all standing within earshot now, lingering to see what he would do next. He tried to unclench his fists first. Back in West-Yield, a verbal confrontation like that did not finish without coming to blows, but the rules seemed different here. Kostian had seemed happy to insult and antagonize Jaeger, then walk away without any further escalation, or closure.

Jaeger wondered if that might make it more difficult to shrug off the confrontation, and considered the possibility that maybe the next time he saw Kostian it might be possible to resolve their issue then. Meanwhile, a petite blonde girl in first year robes who had been sitting nearby stepped forward from her friends to approach him.

"Did you say you're looking for the college office of student administration?" He looked up at her completely free of the frustration he felt moments ago. She was very pretty. She had notably high cheekbones and Jaeger also observed that her eyes were the same blue-green mix that he had. It was something he hadn't seen in anybody else before.

"Yes I am. I have a few questions and was told that was the place to go."

"Well, I have some free time now if you would like me to take you there?" she offered.

"Thank you, that's really good of you," Jaeger had forgotten the name Kostian, and was already pondering the lucky chance that it might be a long walk to the office.

"I'll catch up with you later," she called to her friends, and began walking with Jaeger in the direction he had come into the college grounds from. "Did I hear your name is Jaeger?"

"Yes it, is sorry, nice to meet you," he said extending his hand. She laughed and took his hand with her own, it was smooth and gentle so that Jaeger had to consciously avoid squeezing it too hard.

"Nice to meet you too Jaeger, my name is Aema. If you are new to Conorbatia, would I be right in guessing you are the same Jaeger that has returned from the dwarf realm with Commander Darroch?"

"Yes, I am!" Jaeger exclaimed. "How did you know that?" He was a little shocked by her guess, even though he had been given some warning that the people of the city might have heard of him by now.

"The news of commander Darroch's return from the mountain realm has gone through the city like a wildfire, including your name. I only just heard the stories earlier today. Is it true that you stood above the fallen dwarf king while you fought off an army of the roachkin by yourself?"

"Borgis?" Jaeger said trying to make it sound casual, other than that he had no idea how to respond to the rest of the question. "I don't know that it happened exactly like that, the story was embellished a little in Aridhold as well. I was actually knocked-out pretty quickly so I don't remember much," he lied.

"I didn't know that," she admitted. "How did you survive if you were fighting alone when you were hit?" she pointed out insightfully.

"From what I was told, we were saved just moments after it happened, otherwise I *would* be dead. But I wasn't fighting alone, the king's bodyguards defended him also and were killed, I just rushed in to help them." He had decided that he should try to be as modest as possible on the topic and was hoping that the subject might change now.

"Oh, I see now, so it actually wasn't embellished by much then, you really did hold off an entire roachkin army to save the dwarf king?"

Jaeger couldn't help but laugh, "I suppose it's not a bad thing to have that said about oneself. I just think that the picture I have heard painted makes it sound like I defeated the entire army without any help, when really I only slew a handful of the roachkin, most from behind." Now he was truly certain that talking about it was making him sound foolish and decided he would take the next chance he had to change topics.

Aema had been looking at his face while he talked, and burst out with laughter. "You really do look uncomfortable talking about it you know," she managed to say when the laughing fit had passed. "Most of the boys I know would do anything to have a story like yours to tell."

Jaeger felt a little better. "I guess you're right. So how long have you been at the college here?"

"I began this year, only a few weeks ago. Are you planning to begin soon?"

"Yes, but I only began asking around today, I don't really know how to go about it yet," he admitted.

"Well, you can arrange everything you need to apply in here" she said, pointing inside the building they had just stopped at. "I don't have class again for a couple of hours still, do you want me to wait while you speak to them and show you around the campus after?"

This was immediately the best day Jaeger had in a long time. His heartbeat began to increase rapidly and he carefully tried to calm himself before he spoke. "I'd like that Aema," he said, smiling warmly if not even a little flirtatiously at her.

A coordinator in the office spoke with Jaeger for half an hour, discussing how to apply for the college and making arrangements to sit for the 'matter perception' test later that week. The coordinator was an old lady named Modine who reminded him a lot of his aunt back home. She had taken to Jaeger fondly almost straight away, telling him the realities behind all the paperwork he was reading.

Unfortunately, Jaeger would have to wait an entire year to begin even if he passed the test, now that classes had already been running for a few weeks. She informed him that unless he showed remarkable perceptiveness, (which he told her was unlikely after his brief discussion with professor Worley) or could afford the exorbitant additional tuition fees, he would not be granted exception to this long wait.

All in all though, he was still glad to have put his plans to join the college further in motion, and was even more pleased with his fortune this day because he had met Aema. She took him for a quick tour around the college and showed him a couple of her favourite spots to spend her free time, including a garden with a small stream sculpted through its landscape. The garden was full of thriving plants and flowers that made you feel cooler just sitting there, even in the middle of the hot autumn day.

When he had walked her to her next class, Jaeger chose not to linger long on the college grounds anymore. He felt aware of the stares that he had attracted walking with her, and was a little conscious now of how much the clothes he was wearing made him stand out.

He felt another pang of irritation towards Kostian again, and tried to push that thought out of his head. By the time he had arrived back at the palace, he was once again absorbed in his plans to begin studying at the college of magic.

The next week, Darroch was very seldom seen by his company, who were either taking day trips into the market from the luxury of their palace lodgings, or busy catching up on lost time with their families. Darroch was in constant meetings with the emperor and other military leaders still left in the city, as war raged more heavily than ever before on the southern borders. It appeared that the emperor was expending every resource he could to contain an increasing push from the scaleskins against the chain of fortresses holding the southern line, while rumours spread of battles that had been lost at the hands of a new power wielded by the enemy's shamans.

Jaeger returned to the college a couple of times to complete the paperwork required to apply there, and soon there was only the perception-test left to go before he could enroll. He wasn't lucky enough to come across Aema again and didn't want to loiter around the campus to look for her, although he did remember what time and day of the week it was when he first met her and was quietly confident that if he really wanted to see her, he could just show up in the same place then.

On the day of his test, Marrick and Jaeger began with their routine sword training, before wandering through the markets holding their own counsel on the war to the south. Marrick told Jaeger that the emperor had been contemplating conscription in his meetings with Darroch, who was utterly opposed to the idea at this stage. By the time they had finished the discussion, they had wandered onto the campus grounds and had already passed a few robed students of the college.

"I see you're still eager to join this club," Marrick commented a little sourly.

"You don't seem too fond of the place," Jaeger observed.

"Don't get me wrong Jaeger, mages make some of the most effective inclusions in an army, but the college here is just a reflection of one's status in the community. None of these spoilt brats will be good for anything until they have spent a good year or two touring the frontline after they finish."

"I think I can understand where you were

coming from when we arrived here. I had an encounter with the heir to the silo franchise the other day."

"Kostian!? What happened?"

"Not a great deal. He didn't think much of my attire and I didn't think much of him."

"See that's *exactly* what I was talking about," Marrick declared, getting himself worked up. "Kostian and his father are the epitome of that kind of elitist behaviour, I'd have threatened to run him through if I was there."

"I tried not dwell on it too long, he's just a spoilt rich kid."

"He's not poor," Marrick laughed.

Jaeger stopped Marrick in front of the college office of student administration. "I have to sit the matter perception test here in a couple of hours. I might check in to make sure I have come prepared for it."

When he entered, Modine was sitting there and seemed surprised to see him, "Good morning, Jaeger, we weren't expecting you for a couple of hours yet."

"I know, I just wanted to check that I have done everything and am ready to sit the test. Better to be early than late," he added thoughtfully.

"Wise words. The professors who will be testing you are all here now if you want to sit the test early? I'm sure they won't be upset by your conscientiousness." It sounded like a hint.

"Yes, that would suit me just fine. Where would you like me to wait?"

"Just there should be fine, I will inform them now that you are here."

Jaeger quickly popped outside to tell Marrick

that he would be sitting the test now and not to wait for him. Marrick didn't seem disappointed with the news and agreed to meet him later that day at the palace if he didn't see him earlier. With that, Jaeger went back inside and took a seat in front of Modine's desk. She returned shortly and told him that the testing panel would be out soon to meet him. He withdrew into himself while he waited and tried to tune his awareness into the quiet sounds of the world around him, unsure if it would help, but determined to find something to occupy his focus while he waited.

At length, five professors emerged from a room down the hall to see him. Four of them were old men with white beards that made them appear both magical and wise, one of which was professor Worley. The fifth mage was a short plump lady who appeared to be significantly younger than the other professors, but at the same time Jaeger sensed something about her that told him she was probably closer to their age than she appeared.

Without any pleasantries or introductions, he was led down the hall into an indoor amphitheater, where they placed him at the bottom. They then sat apart, evenly spread so that all five of them were as far away from each other as possible over a semi-circle in the seating before him. Professor Worley, who was positioned directly in front of Jaeger, gave him his first instructions.

"Jaeger, this testing will not take long once we have started, the first thing we want you to do is close your eyes and answer our questions without thinking too much about them." Jaeger nodded, unsure if he was expected to speak straight away, and closed his eyes waiting for the next instruction.

They waited for him to sense the spells around him and use the words 'stronger' or 'weaker' at first, to determine if he could sense the magic at all around him. Sometimes it became so weak that he had to be honest and acknowledge that he could no longer sense anything around him. The panel sounded interested in these comments and clearly an important aspect of the testing, was to determine a young mage's threshold point of sensing magic.

The tests also required him to determine what direction he thought the sensation of pressure was coming from, as well as if he could tell when a new source was introduced from another direction. Other than that, there were no requests for Jaeger to harness the magic or cast any spells himself, just testing his perceptiveness to the forces moving on and around him.

All up, it lasted for what must have been less than half an hour. However, by the time they had finished, Jaeger felt like he had been there all day. He had no gauge to determine how accurate his responses had been, and was sent to sit in the visitors' waiting area while they discussed his results. Again, it was probably not a long time in reality, but the short period of waiting dragged out. Sitting there, he was forced to consider the possibility that he hadn't felt half of what he claimed to have, and may have even been imagining the sensations he was required to comment on. Pushing these thoughts out of his head, he tried to let his mind wander until somebody spoke to him.

At length, professor Worley and the plump older lady entered the room. She smiled at him warmly which he felt was promising, nobody gave bad news with a smile on their face. Worley was the first to speak.

"Jaeger allow me to introduce professor Sharelle"

"Pleased to meet you professor," Jaeger greeted her extending his hand.

"And you two Jaeger. We don't want to keep you waiting so I am pleased to inform you that your application has been successful. There will now only be the issue of college fees and other formalities, but the main point is that you have demonstrated enough ability to gain acceptance at Clouds College of Magic." The pure joy that Jaeger now felt was indescribable, except to say that in this moment he felt utterly content.

Professor Worley then spoke before Jaeger had the opportunity to respond. "The unfortunate news is that the year has already commenced, and we feel that you would be best equipped for your studies if you began from the very beginning next year."

Jaeger did not want to object or appear ungrateful, but couldn't see himself staying in Conorbatia for a year waiting to begin his studies. "That is excellent news, thank you for accepting me, is there any way that I could gain entry a little late this year though? It would make a great deal of difference to me if that were possible."

"Students who are late to commence studies will need extra tuition to catch up," Worley explained. "This extra tuition is expensive and we do not grant the privilege to students unless they can afford this large fee, or display enough potential to justify a scholarship for this tuition."

"I understand, so if I had a means of funding the extra tuition then it would be possible?"

"It would be, but we don't ask this of any students, as the extra tuition is far more expensive than normal learning because it demands a lecturer to teach you individually rather than an entire classroom. Only the wealthiest families offer to pay this fee, and we often see it squandered by rich sons and daughters who are not prepared to accept the extra workload that goes with it."

"Thank you both professor Worley and professor Sharelle. I will do my best to prepare for my first classes next year for now, and if there is any way that I can arrange for the extra classes I will be ready to begin and let you know."

"Your welcome Jaeger and we hope that you are able to," professor Sharelle replied, before they both said their goodbyes, leaving Jaeger to his thoughts.

14 DIVERGENT COURSES

After a couple of weeks enjoying the emperor's hospitality, everybody seemed to finish their own personal business around the same time. The general feeling amongst the company now, was that it was high time to move on to the next thing before they outstayed their welcome.

Kevlar and Korgan had been busy gathering information, both in and around the markets and during discussions at dinner in the palace, and were now eager to return to King Borgisliege with the many updates that had taken place in the capital. Darroch was making ready to depart at the head of the elite guard, to reinforce the beleaguered outposts on the southern border. While Jaeger was still undecided as to which path he was going to take.

He had managed to leave a message for his family with a merchant traveling to West-Yield, but now that he had a year to wait before he could join Clouds College; he had to decide whether he would return home himself, or travel south to join the fight against the scaleskins. Without the proper training or time-in-service, Jaeger was not entitled to join the elite guard under Darroch, who had still offered to escort him to the frontline where he could join the legion.

Other than these options, the only other thing he could do was make a living in Conorbatia for a year while he waited. If he chose to do this, he would do it alone. All the members of his company were now breaking up to go their separate ways and none were staying in the capital.

When he looked further into tuition at the college, he also realized that even the standard fees were expensive and he currently didn't have a coin to his name. This raised another issue of how he could stay at Clouds College once he began, without the backing of a wealthy family like most of the students. The first thing he knew he had to do was look for work in Conorbatia, for one of the farmers maybe, since he had already grown up a farmer. The one thing he was certain of in his job hunting though, was that he wanted to steer clear of any businesses tied to Silo, which was limiting given how much he saw it everywhere.

Jaeger spent a fair amount of the last couple of days in the company of his now-close friend Marrick, while they searched for a job for him together. Marrick had been offered a position in Darroch's elite guard and was keen to join his mission in the south. Something about Darroch leading the army gave everyone a sense that the tide might be about to turn. Even Emperor Hildebrante couldn't help but give that impression when he spoke to them. He hadn't held a dinner with everyone since the first few days after they had arrived, but now he had arranged for another feast tonight before the company split and went their separate ways.

At the feast, the emperor took the time to speak with every member of the company, to find out where they would go from here. He was a shrewd ruler, and after their success in the dwarf realm to the west, everybody involved now shared a certain degree of fame due to their exploits. It appeared that the emperor saw potential in using the current high profile of both the men and dwarves that had traveled with Darroch, and he offered advice as well as positions amongst his counselors and ambassadors. As Emperor Hildebrante enquired at the table one by one, the rest of the company sat in silence, listening to the responses of their companions and the advice of their emperor.

Kevlar and Korgan were currently the closest thing to ambassadors from the dwarf kingdom, but they were returning home now and official communication was soon to be established between the human and dwarf nations anyway. Most of the other dwarves intended to return home to West-Yield and their families, except for Gregcobble-greybeard who had agreed to stay on in the city for a time, as an advisor for dwarven affairs within The Plateau. The rest of the company were set to join Darroch on the frontline. Marrick and Bregan were the only ones who would remain under his immediate command in the elite forces, while the rest would be joining standard posts under different command.

This only left Jaeger, who hadn't put his hand up to take part in any of the roles discussed at the table.

However, in a strangely sudden change of topic, Darroch began discussing their most recent mission again with the emperor before Jaeger could get a word in. Darroch noted Jaeger a number of times in the story, before casually mentioning that he would not be joining them in their mission to the south, and soon the emperor turned back to Jaeger. Darroch's storytelling had brought to his attention the fact that Jaeger had not announced his plans yet.

"And you Jaeger, arguably your actions have had the greatest influence on the events that have come to pass, excluding Darroch of course. I have not heard yet what you intend to do when your company disbands, will you return home to West-Yield?"

"I have been trying to find work in the city here for the next year so that I can save up some money. There is a storeowner in the marketplace who said he might need an extra farmhand if the crop is good."

"Darroch my friend! did you not know of this? All your young soldier had to do was to ask me if he was looking for work!" Hildebrante demanded incredulously.

"He is not one to ask for handouts, a sign of rare good character. Marrick tells me that he has a fascination with the college of magic here," Darroch replied with measured restraint. Jaeger knew that his captain must have heard more about his attempts to join the college, but as always Darroch was calculating with his words.

"Is this true Jaeger?" the emperor asked with interest. "Working for a farmer does not seem to be the most direct path to achieve this, you would need to lodge an application and sit the testing there."

"Yes sir," Jaeger responded a little nervously as he realized what Darroch had been doing. "I have passed the test and filled all my applications. The job is to save enough money for me to begin next year, studies have already commenced this year and I cannot afford the fees for late entry and extra tuition."

The emperor smiled with amusement and gave Darroch a knowing look that indicated that he knew exactly what his general had just done. "Again Jaeger, this is something that could have been resolved in a moment if you had just approached me."

"I didn't want to overstep my welcome. Your hospitality here has been more than enough for me to be grateful for."

"He will go a long way," the emperor remarked to Darroch seriously. Then turning back to Jaeger, he spoke again. "Well, you need not ask now. Besides, your service to our nation has earned you more than just a couple of week's free accommodation in the palace. I will have word sent personally to Clouds College, that your extra tuition and all other fees will be sponsored by the crown, in return for the services you have done for this city."

Jaeger sat there dumbfounded for more than a few moments, everything had fallen into place for him so well that he wondered how it had happened. At length he regained his composure. "Thank you, Emperor Hildebrante, I cannot tell you enough how much this means to me. I don't think I could have brought myself to make such a request of you and the crown," he responded, feeling a little out of his depth around such important people bearing such grand gifts.

"There will be far more legitimacy in your

211

scholarship than most of the heirs who buy their way into the college Jaeger, so don't allow yourself to believe that you are less entitled to be there than anybody else." The emperor held his gaze. "You may not be able to see it yet, but you have earned this. I just hope that you are committed to your studies and may one day serve us again with new abilities."

"I will do everything that I can to make that happen," Jaeger promised.

He didn't remember much of what happened at the feast after that. Once the most important discussions had taken place, everybody got to drinking and eating heavily to celebrate their last day in the palace. He sat quietly eating in a satisfied trance for quite some time at the news he had received, before deciding that now was a better time than ever to join in the festivities. He wanted to enjoy his last night with the men and dwarves who he had spent almost every day of the last three months with.

By the end of the night, everybody was reduced to drunkenness and bawdy singing, with the exception of the emperor who had always seemed quite guarded and a little stiff to Jaeger. At times he would put on a display of comfortable familiarity, but it always seemed somewhat forced. Jaeger suspected that Emperor Hildebrante often wanted to be more like Darroch whenever he was like this.

As he sat back quietly finishing his fifth tankard, Jaeger decided that all in all, being the emperor might not be as luxurious and carefree as it sounded. Many men back home in West-Yield, used the term 'live like an emperor' to describe a better life. But after spending time around a both a dwarf king, and a human emperor, it appeared in reality to be a far more taxing duty than this, and was likely to alienate a man from forming many close friendships in his life.

As the raucous behaviour gained momentum again, these musings were pushed aside, and by the time he had finished his next drink, Jaeger had forgotten ever contemplating his liege so seriously. The night wound on and the company continued drinking and getting louder until the early hours of the morning. At this point, some were faced with the knowledge of how they would feel when they woke in the morning, while others were less concerned as they lay fast asleep around the table they had dined at. It was a night worth remembering for those who could, and those who couldn't still claimed that they had thoroughly enjoyed the last dinner that they all spent together.

Jaeger woke exactly how he expected the next morning, and probably worse for the depressing thought that he would have to say farewell to everybody today. A slight ray of piercing sunlight had also snuck through the closed curtains and now assaulted his bleary eyes. Unable to hide from it by tossing and turning, Jaeger got up and pulled the curtains across at this point, but by the time he had gotten back to his bed he knew that he would not be able to get back to sleep. Instead, he requested some water to bathe with and immersed himself in the hot-tub for the next half hour until it went cold.

Unsurprisingly, Jaeger also found that nobody else was up when he left his room, and ended up pottering around trying to waste time until they were.

Only Darroch had risen before him, but had already left for the military barracks where his regiments were waiting. After a very small breakfast that he didn't finish, Jaeger was glad to see Marrick had risen too and was not looking any better than himself.

"Good morning Marrick, are you all packed to leave today?"

"Who said anything about it being good?" Marrick croaked. "Yes, I was packed before dinner last night, I didn't expect I would want to do any packing this morning and I was right. You look surprisingly well" he said almost accusingly, glaring at Jaeger from behind the shabby hair that was in his face.

"I had a long bath this morning," Jaeger replied simply.

Marrick muttered something under his breath about it being a good idea, then sat down across from Jaeger staring blankly at the bacon and eggs in front of him, before giving up on the thought of eating and leaving the table. They both went up to the social room near their accommodation and joined the small contingent of dwarves and men that were sitting there quietly chatting. There was very little time left now until they would all be leaving on their separate paths, but nobody seemed too interested in doing anything but sitting around until that time came.

Darroch returned at midday, looking unscathed from drinking the night before. He collected those who would be joining him to gather in the town square in front of the palace. Before Jaeger knew it, he was standing on the cobbled streets outside, helping his friends load their luggage onto the wagons ready for departure. He exchanged fond farewells with everyone and stood chatting with Marrick just before they were to leave. They had said very little all morning, but now that the time to leave was here, they seemed to have found their thirst for conversation.

"Keep an ear out for where Darroch is stationed when you get the chance, his name and whereabouts are known well by many and I will be with his regiment wherever he goes." Marrick informed Jaeger. They both realized that the likelihood of catching up again would be low, given that Marrick was not guaranteed to stay in any one place for long. "It has been an honour traveling with you and fighting alongside you Jaeger, I consider you to be a good friend now."

Jaeger gave him a sly grin. "We're certainly not enemies," and Marrick burst out in laughter. They both released the grip of their handshake and walked away still chuckling at Jaeger's final dig.

"Don't forget to track us down whenever you are free to!" Marrick shouted back at him.

"It will be the first thing I do!" Jaeger yelled back, and before he knew it, his now-close traveling companions had all rolled out of sight, leaving him wondering how the departure had crept up on them all so quickly.

15 THE LIFE OF A STUDENT

Emperor Hildebrante's staff had immediately enrolled Jaeger in all first-year classes at Clouds College, and as he read the classes in his learning itinerary, he tried to figure out what each one meant; Fundamentals of magic, Alternate Applications of magic, Magical Cultures, History of magic, and Matter in Practice. One could assume what he would be learning in each of these, but until he began, Jaeger had no idea if he would be good at anything.

It was fortunate that he had already made the necessary preparations for college, because the day after Darroch's departure Jaeger walked alone into his first lecture. Without getting his hopes up too much, Jaeger looked around the room of his first class for Aema. He hadn't seen her again since the day they had first met, and even considered that they may have walked past each other by now without him recognizing her. The class was a descending semi-circle of seats before a stage at the bottom, much like the one where he took the matter perception testing. Without any luck finding Aema, he took a seat by himself towards the back of the indoor amphitheater, trying to be inconspicuous.

The seats around and beside him were soon filled, and three students sat down together beside him on his left. The young man closest to him appeared to be just a little younger than Jaeger. He was lightly built and pale, with the blemishes of youth, overall giving off the impression of somebody who didn't appear to have seen much sunlight. His curly hair reached down to his glasses and got in the way as he spoke quickly and intensely to his classmates. Jaeger contemplated staying withdrawn and keeping to himself for a moment or two, before realizing that he was going to be at the college for a very long time.

"Good morning," he introduced himself in the most confident voice he could muster, unsure of the reception he would get.

The young student flipped his head towards Jaeger instantly as though he had been taken by surprise. "Hello, I am Nasgro," he replied. "I haven't seen you in my classes before."

"No this is my first day here, I was a little late to enroll. I'm Jaeger."

"Hello Jaeger," he repeated without noticing, "this is Berran and Ellis," he said pointing to the two others, who leant forward and gave him a polite wave. "So, did you have exceptional results in the perception test? Or just a wealthy family?" Nasgro asked without stopping to think if the question was offensive, or maybe he just didn't care if it was.

"I've been hearing that a lot since I arrived in

Conorbatia," Jaeger noted curiously. "I am sensing a bit of a trend when it comes to students paying for acceptance here."

"It's an epidemic," Nasgro said dryly.

Jaeger considered this for a moment before answering the question. "Well, my results in the perception test were not fantastic, so I suppose it's closer to the second guess," he responded a little uncomfortably.

"But not quite the same," Nasgro probed.

"No, not quite," Jaeger agreed. "You're quite sharp if I may say so."

"You don't know the half of it!" Nasgro declared without a hint of humour in his voice.

"Don't get him started," Berran interrupted quickly. "He thinks that he was already a magical genius before he even came here."

"And I still am! Have you ever heard of the magical technique called 'feeding,' Jaeger? Or 'fools-feeding' some call it."

Jaeger shook his head.

"Oh, here we go," groaned Berran.

"Shut up Berran, he's new here and he needs to know."

"Know what?" Berran countered. "That he just sat down next to a raving lunatic?"

"Just ignore him Jaeger. 'Fools-feeding' is a technique used to outsmart enemy magic-users. It's a difficult trick that involves creating a counterfeit of DarkLand matter. The whole idea is to lure an enemy mage into drawing on something that isn't there during a duel, rather than allowing them to gather real matter, thus rendering their spells useless. Do you follow?"

"Not really" Jaeger admitted, "I haven't been taught anything yet, this is my first day remember."

"Fair enough. We'll all you need to know is that it was *me* who invented that spell. Not that lying little shit Jates who took credit for it at the time."

"I'll make sure that I remember that," Jaeger promised him seriously, before the classroom hushed and the professor took his place in front of a podium.

"Good morning class," the professor boomed in a voice that was clearly amplified by enchantments, it was professor Worley. "Today in the fundamentals of magic, you will learn about what it is that makes a mage's spells more potent as he develops his skills to become a master." Not everybody seemed as interested in the lecture as Jaeger was, and most of the class continued whispering to each other while the professor spoke. Worley didn't appear unused to this and did not pause to chastise those who weren't listening.

"To me, using magic is a lot like breathing, and to those who become masters of magic, it comes just as easily. You see the air around us is made up of percentages of different things. Some of it we need to breathe, some of it we don't but we breathe in anyways, and some of it is made up of that DarkLand material we call magic. The percentage of DarkLand matter that makes up the air around us is referred to as a 'concentration.' Or a 'contaminant' to those who truly understand its nature," he added cryptically. "But we will go into that another day. The concentrations in the air vary in different places, where they might be stronger or weaker, so logically the greater the concentration the easier it becomes to perform strong spells, yes?

"For humans, our ability as mages to perform strong spells, is measured by how much of the magic around us we can actually channel and use. Training to become mages increases this ability, much like how the men of the mountains learn to extract more oxygen out of the air when they breath. After years of living high up amongst the clouds where there is very little, their bodies naturally develop the ability to draw more from what's there. When you progress, you will learn to feel when there is a lot of magic in the air around you. Master mages can sense the black DarkLand material with the very fibres and being of our wills, much like any ordinary person can feel when there isn't enough oxygen in the air to breathe."

The room was completely silent as the professor paused and looked up. "Some masters of our art claim to have sensed traces of a more-pure form of magical material, different to the black and corrupting DarkLand matter that most of us know. Unfortunately, all reports of this phenomenon have referred to it as the mildest wisp that was so faint and fleeting, that it is hard to be sure if it was ever there.

"You are all here because you can at some level sense this substance when it is around you, some already more than others. With the education you will receive here and the training you undertake in the harnessing and understanding of magic, your abilities will one day be regarded as a weapon and an asset to our armies. Perhaps even a few of you will become masters of the art and serve your people in the frontline on our southern border."

Professor Worley went on like this for the full two-hour period of the lecture. Most of the time he explained the content of his lecture like a story that gave everybody a foundation of understanding as to how magic works, but at times he would pause and tell everybody to make special note of his teachings. By the end of his first class, Jaeger was consumed by a desire to immediately go outside and attempt to harness the DarkLand matter around him, before realizing that he had no idea what a spell really was, or what he could do with the matter once he had tuned himself to sense it.

"That concludes the lecture, thank you for coming and listening to an old man's rant," Professor Worley finished.

Jaeger stood to leave the lecture theatre, already focused on finding the next class which he needed to be at in an hour's time, when he spotted a familiar-looking blonde girl walking up from the lower seating towards him. He immediately realized that he had been wrong to doubt whether he would recognize her. Aema's striking smile immediately brought back the energy that Jaeger had felt slowly seeping away after sitting and listening for two hours straight. He let the students filing out of the theatre move past him while he waited for her.

"Jaeger!" she exclaimed enthusiastically. "I didn't think I would be seeing you here after so long. You got in!" She noted his first-year robes with a nod.

"Yeah, I had to use a little leverage before they accepted me," he joked. "I kept an eye out for you when I walked in but didn't have any luck."

"I know, I'm usually here far too early and sit way down the front," she admitted a little girlishly. "How are you finding the college?"

"This is actually my first class and it's still sinking in that I am a student here now."

"That's cute," she laughed. "Do you have Alternate Applications of Magic next?"

"I have but I haven't found the classroom yet, I might tag along with you if you're going that way?"

It didn't seem like a significant request to Jaeger but Aema's face lit up at the suggestion. "Definitely! I'll introduce you to my friends since you're new. Do you know anybody here yet?"

"I just met a few people in class then, they seemed like a decent bunch."

"That's good, if you see them tell them to join us at *The Pilgrim's Oasis* at the end of the day if you're not busy, it's the local tavern on campus."

"Sounds like a place worth familiarizing myself with," Jaeger grinned mischievously.

Aema led the way to show Jaeger their next class, but they still had quite a while before it started, so they walked back a short way to a meadow that was shaded neatly by the well-kept gardens surrounding it. There they lay back on the grass and chatted, shaded from the direct heat of the sun until class was due to start. Jaeger learned that Aema had initially grown up in one of the outer towns, just north of Conorbatia on the border of the halfling counties, and that before she had moved to the capital, most of her closest friends had actually been halflings.

Without making a big deal of it, Jaeger noted this similarity to his own background, although Aema's friendship with the halflings had led her to a greater appreciation of the serenity of her surroundings and finding quiet gardens. Jaeger's dwarven influences tended to place a greater value on hard work and raucous nights of drinking.

Just lying on the neat lawns in the quiet heat of the day near Aema, gave him the strong feeling of contentment that had been building since he had been admitted to the college. Jaeger was certain that he would one day look back on this time in his life fondly. Before class started, another three girls found them there on the lawn and joined Aema in the shade. She introduced them to Jaeger, who thought he recognized them from the day he had first met Aema.

"Jaeger this is Lisle," she said standing next the tallest girl who had just helped her up, she was even a fraction taller than Jaeger was and had jet black hair that framed her rounded face. Despite her athletic height and build, she still came across as very feminine and her soft voice camouflaged into their quiet surroundings gracefully.

"Pleased to meet you," Jaeger greeted her politely.

"Pleased to meet you too," she smiled and took his outstretched hand.

"And these two are Odette and Dinara," Aema continued, giving the girls a desperate look as they giggled loudly at something Odette was whispering.

"Pleased to meet you both" Jaeger waved, feeling bashful in front of their private joke.

"It is a *pleasure* to meet you, Jaeger," Odette said grandly, smiling at Aema who was blushing furiously at the pair of them. "I saw you the other week when you met Aema, we are both very big fans of yours. I even told my mother that we met you that day and she didn't believe me. I think you are going to have to come around one day and speak to her in person," Odette continued to babble, sounding a little immature. Jaeger figured she was probably showing off a little because she was around someone new.

"Just ignore Odette, she's a little crazy," Aema interrupted, taking her friend by the shoulders and turning her towards the lecture building as everybody made off towards it. Jaeger laughed uncomfortably but didn't say anything, he was looking around hoping that he would see Nasgro and his friends. With no such luck, they filed into to the building together and Jaeger joined them at the front of the theatre for his lecture on Alternate Applications of Magic.

By the end of the next week at Clouds College of Magic, Jaeger had attended lectures for all the first-year components he was enrolled in. He mostly stayed with the small group of friends he had made on the first day, who were in all of the same classes as him, and by the end of his second week he had introduced them to Aema's friends. The two groups all got to know each other quickly, organizing to meet regularly at *The Pilgrim's Oasis* on Wednesdays and Fridays after class.

Nasgro and Odette had immediately fallen to arguing with each other on the first night at the tavern, and before that night was over, something very close to genuine dislike had developed between the two of them. She had begun teasing him over many of the little things that bothered him, and true to form he took the bait every time.

Jaeger found that most of the other students at the college were quite welcoming and friendly also, although almost all of them seemed to possess a certain level of eccentricity. He concluded that in most cases, this quirk must have been an underlying characteristic required for a person to demonstrate talent in the art, after noticing that it was usually common in most of the talented mages from his year group.

The only blatantly unpleasant people were Kostian and his circle of friends, who Jaeger had gotten off on the wrong foot with from the start. It was actually rumored that Kostian had demonstrated some of the strongest matter perception results for years in the pre-enrollment testing. Unfortunately, this had dashed Jaeger's hopes of writing him off as nothing more than an arrogant brat who got in off his parents' wealth. Although there was no doubting that the 'arrogant brat' part was still true.

Another notion that Jaeger was forced to consider, was that he may have encountered the same conflict with other students at the College, had he spoken to someone else the day he first visited. The thought irritated him and he was glad that he had met Aema on that same day.

16 AN UNEXPECTED REUNION

It was a difficult task to fit everything in with the extra tuition he was receiving after class, but Jaeger was determined not to become reclusive as a result of the extra workload. Other than this he found that the scholarly lifestyle suited him well. Even when he was in class he got to be around his friends, unlike farm-work and most other jobs back home. The many well-kept gardens and open spaces provided the perfect environment for sitting around and reducing stress in between classes, and he figured that these fun little aspects to college would only get better once he had caught up on the classes he had missed at the start of the year.

Excluding his practical sessions learning to sense and harness magical concentrations, Jaeger had decided that his most interesting discipline by far was Magical Cultures. Professor Worley also took the classes for this component, which focused on the varying applications of magic that existed in different cultures.

He had been eagerly anticipating a lecture on dwarf applications of magic for weeks leading up to the topic and remembered being told by the dwarf families back home, that blacksmithing was considered to be just a beginner's trade within the ancient dwarven fraternity. Even though back home Karnsmith's skill in forging weapons could not be rivaled by any humans Jaeger knew.

"The most advanced form of blacksmithing is referred to as 'runesmithing', which is not openly known to be practiced by any dwarves here on The Plateau. This art involves forging weapons with special metals that are difficult to work with. These metals must be melted in the perfect conditions by a runesmith, who only gets one chance to do this before the metal is impervious to modification. As you have probably already gathered, this factor alone would make for a very formidable weapon, but the most amazing thing about weapons made from this metal, is that they can also be imbued to give the weapon permanent magical qualities. Can anybody tell me the name for this metal?"

Jaeger expected that in the capital city the name of this metal would almost be common knowledge, but not a single hand in the classroom was raised. He was tempted to just let professor Worley tell them without an answer, but just as the old master mage breathed in to continue, Jaeger raised his hand.

"Yes Jaeger? Have you heard of the metal?"

"I've heard of hydrargyrum, which is used to forge magical weapons and armour in the mountain realm."

"Excellent my boy, did you see this during your

time in their kingdom?" A mild stir ran through the professor's audience. Outside of his close group of friends, Jaeger hadn't been introduced to many of the other students in his year yet. Jaeger was surprised himself also, professor Worley had never acknowledged that he knew who he was until now.

"No sir, I was told by the dwarves from the town I grew up in."

"Truly?" Worley paused for a moment with genuine surprise at this. Then, brushing it off he continued. "Hydrargyrum as the dwarves call it, is produced from the rare ore cinnabarite which we call vermillion. Do you know what the most remarkable thing about the metal hydrargyrum is Jaeger?"

Jaeger shook his head, the simple answer that it could be magically enchanted seemed too obvious.

"The metal hydrargyrum is not a solid substance like other metals. If you tried to hold it in your hand as I am holding these pages, it would ooze through your fingers like honey," Worley explained, holding a pile of parchment in the air.

"How hydrargyrum is extracted from the cinnabarite ore remains a mystery to all but the dwarves. But once they have the metal, their runesmiths smelt it into a mixture with other metals which they then shape into weapons. Runes are then deeply engraved into the metal during this process and these engravings are filled with pure hydrargyrum. The remarkable properties of this metal allow it to absorb any magical enchantments placed on it by the runesmith. The enchantments are then conducted down through the rest of the weapon via the traces of hydrargyrum in its mixture."

Worley smiled in between his sentences, looking

up at the complete silence before him. "So, to explain it concisely; hydrargyrum metal is able to retain magic within its form. Then by mixing it with solid metals, the dwarves are able to run their enchantments through the entire mass of a solid weapon."

Worley went on to explain how the retention of magical concentrations within a solid object was possible because the matter traveled through the air in vibrations. This mode of transport normally caused the matter to bounce off solid objects, but it could be absorbed by the metal hydrargyrum in its thick liquid state. Once absorbed, the dwarves then returned the metal back to solid form, thus trapping the DarkLand matter within a weapon to perpetually power the specific enchantments engraved by its runesmith.

By the time the class was over, everybody was left with a profound new respect for the dwarven runesmiths, along with many secret desires to one day own a magical weapon. Understanding the principles behind the art was one thing, but what seemed most impressive to Jaeger was that some runesmith must have worked the entire concept out by himself initially.

"The understanding of matter he must have had to invent a practice like that must have been incredible," Jaeger went on about this mysterious runesmith after class.

"I've always wondered the same thing about the person who invented milking cows," Berran contributed. "What was that guy doing?"

"Nobody ever congratulated *me* for my discoveries," Nasgro complained bitterly.

"That's because you have never been able to do

it when we asked you to show us!" Berran retorted. "Even the mage who 'stole' your idea has only presented the spell in theory. It still isn't proven that it *can* be done, so if you do figure it out then maybe you can get credit for it again."

"If it still hasn't been done yet, then why did another mage get credit for it?" Jaeger asked pointedly, "Berran is right, you still could prove that it was you're spell if you were the first to perform it."

"No, I couldn't, it would still look like I just worked out how to cast somebody else's idea for a spell," Nasgro grumbled, but with less conviction now. He didn't sound like he would take much convincing if they encouraged him.

"Well, I disagree," Jaeger continued, "you would still get lots of credit for being the first to use the spell at least. And you would have a much stronger argument for claiming it was your idea if you could prove that you understood the concept well enough to cast it."

Nasgro's eyes lit up, "You're right Jaeger! I should go figure this out before anybody else does," he announced, and ran off towards his room on campus as though every minute now was precious.

"See what you've done!" Berran accused, "Don't encourage that man, he's mad."

"It won't do any harm and I kind of believe him anyway, he has no reason to make it up," Jaeger explained trying not to laugh at Berran.

"He's a lunatic! He doesn't need a reason."

Later that afternoon Jaeger left campus for the marketplace to pick up some small items he wanted. His last class finished quite early every Friday, making it a good day to get things done before his evening tuition. Besides, Emperor Hildebrante's treasury had provided Jaeger with a weekly allowance to use, although Jaeger didn't feel comfortable spending more than a fraction of it since the College already provided everything essential if you were living on-campus.

Once he was beyond the campus borders, the tranquility of its gardens and open spaces was lost to the hectic bustle of city commerce. The crowded markets were filled with shouting store owners and customers who impatiently forced their way past the slower shoppers choking the streets. Jaeger did not want to fit into either of these categories, but after he had waited and slipped through the crowds carefully, he realized that he might lose all his free time in here without achieving anything, and immediately understood the driving reasons behind why this booming city was the way it was.

After quickly crossing a few items off his list that didn't seem necessary anymore, Jaeger drifted down to the materials lane for new shoes, which he had not yet gotten to replace the old ones that he had worn through. This street was not so chaotic like the food market he had just come from, and most of the customers were richly dressed women, casually appraising fabrics and clothing. As he looked left and right for the cobbler's store, something strange caught his eye. He looked back again without consciously knowing why.

It was hair. Standing at a fabrics store with her back turned, was a richly dressed young lady. She was wearing a light dress made of fine materials that stopped just beyond her shoulders, exposing most of her arms which were naturally a few shades darker than most people. Her slightly wavy, jet-black hair, looked familiar to Jaeger even from behind and he had actually stopped still in the street, when he paused to double-check why this was familiar. It took a few moments to register who it was that the young lady had reminded him of, and for the first time since starting at the college, he remembered that she had told him that she would be moving to the capital when she left.

Faline turned while Jaeger was still standing there with a foolish look on his face, processing these thoughts. She also froze when she saw him, now looking just as foolish, and for a few slow seconds they both stood motionless facing each other, dumbfounded by such an unexpected surprise. It was Jaeger who recovered first, bursting with laughter at the look on Faline's face. She soon joined in.

"Jaeger!" she nearly yelled running forward and embracing him. "I can't believe you're here! Standing in front of me! I was just thinking about you, you know. Well actually it must have been a few weeks ago now," she told him without any trace of embarrassment, they had always been comfortable speaking openly.

"Really!?" He was even more surprised, "I can't believe I bumped into you either."

"We very nearly did bump into each other then," she laughed. "Yes, your name was the topic of every conversation in the city recent-" she stopped speaking mid-sentence and the same dumbfounded expression from moments earlier returned. "It was you? *You* are the war-hero that everyone has been talking about, Jaeger! It never occurred to me."

He laughed modestly and realized that unlike most times when people brought this up, he was actually glad that Faline knew, before immediately becoming annoyed with himself when he realized this. "I guess so, I'm actually in a bit of a rush today and can't talk long," he blurted, a little more offensively that he intended.

Faline looked hurt and for the first time Jaeger could remember, her smile was replaced by a brief expression of melancholy, which she quickly disguised. "Well, I hope we get to spend some time together while you are here, are you staying long?" she asked.

"Definitely!" Jaeger replied with a little enthusiasm. "I'm studying at Clouds College of Magic so I will be here for a long time. We are having a few drinks tonight at *The Pilgrim's Oasis* if you are free, otherwise you can find me there on most other Wednesday and Friday nights."

"That sounds exciting, I haven't been there before but one of my friends goes to the College, so I can go with him when I come to see you!" She had recovered from Jaeger's sharp response and was beaming once again.

"Excellent, any friend of yours is a friend of mine Faline." And with that they said their goodbyes. Jaeger went back to looking for new shoes, deep in thought about the unexpected reunion until he made it back to his room on campus.

That night after his tuition, Jaeger found himself continually looking up at the entrance to *The Pilgrim's Oasis* for Faline, while he drank with his friends at one of the tables. As he sat with Aema on one side and Berran on the other, he listened with amusement to

Nasgro and Odette across the table from him. Their bickering had improved now and it seemed to have become more habitual than nasty.

Odette was currently baiting Nasgro with insults that he too had come from a rich family like most of the other students at Clouds, and proceeded to quiz him on whether he truly wanted to be studying at the college. Nasgro seemed far less outraged by her teasing now but still argued the point heatedly.

As the pair began to raise their voices at each other, Jaeger leaned closer to Aema so he could whisper in her ear. "Have you noticed that despite these continual public displays of disdain, those two automatically sit down next to each now wherever we go?"

Aema laughed and turned to Jaeger, "I don't think they are fooling anybody."

"No, they're not" he agreed distantly. He was caught off guard by how close Aema's face was to his, as she looked directly into his eyes. For a few moments neither of them said anything, before Aema smiled knowingly. Jaeger smiled back in turn and reached into his pocket to count the coins in there, while wondering how inappropriate it would be to kiss her in a crowded room full of students. He lost the rest of the night at *The Pilgrim's Oasis*, to pondering this quiet exchange.

17 A FRIEND OF YOURS

The next week, Jaeger's studies suffered some heavy setbacks in motivation. As usual he sat next to Nasgro, Berran, and Ellis near the back of the classroom, but no matter how much he tried, he couldn't help but be distracted by Aema. She always seemed to find her way into his line of vision at the front of the classroom no matter what seat he took, and as a result of this, Jaeger found himself drifting off more often than not during his lectures. Incidentally, this week was also the last week of extra tuition before he would be up to date with the rest of his year group, and so Jaeger fought the distraction, determined not to become lax now that he was so close.

By now he had begun to develop his abilities considerably in sensing matter. On the first two days of the week, he had to fight as hard as he could to push his distractions out of mind, while he attempted to harness the matter out of the air and channel it with his palms as he had been taught. He felt completely burnt out now

235

that he was this close to getting through the worst of his workload, and when his last Wednesday of extra studies came around, he was relieved to find out that the class would be interesting and therefore easy to endure. Worley was taking the small class of students today, for tuition on the source of magic in the world and its effect on everything around it.

"Every particle of DarkLand matter in our world flows out of the gates that were opened in the deep south, from the Demon world," the old professor explained. "As you would know by now, this demon world is known as The DarkLands, thus explaining our use of the term 'DarkLand matter' for magic. But what most of you probably *don't* know, is the corruptive effect that DarkLand matter has on all living things it touches.

"The concentrations of matter that reach The Plateau, is but a faint whisper of what emanates from those gates and so we are not noticeably affected by it here. In larger concentrations, DarkLand matter warps and deforms any living plant or creature that is exposed to it over a long period of time. If we lived closer to its source, the power of DarkLand matter to corrupt all living creatures would leave the human race barely recognizable. We would probably resemble the scaleskins, or roachkin, or most likely some other abomination distorted from our own origins." Jaeger thought back to the brutal society he had witnessed in the jungles and shuddered at the thought of life in a world like that.

"So, you see, our service to the civilized races of the world is two-fold. As mages, not only do we use our powers to serve the emperor's armies, but we also consume vast concentrations of this matter with our spells. Our consumption reduces the accumulation of black energy in our world, which would eventually reduce our people to no better than the vile scaleskins beyond our borders," Worley concluded dramatically as he looked around the class before him shrewdly.

Jaeger felt an overwhelming sense of relief as he left his last class of extra tuition, satisfied that he had worked hard enough in this last week. It had been a difficult first couple of months at the College, but Jaeger had still managed to find time to enjoy himself and he had to admit that the majority of his studies had not been overly unpleasant. As he thanked professor Worley on his way out the door, the old mage stopped him.

"Jaeger, I have been impressed with the commitment you have shown over the last two months. I know that the extra workload has been very taxing, but you handled it well."

Jaeger was taken back, feeling a little embarrassed at how transparent his thoughts must have been for his professor to say that. "Thank you, professor. It has been a pleasure learning from you," he responded politely, although Worley's words had meant far more to him than he let on.

He dragged himself home with his last remaining energy, feeling utterly contented, and when he got back to his room, he dropped everything and flopped onto the bed. He needed to get some of his energy back for what was going to be a very big night at *The Pilgrim's Oasis*.

He woke up suddenly with that stuffy sweaty feeling one gets when they have fallen asleep in the heat of the day. It was dark outside and he realized he must have slept for a couple of hours straight. *Knock knock.* The noise made him start and he realized that this was what had woken him up in the first place. He raced to the door knowing that he was already supposed to be at the tavern, it would already be crowded at this hour and Aema and her friends would be waiting for him to join them now.

Ellis was standing at the door looking fresh and ready to go, something that Jaeger only noticed because his eyes were puffy and he felt sticky and unclean.

"You've been sleeping!" Ellis accused when he saw him. "You had better hurry up if you don't want to be left standing all night."

"I know. It was ages ago when I had a lie down and I didn't think I would actually fall asleep," Jaeger explained.

"Well don't stand there telling me all about it, just get ready. We'll be outside."

"I'll be down there in no time!" Jaeger declared, grabbing a towel and racing down the hall to the bath house, disrobing as he ran.

The hot-tubs had been filled much earlier and the only unused one was no longer hot. Jaeger jumped in and immersed himself completely for half a minute, rubbing himself vigorously under the water with his soap. He burst out of the water with a gasp at the cold, and leapt from the tub while wrapping himself in a towel all in one motion, before racing back to his room. His urgency seemed a little bit over the top even to Jaeger, but the running was just as much because he was freezing cold, as it was because he was late. Less than ten minutes after he had been awoken by Ellis' knocking, Jaeger was standing outside with wet hair, ready to go.

When they reached *The Pilgrim's Oasis*, the noise from inside could already be heard and the place was packed with students getting their drinking underway. Aema and her friends had done their best to hold down a few extra seats by chatting to classmates temporarily, but they still fell one chair short of enough for everyone.

"Nasgro doesn't mind standing, do you?" Odette antagonized with an evil grin.

"All right, all right," Aema jumped in before Nasgro could respond, "Nasgro you can have my seat. Besides Odette, we all know that deep down you would be angry with me if I didn't let him sit next to you," she teased.

"Oh yeah, I'd be furious," Odette remarked sarcastically rolling her eyes, although without realizing it, she was leaning back as she spoke so that Aema could rise and vacate her chair.

"Now where will you sit?" Nasgro asked looking guilty, although like Odette; he had already betrayed his words, shuffling past Aema to take her seat.

Jaeger burst out with laughter, unable to contain himself. "I don't think you'll have any luck getting that seat back Aema, you can have mine"

"I couldn't do that," she protested, "I will just sit on your lap if you think you can take my weight."

Jaeger gave a feigned laugh, Aema had a very petite frame. "I'll try to do my best," he nudged her midriff mischievously. Aema laughed and pretended to be offended, slapping him on the arm, then dropped herself down onto his legs as quickly and heavily as she could. "Have you sat down yet?" Jaeger teased, making sure to compensate for his last joke.

The tavern only became louder and more crowded as the night got underway. Everybody at Jaeger's table was drinking fast and consistently, doing more than their part to contribute to the general noise and revelry inside. Even though she was far from heavy, Jaeger still had to shift legs that Aema was sitting on to keep them from going numb.

As he set his tankard down on the table, he glanced back at the entrance for just a moment by chance at the same time Faline walked in. She was wearing another extravagant and expensive looking dress and Jaeger wondered at what she had been doing in the city this whole time to afford those clothes. She was looking around the room and seemed to have come alone.

"Faline!" Jaeger called out to her.

She spotted him and raced over excitedly, "Jaeger! When did you get here? I like the look of this place."

"Oh, it's not too bad," he smiled. "Are you going to have a drink tonight?"

"In a minute, I'm meeting someone here and haven't found him yet."

"Not a worry, we will be here if you want to join us." He looked around at his friends who looked curious. "Everybody this is Faline, we grew up together in my home town," he introduced her, before she was bombarded with a handful of names and handshakes.

Although he tried to watch carefully, Jaeger could not read Aema's expression as the two introduced themselves.

Faline departed for a short while to look around the tavern for her friend, and after some time had passed Jaeger observed she was still standing at the bar not having found him. She did however have a constant chaperone of young male students approaching her to talk while she waited. After a little longer, she was left alone again, leaning quietly on the polished wood of the bar and Jaeger looked over feeling a little guilty.

"Are you going to go and speak to your friend Jaeger? Or just leave her there alone?" Aema laughed as she watched him.

"I probably should," he said, still feeling the need to treat this one delicately. "I only bumped into her briefly the other day and we haven't really caught up yet."

"Well, I'll make sure nothing happens to your chair while you're gone," Aema promised warmly.

Faline looked relieved when Jaeger came to join her, "I can't find him anywhere!" she exclaimed. "But that's okay. So, what have you been doing lately Jaeger? Besides rescuing kings and fighting monsters that is," she added with a laugh.

They talked at length, filling each other in on what had been going on in their lives since they had last properly spoken. Faline was genuinely amazed at the stories Jaeger shared from his travels and the people he had met. She seemed particularly impressed by his description of the dwarf city and the sophistication of the rooms inside King Borgisliege's palace. None of the stories of his battles and hardships seemed to surprise her very much, and she continued to tease Jaeger like she had always done back home in West-Yield.

She reminded him of the time they had narrowly escaped the scaleskin raiding party a couple of years ago and how heroic he had been protecting her. He blushed furiously, having forgotten her skills in blatant flattery, and all the while feeling painfully aware that he had walked away from Aema a long time ago now to speak to Faline.

When he asked about what she had been doing, he found out that she had been living on a local nobleman's estate, courtesy of his son 'Silver' who she had become close friends with. Faline avoided acknowledging the fact, but from what she told him, it was clear to Jaeger that 'Silver' was completely infatuated with her. He had been letting her use half of his own allowance (which was still quite substantial) so that she could explore the city and its surrounding attractions, kind of like a free holiday. The two of them were very close friends now and the story sounded strangely familiar to Jaeger's own relationship with Faline when they were both living in West-Yield.

"You should meet Silver, he really is one of the most talented young mages here, everybody keeps telling me. He kind of reminds me of you actually." Jaeger bit back the obvious response to that. "He is serious but great fun, extremely talented and quite the ladies' man too!" she added with a cheeky smile.

"I don't doubt that! When is he getting here? It's really quite late to be starting the night at this hour."

"He should have been here before me, I didn't look very hard," she admitted, and then seemed to spot something interesting over near the table where Kostian and his friends were sitting. "Silver!" she yelled, and to Jaeger's shock, Kostian turned sharply and jumped up from the table to greet her.

They embraced and immediately began chatting away. "I thought you had decided to brush me off about an hour ago when I didn't see you," he teased, he hadn't seemed to notice Jaeger standing beside her yet.

"I have been here for much longer than that! I couldn't find you. You should have come looking for me, Silver!" she pouted.

"Silver!?" Jaeger exclaimed incredulously.

Kostian noticed Jaeger for the first time and looked at him with disgust. "Those that I like call me that," he said spitefully.

Jaeger immediately had to clench his anger up inside, Kostian could not even be civil in front of Faline. "You sound really tough insulting me in a crowded Tavern Kostian," he threatened in a menacingly quiet voice.

Faline looked horrified, and quickly stepped between the two of them, "I didn't know you already knew each other. Please don't argue, you're both great friends to me," she pleaded.

"I doubt he would ever have been described as 'great'," Kostian continued with a contemptuous sneer.

"Really? Because this whole city has been using that exact word recently," Faline defended Jaeger.

"I'll leave you to it Faline, I'd rather spend my night in other company," Jaeger growled, and walked away to let Kostian say whatever he liked. Tonight was supposed to be a merry occasion and he didn't intend to let Kostian ruin it.

There were a couple of empty chairs back at Jaeger's table, which were being greedily eyed off by other patrons standing nearby when he returned. All of the boys were still there, but of the girls only Odette and Lisle were with them.

"Where abouts has Aema gotten to?" Jaeger asked, returning to the seat that he had been in earlier, much to the disappointment of the many greedy eyes he could feel behind him.

"I think Dinara and her just popped outside a moment ago," Ellis replied, and Jaeger hopped up again to go check, noticing a handful of glances from inside the tavern immediately turning their gaze back to the empty chair.

He found the two of them talking quietly, in an out-of-the-way corner in the outdoor ale-garden. Dinara smiled when she saw Jaeger and made an excuse to leave them to go back inside. Jaeger walked up and leant against the wall beside Aema.

"Sorry I left you alone with Nasgro and Odette's bickering for so long. I was having a great time with you tonight before I had to get up," he said honestly.

"They weren't too bad," Aema smiled, "but I have to admit that I was having a good time too before you had to go and abandon me," she said putting on a pout.

Jaeger couldn't think of any clever response while she was standing there smiling so mischievously, so out of instinct he leant forward slowly. Aema leant forward also, covering the remaining distance between

244

them and meeting his lips halfway for their first kiss. Jaeger closed his eyes and lost himself completely in the moment that he was in; there was no moment in the past to reflect on and none in the future to plan for. For once in his life, he felt like there were no other moments to worry about.

18 A RUMOUR OF SHADOW

Now that he had come to the end of his extra tuition classes, Jaeger found himself with a lot more time on his hands. He now realized that the normal lifestyle of a student at Clouds College, was far less taxing than it had seemed when he was catching up. There were gaps of free time all through his days where tuition classes used to be, which he easily replaced by spending time with Aema.

The two of them were happy to be seen leaving their larger group of friends together, now that they were officially an item. Jaeger enjoyed being around Aema either way and definitely enjoyed the company of all their friends, but being alone together gave him the opportunity to slip her kisses in the garden she had shown him when they first met. They often went here to get away from everything. The river running through it was strong and loud at this time of year, giving the place a fresh energy.

For the next couple of months at the college,

Jaeger's abilities in Matter in Practice came ahead in leaps and bounds. He had even begun to manipulate the matter he harnessed and use it for some of the more simple spells, such as exerting physical force on objects from a distance. He realized that mages didn't just cast spells to do a specific purpose, which was the impression he got from listening to tales growing up. In reality a mage just expressed the forces they drew in through their palms in any way they could come up with, as long as they understood the nature of magic enough to do this.

At first it required intense clenching throughout his whole body and Jaeger would be sore for days after every serious attempt. He had been taught to let this exertion come from the muscles in his pelvis, which was the core of all mages' strength to harness matter. Once a mage had mastered this technique everything became easier, and the simple exertion of force would just be a stepping stone to far greater applications; such as fireballs or lightning bolts of raw energy and many other incredible feats Jaeger had heard of in his lectures.

The lectures in History of Magic were the most fickle, some days their content was exciting to learn, while on other days Jaeger found it hard to stay awake. One of the better topics in History of Magic involved a continuation from the story of the Great Invasion of Evil, which he had heard numerous times by now. Today professor Hillson was discussing how the world was affected on a meteorological level, in the years that followed the opening of the DarkLand Portal.

"It took a full week for the demon princes of the DarkLands to finish opening their portal to this world, and during this time our lands were ravaged by thunderstorms and earthquakes from the upheaval it caused. The effects this had on the weather of our world, lasted far longer than just the initial week though."

Professor Hillson spoke in a deep throated monotone voice, which could make even the most interesting lectures roll out of his throat as if he was reciting the words mindlessly from an invisible page in front of him. Interesting topics like this one helped a little, but Jaeger still had to focus hard on the noise that he was translating into information.

"Our most reputable theories claim that the marauding creatures who invaded our land, were not actually from the DarkLands like the demon princes, but from a separate land mass across the sea that was connected to our own continent by an ice bridge. The ice bridge was hundreds of miles long, and formed at the southern end of the world near the gates of hell. Learned men in this field believe there is still a land-shelf remaining today just a small distance below the water's surface, and that this shelf acted as the foundations for the ice bridge.

"The shallow water above the shelf was more susceptible to the temperatures of the world above, which is what caused it to freeze, creating the solid bridge for the roachkin and scaleskins to migrate across."

Professor Hillson went on to discuss the theories of a migration across the bridge, which had been many miles wide. He described how the scaleskins and roachkin had slowly moved further and further north, after years of exposure to the thickest concentrations of dark matter in the south closest to the portal.

"It is highly probable that the beasts we now know today as roachkin and scaleskins, were mutated from a more civilized species not unlike ourselves, or the dwarves, or elves, or even halflings. We have since tried to learn from this, and so it happened that nearly a hundred years ago; the emperor of the time ordered that before any new towns were built, approvals had to be given by his mage advisors, to determine whether the population would be exposed to dangerous levels of DarkLand matter in an area."

By the end of the lecture, Jaeger felt exhausted from the mental strain that had gone into absorbing the professor's baritone noise of information.

"Yet another two hours of my life that I won't get back," Berran commented dryly as they stood up to leave.

"I actually found the content quite interesting when I listened," Jaeger admitted. "The problem is Hillson's voice, it is nearly impossible to focus on anything that comes out of that man's mouth for more than a few minutes."

"I wouldn't be able to comment on the content of his lectures unfortunately. As soon as he starts talking, I go to sleep."

"We noticed that," Ellis added with a sly grin, he had been lightly brushing ink across the end of Berran's nose while he slept, until it was black like a dog's. Jaeger chuckled to himself inwardly and let Berran leave the lecture theatre unaware of his new look.

The most momentous news Jaeger received during his studies, came around halfway into the year. Rumors had been spreading of a new threat in the world since before he even left West-Yield and there was now a growing belief, that something dark and powerful had been taking power beyond the borders of The Plateau, driving their enemies with more purpose than ever before. Darroch had alluded to it when he first addressed Jaeger's town, and on a number of occasions afterwards, while The Plateau and the Stronghold Ranges had been working tirelessly to piece together the source of this new shadow before it rooted itself deeper in the world and spread.

Professor Harbold was taking the opportunity of a relevant topic in Alternate Applications of Magic, to discuss his own speculations on what this source may be. The lecture today was about the elves deep to the southern island below the continent of Thylacine, and how they may be playing a pivotal role near The DarkLand Portal in holding its influence at bay.

"I do not intend to bore you by telling you again, that if our lands became flooded with DarkLand matter -or saturated by it may be a better term- then we would all live the same sad existence as the scaleskins and roachkin. However, despite the relentless tide of DarkLand matter through the portal into our world, we do not find ourselves in that predicament. Can anybody tell me why?"

A number of hands shot up immediately, clearly the answer was no secret. Professor Harbold pointed to a student in the middle of the classroom who must have raised his hand first. Even when there had only been a fraction of a second between students, the professor never hesitated to decide whose hand was the first in the air. Jaeger liked to believe that he always knew.

"Because all races have their own mages that use the matter up," a voice echoed out of the group.

"Yes, there are mages, runesmiths, shamans, seers and warlocks all from their respective races, who use this matter and therefore contribute to the consumption of it. But helpful though that may be, it is not likely to be the main reason that DarkLand matter concentrations are held at bay." He let his comment sit there as the majority of his students lowered their hands only leaving a handful still raised.

Kostian was one of these, "The elves have discovered a way to block the matter from entering our world."

"Correct to a certain degree. The elves long ago mastered the ability to gravitate large concentrations of DarkLand matter from their surrounding areas. And so, the pivotal question now is what do they do with it?"

Nobody raised their hands this time and Harbold did not wait long for anyone to figure it out. "You know no less than I do on this matter," he admitted. "It is suspected that they have converted their archipelago of islands into a web, to capture and obstruct the influx of DarkLand matter, but that is about as much as we know. What we also know is that they stand guard over everything else that comes out of the portal, a gateway that connects our world to another world of demons and dreadful evil."

It dawned on Jaeger as he listened, that the entire existence of the elves was just one great terrible burden. One which now seemed to dwarf the problems of his own people who only had mortal enemies at their borders to deal with.

"The latest intelligence on the war, is that the scaleskins and roachkin may possibly be collaborating for the first time to work together against us and the dwarves. Rumours have also been heard that demons have been present on this continent. That the elves have been forced to allow many invasions to pass by unchallenged, unable to stand against The DarkLand Portal indefinitely.

"If there is truth to both the intelligence and rumours, then it would be grave news indeed. I suspect that the two are linked, and that it is demons who are responsible for coordinating the latest spree of attacks on the human and dwarf realms. Until now, our biggest advantage against the savages has been their lack of discipline and tendency to fight each other almost as much as they fight us. But under the command of DarkLand demons, they may soon coordinate a full-blown invasion to wipe out the civilized races of our world forever."

Harbold decided he would leave them all on that grim note at the end of his lecture. Evidently, he had been harbouring these concerns for a long time and probably felt that the carefree youth of the world today could do with a shake-up, to make them think beyond their own plans for the tavern on Wednesday nights. It had certainly affected Jaeger, he had spent his life in a border town under the shadow of constant scaleskin raids, and had witnessed the devastation that they caused first-hand. And now this shadow was lengthening.

19 OF MONKS AND MOUNTAINS

Jaeger had not seen or spoken to Faline since his argument with Kostian at The Pilgrim's Oasis, although he had seen a lot of Kostian around the College. He now had more reason than ever to dislike Kostian and felt that he saw far too much of him wherever he went. Faline on the other hand was unlikely to see Jaeger unless she came to the tavern again to find him, but Jaeger was still undecided on whether he wanted to see her straight away even though he knew it was not her fault that two of her closest friends didn't get along.

Despite how long it had been since that night, Jaeger had been so caught up with his business that he hadn't been able to give it much thought. Between classes, friends, and Aema, he had most days fully occupied and was content with how everything was going. It was on a Tuesday night after class, when suddenly out of the blue Jaeger was reminded of Faline and the last time he had seen her. He had been lying on his bed staring at the ceiling when his thoughts shifted topic to her. It was like the reminder one gets when they realize they have forgotten to do something.

In the same moment, he felt his palms pushing lightly against the DarkLand matter in the room like magnets. This was how his palms always felt when he was harnessing magic, although it had never happened spontaneously like this before. Jaeger wondered if perhaps this was normal and that his abilities were growing, before concluding that whatever it was; it seemed to have started at the exact moment that thoughts of Faline were suddenly thrust into his head.

Sitting up on his bed, he closed his eyes and tried to harness more DarkLand matter. He had no idea if this would achieve anything, but decided to run with this new sense to see where it would take him. Slowly he gathered all the matter in the room with his palms, rotating them slowly to scan for more, like an old man cocking his ear towards a conversation to hear better. The magnetism inside his palms was now enormous, he could no longer point them towards each other without his arms flying apart from the force and straining his shoulders. He was more focused now than he had ever been before during Matter in Practice.

Once the charge of DarkLand matter had filled his body, Jaeger realized that he had not yet decided what he was going to do with the energy and looking around the room, he tried to find something he could use magic on. He faced both palms downwards in the meantime as he had been taught in class, pushing against the ground with the matter as though his hands were resting on two invisible walking sticks.

This was one of the first tricks taught to young

mages, and once mastered, they had learnt the foundation to potentially to thrust themselves from one place to another, or high into the air. He decided against trying this after noting how low the ceiling in the room was, and continued looking around until his attention eventually settled on the door. He could blow it outwards with this force? Again, probably not a wise decision, but he couldn't stop staring at it. Suddenly it knocked.

Hearing the door knock was the last thing Jaeger had been expecting and he nearly *did* jump into the roof, palms still facing down. This had had nothing to do with him or any of the energy in his palms which he had not yet released, and as he sat there considering this, he began to wonder if he had just imagined it. Then another louder knock came, nearly making him jump all over again. Somebody was outside the door of course. He raced over to the door, still tense with the build-up of energy inside him and opened it. Faline was standing in front of him with her hand raised to knock again.

"Jaeger, I'm sorry to surprise you but I couldn't think of any other way to get a hold of you without going to the tavern with Kostian again. And that didn't turn out wonderfully last time," she added with a nervous laugh.

Jaeger was at a loss for what to say, still dumbfounded that some supernatural force had informed him that Faline would be visiting. He was still trying to unravel what the magical implications of this would be if it was not a coincidence, when he realized he hadn't responded.

"Yes, that's fine. I mean you're right, it didn't. Do you want to come in?" he asked, fumbling terribly with his words.

"Is everything alright? I can come back another time if you don't want to talk to me," she said a little accusingly.

"No, come in, I just got caught up in my own thoughts then, it is nothing to do with you. Then again it kind of is." He said awkwardly still trying to unravel his thoughts.

"What do you mean?" Faline asked, unsure of what he was getting at.

"Ah, it's complicated, can you open that window for me please?" he asked, holding his hands down carefully trying not to touch anything. He felt as though he was about to implode.

"Sure," she laughed nervously, and jumped onto his bed pushing the window above it open. Jaeger motioned with his head for her to stand clear and slowly raised both palms until they were facing the open window. He clenched his entire body and felt the surge of energy racing down his arms and out of his palms, creating a painful burning sensation and making him shiver all over at the same time. An incandescent purple ball of fire ignited the air in front of him and went hurtling out the window. Ignoring gravity, the fireball maintained its direction without falling until it burnt out a hundred yards away.

Jaeger gasped and looked at Faline who shared the same look of wild-eyed shock as him. "You didn't know that was going to happen?" she exclaimed sounding a little bewildered.

"No, I've never cast a fireball before, they haven't even started teaching it yet. I'll have to remember how I did that," he added, feeling a little pleased with himself now that it was over.

Faline took a seat at the foot of his bed while Jaeger sat at the other end. They were both a little tentative to say anything at first, but once they had moved on from the fireball incident, they both began to chat away until the hours flew past. It was the first long, genuine, conversation Jaeger had had with Faline for a long time and it reminded him how they could spend an entire day alone together in the sun by the river back home.

It also reminded Jaeger of how strongly he had felt for Faline when they both lived in West-Yield, and he felt a little guilty that he had made so little effort to see her in Conorbatia since the night at the tavern. For some reason he had resented Faline after that, or maybe he had resented her even before then, he considered, remembering how he had snapped at her in the marketplace. Right now though, while they were talking, he couldn't have felt further from resenting her and it made no sense that he had before.

They talked about anything and everything, from what each of them enjoyed about living in the bustling capital city, to their plans to see the family and friends they had left behind. Jaeger was bothered that he had made the decision to continue life away from his home town without going back there first. It was likely that Tevin, Mendel and little Bellan, had been expecting him to come home and return to his old life once he had completed his quest with Darroch. He hoped that his letter had arrived at least, and that they knew he hadn't been killed.

"I will definitely be sure to go home at the end

of my first year," Jaeger declared. "There is enough time before second year starts, for me to travel to West-Yield and back in between. Also, I'm hoping Aema might like to come with me to meet everyone back home."

"I remember her from your table," Faline surprised Jaeger. "She was the blonde girl with the green eyes, she was very pretty," she teased.

"Yes, she is," Jaeger laughed comfortably. "What about you? You don't have anything that you're tied to before you can go home do you?"

"No," she said thoughtfully, "but I don't feel like I am in any rush to return. If I were to go home anytime soon, it would only be because I feel guilty that my family are missing me."

"Yeah, that's the way I see it too, although I do really want to see them as well. I don't know, is that still just because of guilt or because I miss them?"

Faline laughed, "I'm not sure, I think it could still be a little bit of guilt. But I think that missing someone and feeling guilty that you haven't seen them for a long time can feel very similar."

"Exactly, so it's probably guilt. No, it's a bit of both," Jaeger concluded. "Are you getting tired yet?" he asked, watching Faline yawn. He couldn't help but yawn himself and was reminded of how Tevin used to always tell him that yawning was contagious.

"I am, yes. I think I had better go, it must be well past midnight now!" she said, realizing how long they had been sitting there.

"It is, I don't think dawn is a long way off actually," Jaeger agreed, "I will walk you back home."

Faline protested a little, but Jaeger refused to let her walk back through half the city on her own at this hour. They said their goodbyes when Jaeger reached the entrance to Donagarn's estate, and promised to make sure they would see much more of each other now. Jaeger watched Faline disappear on up the private pathway to her housing, before he turned around to walk the path he had just come by.

As he made his way home, Jaeger was struck by how differently he viewed Faline now that he was no longer infatuated with her, but chose not to analyse that observation too deeply. Dawn really was on its way by the time he got home and he noted the black night sky was a lighter shade. The morning birds had begun their chirping now in the freezing cold at the start of a new day.

When Jaeger woke, he felt like he hadn't slept at all. His eyes stung from lack of sleep and he contemplated the idea of trying to get away with skipping class today. But in what felt like a superhuman effort, he conquered the temptation to go back to sleep and forced himself to stand and wash his face.

The sun had been up for only a couple of hours, which was all the sleep he had had since it was just breaching the horizon when he got home and closed his eyes. Despite the drowsiness he still felt great. For some reason everything seemed to be turning out just perfectly for him lately, which fueled his motivation to do the right thing by going to class.

The lecture today in Magical Cultures was about the monks of the 'Thin-Air Peaks', which were located in the middle of the desert far south of The Plateau. Jaeger had heard very little of the monks before and knew this lecture would be the best opportunity that he would get to learn about them, which was another telling factor in convincing him that today wasn't the day to be skipping class.

Professor Worley stood at the front of the class and waved them down for silence. Everybody slowly hushed and Jaeger felt his mind drifting off as he nearly dipped into sleep where he sat. The sound of Worley's voice drew his attention back and he clenched every muscle in his body to stay awake.

"Today we will explore a magical culture that is unlike any other, both in its structure and its nature. In my final year as a student mage, I specialized in the lore of the monks. This particular field turned out to be one of my personal favourites from my time as a student at Clouds College of Magic," he said grandly.

"The first distinctive characteristic of this culture, is that it is not made up of any one race. Our demographic on The Plateau is also made up of various races including; humans, dwarves, and halflings, but each maintain their own culture within this society. The monks on the other hand blend these same races into one culture, until they no longer identify with each other as being from different peoples. They all fall under one single title together, which they refer to as *one who has heard the call*." This didn't really make sense to anybody and Jaeger pricked his ears up to see if Worley was going elaborate on the term.

"You see, reaching the 'Thin Air Peaks' is considered to be virtually impossible," Worley explained. "The journey leads through a harsh desert with no paths and it is rumoured that any who attempt this journey without having 'heard-the-call', are destined to perish before they find their way. Some believe that a higher power beyond the magic of mages or shamans, protects the monks from the violence of the outside world, and that this power is what sustains and guides those who were intended to come there.

"So, if this is the case, then how is it possible for any of us to know anything about their culture?" Worley asked, putting everybody on the spot to consider his question. "With great difficulty!" he laughed after a short pause, and Jaeger wondered if he was referring to his own research when he said this.

Jaeger had heard a few times now that Worley had gained great renown for his studies of the monks in his final year at Clouds. All students at the College were required to specialize in a single area of magic in their final year and complete this learning without lectures or guidance. It was a clever system devised long ago by the founders of the College, to ensure that advancements were continually being made in the human study of magic.

"As I said," Worley continued, "the monks are a mixture of humans, dwarves and halflings who had heard-the-call. After which they were compelled to undertake their journey through the desert, sustained by what can only be described as some higher power or force of magic, until they reach the peaks. Once among the peaks, all monks choose to live without the luxuries and frivolity that is such a core part of our lives on the Plateau.

"Instead, they practice a simpler life, consisting of their valued necessities, such as; food, water, shelter and inner-harmony which they value as the greatest necessity of all. This they gain through daily meditation and by undertaking activities that they believe nurtures one's soul, such as tending to plants and all other living things that share their habitat with them.

"Interestingly, it is these activities that have developed them into most accomplished Clerics. The monks are considered to be among the most magically gifted people in the world, as a result of their centuries of inner silence and single-minded commitment to their abilities. Our emperors and other military advisors have often tried to seek them out for alliances throughout history. Unfortunately, as I said; the journey to the Thin Air Peaks is virtually impossible for those who were not meant to make it.

"Another problem these commanders face if they ever could make it, is that the monks refuse to use their magic for any other purpose than to maintain harmony within the world they have created for themselves. This world of theirs is almost completely separated from the world that the rest of us live in, and is definitely separated from the troubles we face."

For all the sense that this made, Jaeger couldn't help but question the one thing that frustrated him most about their resolve of indifference.

"But can't the monks see that if they helped us to destroy all the evil creatures in this land, then the entire world would be free to live peacefully, just like them?" Jaeger immediately felt foolish once he had spoken. Somehow, he felt he should know the answer to this.

"As you will all someday realize, it is not just roachkin and scaleskins who stand in the way of peace, but humans too," Worley replied with surprising decisiveness. "Did you know that all monks have the ability to instantly heal wounds and ailments? And that they also refuse to use this magic to tend any hurts to themselves?

"They do this because of a commitment to their acceptance of suffering, believing that this is a necessity for enlightenment. Instead, the monks only use these powers to nurture the lands, plants, and beasts around them. In fact, it is believed that the fabled aves-caprinae -enormous winged goats the size of horses- live in the thin air peaks. The bond between these creatures and the monks is said to be so close that they even allow the monks to ride them when the occasion demands.

"So, if you listened carefully, you will see that it is because of their belief that suffering and enlightenment lie hand in hand, that the monks refuse to change the violent suffering in our world. They acknowledge that roachkin and scaleskins are evil, but see no difference between suffering from physical torment at the hands of these creatures, to suffering from the spiritual degeneration at the hands of selfish and decadent living."

The old but stern looking professor waited and assessed his students for any more queries on this topic. Nobody spoke up, but the quiet buzz of many conversations now filled the lecture theatre. It was a lot for Jaeger to take in, but as tired as he was, he was listening. After a short pause Worley continued.

"So now we return to the reason that monks are so sought after for their prowess in battle. I have already mentioned that they have extraordinary powers of healing, which on its own would make them an invaluable asset in battle. But it is because of a monk's broad variety of magical abilities, that our battle mages consider them to be such a well-rounded package.

"As mages we possess the ability to manipulate matter which they too can do, but they are also adept to other powers more similar to that of a seer. They do not claim to be able to hear other's minds, but it is said that they can read a person and their true intentions without having to listen to what they are saying, or *despite* what they are saying more often than not. They can also sense the future, not like folktales would have you believe of old mages standing over a crystal ball, but they can feel events before they happen. Far less clearly perhaps, but the nature and proximity of the event is clear to them."

"How is it that all this is known if the only people who can reach the peaks, are those who become monks and stay there?" someone on the other side of the classroom asked. Jaeger looked across. It was Kostian.

"With great difficulty as I said," Worley laughed, and again Jaeger suspected the old professor had just made some personal joke to himself. "Many ordinary humans other than those pilgrims who heard-the-call, have attempted to reach them for various reasons. Some want to ask for the healing of a terminally ill loved-one, others have attempted to convince them to take a stand and join the battles that engulf this continent.

"Our history has no records of any such people who have ever returned or been heard of since, and although the monks are a peaceful people who would do no harm to others, it is still considered perilous to try to reach them. Those without an iron-resolve to reach the peaks, should probably consider that there are many other more-productive causes to die for than that."

"That still doesn't really explain how we can know anything about the monks," Kostian complained.

"Doesn't it?" Worley replied, still sounding amused. "Well, everybody that concludes our lecture on the monks of the mountains, thank you for listening to an old man rant again today."

Jaeger nearly fell asleep where he sat the moment professor Worley announced the end of the lecture, as though only his will had been keeping him awake and focused during the class. With this will now withdrawn, Jaeger didn't feel he had the energy to even make it back to his room. He did indeed slump down in his seat and let his head drop onto Ellis' shoulder, who was sitting next to him.

"What's wrong with you?" Ellis immediately recoiled, leaving Jaeger's head with nothing to rest on. "That was one of the best lectures we've had so far this year," he declared, mistaking Jaeger's exhaustion as a display of boredom.

"No, I agree," Jaeger said dreamily, trying to shake his mind clear. "I just had no sleep last night and that lecture was the only thing keeping me awake."

"*Reeeeally?*" Ellis said with exaggerated interest, "and why were you awake all night?"

"I just didn't get any sleep is all," Jaeger answered, omitting unnecessary details that would sound suspicious to his friends. Aema and Odette came walking up the steps from the front of the theatre towards them.

"Hello!" Aema greeted them chirpily. "That was a great topic."

"We were just saying the exact same thing,"

Ellis agreed as the whole group of them started filing outside together.

"What are you boys doing now?" Aema asked, mainly directing the question at Jaeger.

"I am going to go to bed and sleep," Jaeger announced, "I am so tired that I will fall asleep wherever I am, so I might as well find somewhere comfortable."

"He didn't get any sleep last night," Ellis nudged Aema suggestively. She gave Jaeger a questioning look and he just rolled his eyes.

"You can join me if you like, I'll be asleep but it would still be nice to be with you anyway," Jaeger offered, which drew a number of cat-calls and suggestive whistles from everyone. Jaeger had been too tired to realize how his offer sounded.

"Ignore them Jaeger, I know what you meant," Aema laughed putting her arm around him and kissing his cheek.

This drew even more teasing from their friends, before Odette decided to start goading Nasgro into an argument about maturity. Jaeger and Aema then parted ways with their friends and strolled across the quiet grounds towards the haven of his room. When they finally got there, Jaeger dropped onto his bed and Aema nestled in alongside him, where they both fell asleep for the better part of the middle of the day,

20 THE SHADOWS LENGTHEN

Towards the end of Jaeger's first year at Clouds College, reports began to flood into the city that the war on the southern front was not going well, and that the series of forts and settlements along this front were now battling to survive on a daily basis. In the past, every human casualty was rewarded with numerous scaleskins killed, on account of their heavy fortifications and other tactical advantages associated with defending the high ground.

But the traditionally disorganized mobs of the scaleskins, had now been replaced with military discipline as they closed this gap, only conceding twice as many of their kind for every human lost. Similar stories were continuing to emerge from the dwarven kingdom, where the roachkin had continued to become more and more cunning in their attacks, following the ambush inside Aridhold that had nearly claimed their king.

There had been a temporary stall in the scaleskin

advance and maybe even a little progress was made when Darroch had taken command at the frontline. However, reports continually came in now, that the battle mages were being consistently out-mastered by enemy shamans, and no reported solution had been found yet to tip this balance of power back.

The news seemed to be taking its toll on almost everyone. Even the carefree students at Clouds College who had lived their lives sheltered from the threat of invasion, were beginning to express concern and discuss their fears. Normally the most serious issues they had to talk about was the effect that lectures and assessments had on their social lives, but nobody was able to escape the almost daily reminders. It seemed like the entire existence of the human race was hanging on by a thread.

Every year around this time at Clouds College of Magic, first year students also started to become excited for their annual field trip. Under the supervision of the head mage lecturer and a handful of master mages, all first-year students were invited to attend a field trip to the southern frontline, for their first taste of the world they were ultimately training for.

It was something everybody had been looking forward to, but like everything else, the trip had now come to serve as another reminder of the gloomy tidings from the warfront, as discussions were underway to determine whether it was safe enough to hold the trip this year. It would only be a couple of weeks away now if it was to go ahead, and even then, everybody knew that the experience was going to be severely restricted compared to previous years.

"I think that now more than ever it is a good

idea to send us down there to help," Jaeger declared to his friends across a table at *The Pilgrim's Oasis*. It was quieter than usual for a Wednesday night, which had been the case for a while now.

"The field trip isn't designed so that students can go down and help, they wouldn't be sending first-years if it was," Lisle disagreed in her soft voice, which was calm and friendly even when she was arguing.

"I still think that we have learnt enough this year to be of some help if we all stick together," Jaeger maintained stubbornly. It still hadn't escaped his mind, that he might possibly see Darroch and Marrick down there with a little luck.

"I'm sorry but I have to agree with Lisle," Aema responded after Jaeger looked at her enquiringly. "I definitely want to go on this field trip, but only as a learning experience. If there is fighting going on, then I don't think any of us should be anywhere near it."

"Fair enough," Jaeger conceded. "I just hate hearing all this bad news about the war, when all I can do is listen and wait here while it gets worse."

"You've seen and done a lot more than any of us though," Aema said encouragingly. "You have to understand that most students at Clouds College, have grown up in Conorbatia away from the threat of attacks and raiding parties," she explained putting on a girly display of innocence. "And *none* of us have journeyed through the wild jungles, fighting scaleskins, and roachkin, and rescuing kings!"

"Now you're just making fun of me," Jaeger accused.

"Yes, but the point I was making is still true. We are not ready for any fighting yet. You have the advantage of knowing that if all else fails, you can just grab your sword and hit things with that. Can you imagine any of us being suited to that?"

"Not everyone," Jaeger admitted, "but they could just stand behind us," he laughed, nudging Berran and looking at Ellis and Nasgro who smiled and nodded confidently.

"Don't lump yourself in with them Nasgro!" Odette roared with laughter. "You definitely fit into the skinny academic category, hiding behind the fighters!" She continued laughing uncontrollably.

"You're right, I would drag you to the frontline first as a sacrifice and then hide behind you," Nasgro retorted. He had been getting a lot better at returning her insults.

"How very un-chivalrous of you," she huffed.

"I'm confused? I've always been told that chivalrous knights got rid of monsters."

It wasn't long after this, when everyone was put out of their anxiety from waiting to find out if Clouds College would still hold the field trip. On the Monday following their discussion at *The Pilgrim's Oasis*, Professor Worley addressed the entire grade before their early morning lecture in History of Magic. The lecture for History of Magic held the entire year group in one sitting unlike the other components, which held the same lectures at different times to spread the large student numbers into smaller classes.

The old professor waited until after the normal start time for the lecture, allowing any latecomers to arrive for his message, before raising his hands for silence.

"As you all know, we have been holding some serious discussions recently to determine whether or not our annual field trip to the southern front would go ahead this year" Worley announced, cutting straight to the point. "We have decided that the trip this year should still go ahead, but will have to be limited to the chief military fort of Grantanmar, in order to ensure the safety of all students.

"Grantanmar is the headquarters of all operations on the frontline and is the most secure hold we have down there. Nevertheless, it is still in the thick of the war-zone now, so none of you should worry about missing out on getting some real hands-on experience out there." A little grumbling could still be heard around the lecture theatre, but for the most part, everyone seemed to just be glad that their excursion had not been cancelled altogether.

"We have also managed to secure an additional contingent of master mages to accompany us for extra protection. So, at the end of this lecture, I want everyone to come to the front and put your names down for the groups you will be separated into. Now if there are no questions, I suggest you all start preparing for the excursion as you will be leaving on the second Monday from today. Thank you and enjoy your lecture," Worley finished simply, and exited the lecture theatre as it erupted with a chorus of chatter, leaving the noisy room to professor Hillson.

When the Monday arrived, everyone was relieved to find out that they would be traveling the long roads to Grantanmar in a convoy of wagons to make the trip easier. Many of the students from the estates in and around Conorbatia, had even brought their own horses to ride upon which the College had allowed for years, as it reduced the demand for wagons as well as the crowding in the ones supplied.

Most of them rode at the head of the two-hundred-strong convoy now, dressed in their finest riding clothes. It seemed a little typical of their haughty nature, but Jaeger didn't give much time to think about it. He was instead preoccupied by a strange feeling of dread that had been tugging at him ever since the convoy started moving south. He now sat pensively in his wagon as they rolled on.

The wagons were primarily used for transporting goods not people, and around eight to ten people had been fitted in each one, sprawled out across the tray inside under the semi-circular canvas roofs. Aema sat next to Jaeger against the side wall in their wagon, with her head on his shoulder resting quietly. Beside her was Odette and Dinara, while Nasgro and Ellis sat opposite them against the other side. Berran and Lisle were lying comfortably on the piles of blankets in the middle. Everybody seemed relaxed and calm and most of them were either asleep, or dozing in that comfortable place on the verge of sleep.

Jaeger was the only one that did not feel at ease. Since he had begun to develop his abilities in harnessing magic, he had also started noticing that he would get a tingling sensation which affected his mood before significant events occurred to him. At first this had made everything seem like a strange coincidence when it actually happened, before he began to suspect there may be a connection between the two. Nobody else could relate to this when he described the sensation though, so he assumed it was not common in mages and tried not to let his own sense of dread affect the others in his wagon by mentioning it.

The season of spring was well underway now and the weather had begun to hint that summer was not far off before they left Conorbatia. But on the second day of their journey south, the sun had disappeared behind thick clouds and hadn't returned. These clouds had become increasingly thick and dark as they moved south and it had now been raining for three days straight under them.

Sitting uncomfortably in the dripping wagon under the dark relentless storm clouds, Jaeger couldn't help but think that an ominous shadow was now stretching out across the land, and that now they had entered it they would never come out again. Unlike everyone else in his wagon who were happy for the wet change, the weather only pushed Jaeger's sense of dread into a strange melancholy, making him uncharacteristically quiet while the rest of them chatted.

"What's the matter?" Aema asked Jaeger, who was barely mumbling a reply to anybody who spoke to him. "You don't seem to be too happy about this field trip anymore."

"Not at all! I can't wait to get to Grantanmar," he lied, trying to force some enthusiasm into his voice. "I think that being cramped up in this wagon is just making me feel lethargic."

"You can always jump out and jog alongside us if you need some refreshing," Ellis suggested.

"I'll keep that in mind as a backup plan," Jaeger promised dryly. "This is unusual weather for this time of year don't you think?" he probed again to see if anyone had started picking up on general feel he was getting from the environment.

Nasgro considered the question seriously, he seemed to be the only one who had gathered that Jaeger was not making an offhand comment. "The rain does seem a little heavy for the end of spring I suppose, but other than that everything looks normal and green out there."

"It is very rich and green out there isn't it" Jaeger agreed.

The rain eased down to the occasional light drizzle over the next couple of days, but the clouds did not go away. On the seventh morning of trotting along, the group's mage supervisor Renold, leant back from his seat as he drove the wagon, to inform them that they would probably reach Grantanmar before the evening set in at this pace. Renold was young for a master mage and didn't even look to be quite thirty yet. He was charged with the safety of around twenty students on this trip, which covered the wagon Jaeger was in, as well as another group who had been assigned to him. Jaeger hadn't been surprised to find that it was just his luck to have Kostian and his buddies in the other group randomly assigned to Renold's supervision.

The entire convoy maintained a slightly faster pace than usual throughout this morning. Evidently the other wagon drivers were also aware that they were close to the military base now, and were all trying to make it before nightfall. By midday they began to pass the first outlying settlements attached to the network of forts. Everybody was caught off guard by the condition the settlements were in.

The houses were filthy and any repairs that had been done on them clearly stood out by how shoddy the work was. The fields were disorganized and grew a poor stunted crop, while the livestock were severely malnourished. Jaeger looked out with disgust. Farms like these would go out of business immediately back in West-Yield, but he figured that the demands of the war must have been the reason why everything was so substandard, and tried not to judge.

This entire region was also notorious as a turbulent magical catchment, and Professor Hillson had surmised in his lectures that this was a result of the general shape of the lands around it. The bowl-shaped hills of The Plateau, acted as a funnel for the currents of DarkLand Matter that flowed up from the south. This combined with the unwholesome scaleskin activity near the area, had caused much of the land to die out and join the Great Desolation.

Hillson had explained how the Great Desolation was a blighted corridor of land ten leagues wide, which ran south from the borders of The Plateau, passing through the central jungles and onto the scorched volcanic deserts beyond. Looking at the general state of the lands they had just entered, Jaeger was also reminded of what he had been taught about DarkLand matter affecting its environment, especially in strong concentrations.

The afternoon was pushing on when they finally rolled in through the tall spiked gates that marked the entrance to Grantanmar. The town had a cold, dark feel to it and reminded everybody of the fireside tales they were told as children, about vampires and ghouls and the eerie ghost towns they haunted. Of course, these stories weren't actually real and had only been designed to scare young girls and boys out in the woods at night, but everybody seemed to be making the same comparisons.

The puzzling thing to Jaeger though, was that he had been told that Darroch was supposed to be in command of the region now. Surely Darroch would not have allowed a place to remain like this for long if he came through here. Something told him that he was not likely to bump into the commander or his close friend Marrick while he was here.

Their accommodation was in the centre of the large military city and was a square of barracks specifically built for students from the college, who had been coming here for years now. The barracks were the best-kept buildings they had seen so far in Grantanmar and everybody looked relieved when they finally checked into the large two-storey building. It was as if it represented some kind of safe zone from the rest of the city.

The rooms were all on the second story and each one was designed to lodge four people, which suited Jaeger and his three friends perfectly. The top storey of the building was divided into two separate wings that did not connect, ensuring that the girls' quarters were kept safely apart from the boys.

By the time everybody had unpacked into their rooms it was getting dark, and they did very little after that other than have dinner before they had to retire for the night. Professor Worley silenced everybody in the dining hall just before they left, to make what appeared to be an important announcement.

"I would like to take this last chance to address you all privately and deliver some words of caution, or maybe even a warning, however you choose to take it. The area you are now in is considered the front line for much of the heaviest fighting seen by our people. It is run by just a few battle mages who rule the city and defend it with the help of the emperor's soldiers." He looked around the room to ensure that everybody was taking his words seriously.

"This year, additional professors and master mages from the college have been brought along to provide extra security for the students, given the unprecedented instability in the region. But what is most important for everybody to realize, is that although you may be traveling under the supervision of your professors, we are no longer in control of your fate should you step out of line down here.

"The battle mages have very little patience, and have become what some may call 'an acquired taste' as a result of their long exposure to this region. Mind what you say and do here and try to learn as much as you can from this experience. I guarantee that you will all have a lot more perspective by the time you leave."

Nobody seemed to know what to make of the professor's speech, but the combination of knowing they were closer than ever to the frontline of battle and being caught off guard by the atmosphere in this alien city, gave the old professor's words a chilling sense of omen. There was little else to do now other than return to their rooms for sleep and see what the morning was going to bring.

21 THE EYE OF THE STORM

Morning was freezing and Jaeger woke well before he had to because he didn't have enough blankets. He lay in bed trying to gather his sheets more tightly together without waking himself up anymore, but knew that he would not be warm until he got up and threw on another blanket from his pack. Eventually he did this and laid back down feeling fully awake now.

He remained in this limbo until the sun rose outside, and to his frustration, felt himself drifting back towards sleep only minutes before he knew he would have to get up again. He wasn't wrong and soon Nasgro could be heard bustling around the room, followed shortly by the others. They still had a little time for a quick breakfast, before being formally addressed by the head battle-mage of the city in the cold streets outside.

Jaeger discovered that although Darroch was the commander here now, he had not been stationed in Grantanmar and had little to do with the running of this city. The city's head battle-mage Charnel, who had been serving on the frontline for nearly a decade, controlled everything that went on in the base. Charnel was considered to be a hero back in the capital where his reputation was well known, but the man who stood before them this morning didn't match the depiction that had been made of him at all.

What hair he had left from his receding hairline was dirty, and looked like it would fall out if he ran a brush through it. His teeth were yellow and the veins in his face showed up just below the skin on his temples and cheeks. Everything about the man said that he had given up on personal presentation years ago, and appeared to have lost a lot of the physical qualities that defined a human being. However, the scariest thing about him was his eyes.

His eyes seemed to be the only place left where any form of self-expression remained, but what they said did not improve his appearance as a human being. When anybody from the College spoke to him, those eyes watched fiercely as though he was intensely interested in every word that was said. At the same time his reactions to what he heard didn't change, no matter what was said to him, like a man who does not believe any friendly gestures towards him could be genuine.

His tone was also very authoritative when he spoke to the year group before him. It was as if he didn't trust them to follow instructions without trying to twist his words. The expressions of the professors and master mages from the College remained unreadable the entire time.

"Grantanmar is the only fortress along our frontline that is *not* perpetually under siege, this is a place of governing not war!" Charnel yelled as if somebody had contradicted him.

"In this place we process soldiers who are beginning their tour of service before they join our ranks, and those who are concluding this service before they leave. Other than that, we use Grantanmar to hold enemy prisoners for interrogation, a *tactic* that has done a lot to keep you all safe at night. So, I am warning everybody now, that I will not tolerate criticism from first year student-mages on our methods while I am allowing you to tour my city!" Again, his preemptive strike on the audience seemed completely unnecessary, but Jaeger figured he must have been referring to students in past years, who might have obnoxiously overstepped the mark. Youthful self-righteousness and entitlement probably wasn't a popular trait in a place like this.

Once Charnel had concluded what could only be described as a long rant, he led the entire congregation from the student barracks to commence their induction of Grantanmar. As his battle-mages led the students through the city, the supervising mages from the college seemed to be making a conscious effort to place themselves between the battle-mages and the student groups while they walked along. The first building they entered was the Weapons Development and Testing Laboratory, which Charnel used to hold scaleskin prisoners who were squashed into cages that would barely fit a dog.

"This place is used by our battle-mages to test new techniques with DarkLand matter, on soldiers of the enemy that we are able to capture alive from battle" he explained with a proud grin, pausing to look around as if expecting a sea of impressed faces looking back at him.

Nobody said anything so he continued. "It is no easy task to capture scaleskins alive in the midst of battle, and we have to tread a fine line between winning the battle and ensuring that we obtain a fresh supply of live prisoners at the same time.

"To combat this dilemma, our mages have perfected an instrumental spell for this very purpose. The process involves harnessing thick concentrations of DarkLand matter, before directing it into the muscles of an enemy, saturating them with the stuff and subsequently paralyzing them. Ironically that very spell was developed here in these laboratories to make our work easier," he chuckled. He seemed to have been looking forward to giving this speech for a long time, but only got a few murmurs of congratulations from the students. Jaeger did not fail to notice that Kostian was one of them.

Charnel also went on to describe in detail, some of the other spells that were practiced on a daily basis by the battle-mages in Grantanmar. Each of these spells was as sadistic as the last and none of them really sounded like they were of any value. Jaeger began to wonder how much use the battle-mages were on the frontline, if they spent most of their time gratuitously experimenting in this military capital rather than in the fortresses that were under attack.

"In the coming days, we may be able to give some of you the opportunity to take part in this hands-on training. If time allows this, then I will select those of you who I am most impressed with to receive the privilege." Nothing appealed less to Jaeger than being forced to take part in the sadistic experiments, and the fact that Charnel offered the opportunity as though it was a treat seemed to confirm a lot of the suspicions Jaeger had begun to have about him. Jaeger looked around his peers, checking to see if anybody else had caught onto the fact that the head battle-mage of Grantanmar was borderline insane.

"Most of those spells have been around for decades and don't require practice," Nasgro whispered to Jaeger quietly as they left the laboratories.

The extent of the evil in Grantanmar continued to take them by surprise as the tour went on. Jaeger and the other students were shocked to see that the pride of the emperor's entire magical warfare unit, were blatantly cruel people who had little or no remaining grasp of compassion or ethics. Their torture of prisoners wasn't the only sign that sinister forces were in effect here. Other than the student barracks, none of the streets and houses were maintained like they would be if you walked into any other town or city on The Plateau.

Even the management of their deceased was substandard. As the class walked past the graveyard, they could see that bodies had been left lying next to half-dug graves, without wrappings or any dignity. Some had even been propped up into a sitting position against their gravestones, holding items like knives and forks in their hands, as though their undertakers had found some kind of tasteless humour in this vile puppetry.

It appeared that in this secluded part of The Plateau, the normal ethics and way of life that separated humans from their enemies didn't exist. Everything about it disgusted Jaeger and a part of his mind hoped that if his people and their allies ever did conquer their enemies, that this place and everyone in it would be destroyed before it happened.

By the evening, Charnel announced that he would be finishing the tour on the crest of the hill, where the border of The Plateau overlooked the desolate plains below. It was just a few miles south of Grantanmar but the professors seemed uneasy at the news. Evidently, he had not notified them that this would be part of his tour and there was some discussion as to how safe it would be. Charnel was prepared for this and had promptly presented ten of his most experienced battle-mages as extra security for the excursion.

"There is no shortage of magically adept people here already Charnel, but any trips to the border would be better served if we had a military escort with us." Worley criticized.

"Pah, the only use soldiers have is patching up the gaps left when good mages are in short supply!" Charnel spat. He was clearly more willing to let the disagreement turn into an argument than Worley, who seemed to be weighing the evil of putting his students in harm's way at the border, against putting them in harm's way with the battle-mages.

"I'm not here to argue the value of having soldiers, so I will trust in the strength of your battle-mages, but please show me the respect of informing us about these decisions earlier next time." Worley was clearly choosing his words carefully, to avoid challenging the erratic battle-mage.

"I'll be sure to defer to your wisdom from now on," Charnel assured him half-mockingly, before proceeding to lead the crowd out through the southern gates of the city towards the border.

Once they reached the edge of the ranges, they were allowed to pass a low wall which stretched into the distance across the entire southern front, broken up intermittently by sturdy guard towers twice every mile. They could now see for miles into the plains below, which were completely barren, even the land at the top of the ranges where they stood was dry and cracked.

Below this, the lights of enemy camps began about a mile from the foot of the ranges, continuing into the distance until they were only tiny specks, also spanning outwards in either direction as far as the eye could see. Every human fort and settlement along the many leagues of the southern border must have been confronted with this same view every night.

"As you can now see, launching a counter-attack on our enemies is no longer an option. If superior numbers were the only factor in our war, then we would have been exterminated long ago," Charnel explained grimly. "Instead, we are forced to sit and wait, defending our ground whenever they choose to come at us, which has been more and more often of late." For the first time since Jaeger arrived in the city, Charnel had started to show signs of humanity, as he explained the desperate situation to the students.

"It is not all a lost cause though. Our significant high ground advantage and heavy fortifications, allow us to extract heavy casualties from the enemy when they do attack." He grinned viciously and the brief moment of humanity was replaced again with his regular cruel disposition.

Jaeger also felt a similar sense of satisfaction as he pictured their defenders butchering the scaleskin attackers, and immediately realized the effect that a place like this had on a person over a long period of time. The combination of exposure to constant war, and the influence of heavy concentrations of DarkLand matter, was like a poison to the soul of any man who was forced to live here. It was entirely possible that Charnel had at one time been more than worthy of the praise and reputation he had as a hero battle-mage.

"I can't stand this place," Aema complained with a sick expression once they were walking at the back of the crowd again, as far away from Charnel as they could get.

"Don't worry, nobody can," Jaeger assured her. "I'm surprised the professors even see value in taking us here."

"I wouldn't say *nobody* can stand it, Kostian seems to be in his element," she said, pointing ahead to Kostian who was following along at Charnel's heels like an eager pet.

"He's just a poisonous chip off the old block, he thrives in nasty situations like his father," Nasgro added. "A few years ago, his father lured the halfling lord into engaging in some underhanded dealings with him. Lord Barnaby was dishonourably removed from power for his part in it, while somehow Donagarn received compensation for the failed venture and nearly caused the entire halfling province to go into depression! There is something about unwholesome environments that appeals to that family."

"I think you have hit the nail on the head," Jaeger agreed.

The group was led back behind the safety of the low wall not long after, and everybody looked more than ready for sleep after the long day. Charnel had been determined to push them from place to place all day without breaks, in an effort to exhaust his inexperienced guests and exert his authority over them. A lot of the less durable students had begun whispering their dislike for the head-mage throughout the day and had been deliberately standing far back out of earshot during his long rants.

Jaeger had also made up his mind that he wasn't fond of Charnel, but refrained from saying anything. Something about this place wasn't right and he was sure that his classmates were in far more peril than they realized by showing outward displays of disdain for the man in control of the city.

Once they were back within the homely compound of the student quarters, everybody sat down to dinner quietly after the long day. Some skipped the meal altogether and retired immediately to their beds as soon as they returned. Jaeger deliberately sat down with Aema near to Worley and the other professors, to hear what they had to say about how the day had gone. The professors made no attempt to keep their discussions secret and didn't seem bothered by the fact that Jaeger had gone out of his way to eavesdrop.

"The Scaleskin camps have reached their closest position ever to invading The Plateau," Harbold continued as Jaeger sat down. "Some of you may not have noticed, but there are also many tribes camped on the shoulders of the rise, that do not light fires at night and couldn't be easily seen."

"I was aware of them," Worley noted calmly.

"And reports say that they had taken a number of positions on the open plains of The Plateau towards the eastern peninsula, before being driven back off when Darroch took charge early this year. After looking at the state of things down here today, I am sure that it is now only a matter of time before they secure a permanent position within our borders." Harbold's tone was alarming and Jaeger could feel Aema becoming tenser beside him.

"It does appear that events are moving in that direction," Worley again agreed without giving anything else away.

"Something must be done before we face complete obliteration!" Harbold demanded, seeming irritated by Worley's obtuse demeanor.

"Harbold, there is little else that can be done for now. Many of our soldiers have been asked to extend their tour of duty here already. The dwarves are overwhelmed, the halflings are not capable of turning the tide, and the monks refuse to involve themselves in our problems."

"What about the elves?" Jaeger interrupted without thinking. The professors were all startled by his outburst, only Worley seemed unsurprised that he had been listening.

"The elves are in deeper than any of us at the bottom of the world next to the DarkLand portal. We fight scaleskins, dwarves fight roachkin, and elves fight demons. If anything, we should be sending them help. No, the only civilized power left in this world where help could come from, is the monks of the mountains. Unfortunately, they do not see the same logic in fighting our enemies and probably never will."

"So, if they *could* be convinced, they could help us?" Jaeger asked.

"I wouldn't even entertain the idea Jaeger, those who seek the monks to go to war never make it to their mountains," Worley warned him, sounding uncharacteristically serious.

"Then conscription will be our only option soon" Harbold declared, and they continued to discuss the predicament while Jaeger buried himself in his own thoughts next to Aema, who watched him with concern.

For the rest of the week in Grantanmar, the separate groups of students were rotated through the different areas of the city, spending an entire day at each. They had begun to accept and ignore the vile decorations of the city by now, too scared to say anything to Charnel about it. Most of the activities Charnel's battle-mages took part in, seemed to have no value to the war that was going on around them and Jaeger grew increasingly frustrated as he realized the amount of resources Charnel was squandering here.

To add to this frustration, Charnel had also taken a liking to Kostian who seemed to fit in perfectly, especially in the abominable laboratories where he eagerly took part in spell testing on scaleskin captives.

"I am going to be sick if I have to see him show off again killing prisoners," Aema whispered to Dinara with disgust.

"Just stand behind us and try not to look," Jaeger suggested sympathetically.

He too was appalled by the foul practice. Being forced to watch filled him with rage and made him feel sick at the same time. Aema hid behind Jaeger and slipped her arms around his waist, burying her face into his back. The gesture temporarily dragged him out of his angry thoughts, allowing him the brief insight into how unhealthy this place was.

The influence of DarkLand matter here seemed to seep right into a person's very being, forcing them to fight the evil within themselves as well as the evil that was camped below their borders. At length, Charnel and Renold both left the room for a short period, leaving the two small groups of students to themselves.

"He's a great leader that Charnel," Kostian declared smirking at Jaeger. It was bait and Jaeger knew it.

"You have a bit of a crush on him, do you?" Jaeger responded, trying not to get worked up. For some reason he knew that everybody else expected *him* to be the one to say something.

"You don't have to have a crush on somebody to admire their greatness, this is an inspired program he has here. Did you see how much I have improved since I started practicing on prisoners! You should really give it a try if you don't want to be left behind Jaeger."

This was all he could take after spending the entire day enduring Charnel and his new sidekick. Kostian had a talent for finding the right thing to say to push a person beyond their limits. Jaeger dropped his act of indifference and lunged forwards, grabbing

Kostian by the front of his tunic with two hands and nearly lifting him off his feet before throwing him to the ground. Kostian had not expected such a sudden response and tried to scramble to his feet, but Jaeger grabbed his shirt with one hand before he was fully standing, and ran him backwards into a wall, pinning him to it with his forearm across Kostian's neck.

"Not so clever now, are you," Jaeger snarled from behind clenched teeth, the angst that had been consuming him for the last week had finally gotten the better of him.

He felt the tingling sensation of DarkLand matter swirling around him and realized that Kostian was drawing it in to unleash, Jaeger drove his forearm in harder and grabbed Kostian's right arm to point his palm in another direction. Kostian wrestled against him, but despite being slightly taller than Jaeger, he did not have anywhere near the same physical strength. Moments later a blast of cold shock ran up the right arm Jaeger held to Kostian's throat and he was thrown to the ground. His is entire arm was numb from the fingertips to the shoulder and he was frozen where he lay. But it was not Kostian who had directed the matter-attack that paralyzed him, it was Charnel.

The scowling battle-mage stood over him with a wild look in his eyes, and Jaeger realized that he was still being held to the ground by the flood of force that was being channeled into him.

"You might fit in better carrying a sword alongside all the other minions in the emperor's army!" Charnel mocked. He didn't seem the least bit interested in what the fight was about. "Or is it that you were afraid to commit to harnessing matter against someone who can do it better?" he sneered. The fact that Kostian was far better at harnessing DarkLand matter didn't bother Jaeger, but Kostian was smirking from ear to ear as he stepped forward to stand over Jaeger beside Charnel.

Charnel continued to hold Jaeger down and looked across at Kostian with an encouraging look. Fear took Jaeger as he realized the peril he was in. He could feel the enormous concentrations of DarkLand matter swirling through the room in many different directions. Charnel sharply turned his attention to Jaeger's group of friends who had now stepped forward from their quiet corner of the room to face him. Nasgro of all people was at the front, with Aema beside him looking scared but resolute.

"Would all of you consider yourselves a match for me together?" Charnel mocked, easing his grip on Jaeger. "I suggest you all stop collecting the matter in my city before I turn on you too."

For a brief moment the scene above Jaeger reminded him of when Marrick had explained scaleskin society to him in the jungle. How they constantly fought amongst themselves in their never-ending quest to establish dominance over others. The situation looked like it was about to deteriorate rapidly, when Renold stepped back in. At first the studious looking master mage looked as though he was in over his head, before he composed himself and walked forwards slowly.

"What has happened here Charnel?" he asked calmly in the least-accusing tone he could use.

"Don't try me boy, I could destroy you too if I

had to," Charnel threatened without taking his eyes off Aema.

"Surely we can resolve this without it coming to that, think of how many good mages we would lose if we started fighting amongst ourselves."

"Spare me your patronizing, besides I doubt that your band of brats would be any great loss," Charnel continued to antagonize everybody around him, like a cornered snake lashing out.

"With your permission I think we will all leave then and get out of your way," Renold suggested.

There was a long pause as the room hung on Charnel's response. Everybody was silent and frozen still for what seemed like many minutes, the tension in the room almost made breathing sound loud.

"Go" Charnel growled menacingly, and everybody moved slowly past him while he stared each of them down with a look of pure hatred.

Nobody spoke as Renold led them down the halls, further away from the scowling battle-mage they had left behind. Even Kostian knew better than to say anything while they made their way out of the Testing Laboratory building.

"He's completely insane!" Jaeger burst out once they were finally outside, he was now furious with both Kostian and Charnel for what he had just been put through.

"I know, just go straight to the student quarters. This is our last night here anyway," Renold said, still fighting to maintain calm.

"We need to tell professor Worley about this!" Aema pressed. "He can't just attack and threaten us like that for no reason."

"I wouldn't worry about that right now young lady. I intend to get full details of the entire incident from all of you and will be speaking to the professor tonight. But for now, we have to be calm and not react in this place, it is not safe here."

They all did as they were told. Evening was not far away now and the heavy rain clouds overhead had already darkened the cold streets as they walked. When they returned to their quarters, Renold took Jaeger, Kostian, and a couple of other students aside, and made them recount what had happened to cause the incident. He seemed unconcerned with the altercation between Jaeger and Kostian and was more interested in what had happened once Charnel had entered the room and intervened. He spoke to Jaeger first and gave away little of what he was thinking while he listened, then asked him to return to his room while he spoke to others.

Jaeger had been sitting there talking to Berran and Ellis for less than an hour, when Renold burst in with the rest of the group behind him.

"Come with me! We are not safe here anymore," he demanded, and they all leapt to their feet. Jaeger had just enough time to belt his sword on before they rushed out of the room.

Nobody knew what was happening, but Renold's sudden change of mood worried them all. He rushed them out the front of the student quarters where it was quite dark outside. For some reason none of the lamp posts in the street had been lit. They raced down the street moving south, unsure what it was that they were running from and looking side to side the whole time, as if they expected to see Charnel and the other battle-mages had formed a lynch-mob to come and get them. When they came upon a small handful of soldiers on night patrol, Renold stopped to speak to them.

"What is the hurry sir?" one soldier asked, drawing his sword and looking past them to see if they were being chased.

"We need to find professor Worley of the College of Magic if you know where he is or have seen him," Renold insisted.

"I believe the professor and his students are being escorted by our soldiers along the southern wall," the soldier replied, still looking around uneasily. "What is the trouble?"

"I can't quite say right now, but we must keep moving," Renold replied, and continued to lead everybody further south with the soldiers now alongside them.

22 THE STORM BREAKS

They were now at the southern wall and still Renold had said nothing to his students, but kept looking back at them, counting to be sure that he hadn't lost anyone. The gates were open and the guards were both leaning against its walls on opposite sides with their heads down, as though they had managed to fall asleep standing. Renold walked towards the closer one cautiously.

"Excuse me, is professor Worley beyond these gates with a class?" he asked, pointing into the darkness beyond. The soldier didn't move or respond and Renold moved closer. "Excuse me soldier!" he demanded, grabbing the guard's shoulder and shaking him.

The guard did not respond or even change his stance as the movement tipped him off balance. His rigid body fell to the ground like a tall tree that had been cut down. Renold immediately spun around facing the darkness beyond the gates, throwing his arms wide to harness the matter around him. But it was too late.

An incandescent, purple and black ball of fire came hurtling out of the darkness beyond his vision, striking him full in the chest. He fell to the ground coughing and spluttering, as two soldiers raced past him to shut the gates. Another two rushed to their knees to drag him to safety behind the cover of the wall, and the fifth soldier, the one who had addressed the group earlier, drew a small horn from his side and blew it loudly. A series of responses came from further down the wall, but there were no soldiers to be seen in the immediate vicinity.

The gates had been designed to open outwards and the two soldiers running them closed, had been forced to enter the darkness beyond the safety of the walls to shut them. They were running blindly and had almost made it, when they realized what still stood in their way. Between them as they ran towards each other, stood three hideous scaleskins that Jaeger immediately recognized as shamans by the sheepskin coats they wore.

The coats ended with the skulls of sheep still sitting atop their heads like gruesome hats, and each of them carried a staff adorned with animal teeth and topped with a small animal skull. The middle shaman raised his staff before any swords could be drawn. Blinding rays shot from the eyes of the small animal skull, directly into the face of one of the bewildered soldiers, who dropped to his knees screaming and clutching at his face. The second soldier charged towards another shaman but was thrown backwards by an unseen force, before the shaman finished him off with another spell.

Everyone else had managed to take cover behind the wall next to the open gates, so as to stay out of the direct eye-line of the advancing shamans. Renold now lay dead at the feet of the two soldiers, who had drawn their swords and moved in front of the students to protect them. Jaeger drew his sword also and stood beside them. The three shamans moved unchallenged through the open gates, to set foot for the first time within the most secure human fortress on the southern front. The lone soldier on the other side of the entrance rushed at them first but was struck down by another dark fireball, before the three shamans turned to Jaeger and the remaining two soldiers.

Of all the things to happen at this time, it was Nasgro who pushed his way straight through the middle of the armed defenders and paused still, with his eyes closed. Jaeger felt the air pressure in front of him building, which indicated that the DarkLand matter around them had apparently just grown exponentially. The shamans raised their staffs and waved their hands looking puzzled, then began to do so more and more wildly.

Suddenly Jaeger realized what the source of their confusion was. Without waiting a moment longer, he raced past his entranced friend with his sword raised and began systematically hacking at the dazed and poorly armed shamans, leaving a bloody pile of bodies and animal skulls at his feet. Nasgro opened his eyes to stare at the scene that he had just missed, for a moment a look of disbelief crossed his face before it was quickly replaced with a victorious grin.

"Who wants to take credit for my work now!"

he shouted, capering about in relief and ecstasy. "Fools-Feeding indeed! I fed those filthy shamans rotten matter and I'll be feeding that imposter Jates his own words too when we get back home!" he declared triumphantly, and continued capering about foolishly.

Jaeger looked sideways at Odette and to his surprise, rather than shaking her head at the display, she was beaming with admiration at the scruffy young student who continued to dance and caper, unaware of anything or anybody else around him. She ran forwards grabbing his shoulders to make him stand still and Nasgro froze, looking embarrassed at getting so carried away. But before he could say anything, Odette threw her arms around his neck and planted a kiss on his lips in front of everybody, right in the middle a looming battle.

The two remaining soldiers ran to the gates and finished drawing them closed to the hostile world outside. Scouts with bows slung across their shoulders and long spears in their hands, came running across the pathway on top of the low wall from both directions, as more horn calls could be heard back across the large field towards the city, getting closer to the gate. A small contingent of about twenty mounted soldiers were the first to reach the defences, and not a moment too soon. Hordes of scaleskins came howling against the gate out of the darkness beyond, as arrows swept the tops of the walls and came hurtling through the gaps in the gates.

Jaeger could see hundreds of scaleskins within the light of the walls and guessed that there must have been thousands beyond, still flooding in. The attackers had obviously prepared for the unlikely event of their shamans failing, because they had also brought a large battering ram as a backup plan. It was carried by a crowd of burly mucks, who trotted along with it on their shoulders as though it was weightless.

Under the hail of arrows, the soldiers were unable to approach the gates to defend them. Any more reinforcements to come, were now running out of time. Jaeger stepped out from the cover of the wall a short distance back from the gates and began harnessing matter to force back the arrows. He didn't have any fancy spells for doing this, and instead just began exerting the matter he held, pushing outwards in the direction of the arrows which were coming from the south.

The concept seemed to be working and the arrows quickly lost velocity once they had cleared the gates, as though they were moving through thick water. Aema and Nasgro ran in beside him to help and soon the entire group of students had combined their powers to repel the missile attack. Jaeger closed his eyes and focused hard to harness as much matter as he could hold without releasing it, before using the force of the black magic to crush down on the battering ram and its operators. He felt the battering ram crack mildly beneath the force of the manipulated DarkLand energy, as its long length worked against it making the centre a weak link. The mucks carrying it also cowered down, releasing the ram and letting it fall to the ground in pain.

It was then that Jaeger realized that his spell was pressing down on the Mucks also, slowly crushing them to death. He could feel the dark energy in his palms encouraging him to enjoy the pain of his enemies, tempting him to prolong the spell to drag out their suffering. Jaeger recoiled in disgust, letting go of the handfuls of magic he was holding with his will as if it were diseased. The exhausted Mucks fell to their knees, relieved at the sudden respite.

Out of nowhere, Charnel leapt past Jaeger and ran right up to the gate, reckless in his desire to finish the cruel job that Jaeger had started. He looked back with an evil sneer on his lips, then raised his arms emphatically. The cluster of recovering mucks were now struck by a second bout of unnatural pressure, and doubled-over screeching in agony. Jaeger was even more disgusted with Charnel now than he had been with himself moments earlier. The small group of mucks had already been incapacitated and no longer posed any threat. With Charnel's powerful abilities he could have finished them off instantly and focused on other enemies in the massive host before the gates.

But having briefly succumbed to it himself, Jaeger now fully understood the corruptive influence of the DarkLand matter. Charnel had lived and breathed war in Grantanmar for years now, he had grown to hate his foes, after spending a lifetime fighting them. But more than anything, the DarkLand matter that accumulated in this unholy place had warped him. He was now a completely different man to the young master-mage who had been deployed to the region so many years earlier. That man had slowly mutated into the evil creature he was today, fighting against other evil creatures just like him, to protect those who were still inherently good.

Five of the Mucks fell unconscious under the supernatural pressures, dropping to the ground with broken limbs and blood flowing from their ears, mouths, and noses. The rest were on all fours gasping for air and coughing up blood, when Jaeger felt a new force rushing towards them. The concentrations of DarkLand energy it controlled was colossal, and it felt like a cyclone to the senses he had been tuning all year to perceive matter. Jaeger immediately began drawing more matter in to create a shield for himself and hoped that it would be enough to protect him, but for Charnel it was too late. He was still too preoccupied to notice this new threat.

Moving in from the edge of sight, an enormous scaleskin had been walking forwards. Its fellow tribesmen moved clear of its path when they saw the creature's eyes glowing with unholy fire. Even though he had little experience with scaleskins, Jaeger knew that descriptions of such a creature would be well known if any shamans like this had been seen before.

A dark shadow twice its height flickered in the same space occupied by the shaman, as both entities advanced as one. The students watched in horror as black and purple colours tore open Charnel's body and thousands of tiny little detonations burst outward from his skin. Every hole created by these detonations bubbled with sizzling flesh, as though he was being boiled from the inside. Charnel had an agonized expression on his face but was unable to make any sound. After what seemed an eternity, he eventually fell to the ground, lifeless, but free from the terrible torture as his killer looked down on his body giving it a kick.

Looking up from the smoking corpse, the

shaman-figure then turned its attention to the students, with eyes that were now burning so intensely red that they were creating a second light source in the dark. The monster raised its gangly arms above its head cracking the gate open, before it froze looking beyond Jaeger and his classmates as though they were transparent.

Worley had arrived, surrounded by a glowing white nimbus. He began hurling balls of fire at both the shaman and the evil shadow occupying its space. Each of his fireballs gave off a slightly different sensation to most matter, as though they were made up of a different form of energy that was not of the same origin as the DarkLand stuff. And with every ball that impacted and exploded on the shaman's defences, the shadow flickered and shrank.

Like a ship furling its sails in the wind, the driving forces behind the shaman were quickly disintegrating, until Worley hurled one final enormous white cloud of magic at his enemy. The shadow around it burst, leaving only the trembling shaman standing before Worley as its bodyguards retreated in fear. It was dazed and confused and for a brief moment, Jaeger almost thought he saw a look of relief on the creature's ugly face, before Worley promptly finished it off.

A flood of soldiers now poured in across the mile-long stretch of open land from the city to its walls. Patrols of as few as five soldiers, to units as large as fifty converged together, until almost five hundred soldiers were fighting to overcome any enemies that had breached the walls. Many scaleskins had scaled the unmanned walls with ladders, and over a hundred had filtered in this way, while more pressed against the defense of the broken gates to let the bulk of the force through.

"All of you students are to leave immediately! This city is now leaderless. I must remain here to govern the defence until reinforcements arrive," Worley shouted at them above the mayhem.

Nasgro had already begun leading the magical assault on those scaleskins standing atop the city wall just west of the gate, with the help of Berran, Ellis, Odette and Dinara. Kostian had run off as soon as the battering ram appeared and Jaeger had just assumed that he was spinelessly trying to escape to save his own life. He now saw that Kostian had spotted scaleskins entering the city over the wall to the east of the gate, and with the help of a handful of other students, he had been systematically destroying each one of them as they came within range.

"This city needs all the help it can get," Jaeger protested, still following Worley.

"You have all helped tremendously, but this is a frontline warzone and I would not lose the next generation of upcoming mages for the sake of what little help you could be."

"But we could almost have them on the run if we press them now!"

Worley turned to Jaeger and took precious time to walk back from the fighting to speak sternly to them. "They would still be back soon. Their numbers are too great and they won't pass up this opportunity to take the largest keep in the province while it is within their grasp."

Jaeger and Aema both gasped at what his words

meant, but Worley did not relent. "Go now and collect whatever is precious to you before you leave, but do not linger a moment longer than you have to. We have encountered forces tonight that even I do not understand, and although I remain, I do not believe we can keep this city from falling tonight. This is damage control! The best I can do is save as many of our forces as I can before we evacuate, which includes you. Now good-bye!" Jaeger argued no more, and with Aema he collected everyone he could, dragging them away from the fighting to flee the city.

23 GRADUATION

Throughout the night, Jaeger's dreams had been haunted with the vision of buildings burning and the sound of loud explosions. These had been the last things witnessed by the year group, as they escaped in their convoy through the north exit to the city. They had now left this scene and all the other bad memories of Grantanmar behind and were unlikely to ever return again if the city fell, which seemed inevitable now.

Jaeger regretfully recalled how he had wished this fate on the city only days earlier. He hadn't fully comprehended at the time what this meant. The emperor's most powerful fortress had now fallen to the enemy, giving them their first ever foothold on The Plateau and leaving no line of defences standing between them and the rest of the vast country. This was the beginning of the end and the thought of it made Jaeger feel sick. Their escape from the carnage of Grantanmar didn't change the fact that there would soon be nowhere to hide.

Nobody spoke, while Jaeger could hear Dinara sobbing quietly to herself, as they fell asleep to the consistent bumping of the wagons over the road. Jaeger even pitied Kostian a little when he saw the look on his face as they left the city. All the walls and safety nets he had lived with all his life had just been torn down around him. He now looked like somebody who had opened their eyes for the very first time, to see how fragile their existence in this world really was. How shamans had killed the scouts on the walls without raising the alarm was a mystery, while Jaeger also had to admit to himself that Kostian had helped immensely during the assault.

In the days of slow travel that followed, everybody constantly looked back over the path they had come from with angst. The general fear was that they would soon see an enormous army of scaleskins just over the horizon behind them, ready to come flooding across the plains in pursuit of any fugitives from the fallen city.

A few of the master-mages who had been supervising their field trip were with them now, leading them north along the emperor's roads back to Conorbatia. The rest had stayed behind to help carry out Worley's commands, and facilitate the evacuation of Grantanmar.

After a couple of days, the sun reemerged from the heavy overcast that everybody had become so used to, and the spirits of the entire convoy rose at this reminder that the world had not completely fallen into darkness yet. They were not far away from home now and time seemed to move a little quicker, or easier

Jaeger concluded, now that traveling wasn't so grim.

Everybody started talking a little more in the wagons and Jaeger felt the tight stress in his stomach unclench for the first time in days. By the time Conorbatia came into view across the broad flat plains, they had all pushed their troubles out of mind and were now joking and laughing again like nothing had happened.

Upon arrival, they found that Conorbatia was a hive of activity, but not the normal buzz of busy market places and major industry like usual. The entire population was preparing for the army to mobilize and move south, leaving only a small guard behind to police the city. Many fast messengers had overtaken the convoy of students while they meandered home, and Emperor Hildebrante was now even better informed on Grantanmar than they were, despite them being the ones to have just come from city. He had ordered a levy on all businesses to provide a percentage of their goods to the army upkeep, as well as to state-owned storage, in order to prepare for any further events that may disrupt their nation.

The order had been relatively well received by most people and Jaeger knew that back in West-Yield the population would be more than understanding of this necessity. But here in Conorbatia some of the more wealthy and selfish merchants were not happy, demanding to receive compensation when the crisis was over. It was no surprise that Donagarn led this call and Jaeger had his own private suspicions that if it was looked into, they would probably find that he was the *only* one with any objections to the order.

Everybody returned to their studies a week after arriving home without their two most senior professors, while messages continued to roll in from Grantanmar. The most recent word to reach them was that the military headquarters had inevitably fallen, but the losses had been nowhere near as bad as expected thanks to Harbold and Worley.

The two professors had taken complete command of Grantanmar now, bolstering the settlements nearby with fugitives from the assault and managing to hem the fallen city into a geographical siege. The surrounding settlements had also been surprisingly well prepared for this outcome and Emperor Hildebrante seemed secretly confident that they would retake Grantanmar when the army arrived, thus removing the scaleskins from their only foothold on The Plateau.

Their last few weeks of the year at Clouds College of Magic went by quickly, as most of the focus of the city was on the emergency in the south, taking the pressure off Jaeger's last classes. With the exception of a few classes taken by replacement teachers while Worley and Harbold were gone, nothing had really changed and a level of calm slowly settled back into the city, as the reports coming back grew more and more positive. Jaeger wasn't sure if this was just to keep the greater population from panicking, or if Emperor Hildebrante really was confident in something that nobody else knew of. Either way the composed demeanor he presented each day had a reassuring effect on the population.

Just a week before exams, news arrived from the

most reliable source yet that Grantanmar had been retaken, and by the morning of their Wednesday Magical Cultures class, Worley had returned and was waiting to greet the year group as they entered the lecture theater. He had stayed in Grantanmar for just a few days after retaking the city, to ensure that it was properly fortified by the army, but hadn't stayed any longer when he realized that Darroch could take care of everything.

The old professor was immediately flooded with questions from his students about what had happened after they left, although none of them could be heard above the chorus of different voices. Realising that he would not be able to begin the class until he gave them a full retelling of what had happened, he decided to be generous and started from the beginning.

"To be honest, most of what you all missed could be easily guessed," he began modestly. "After their possessed shaman fell, there were few other surprises and despite overwhelming us by sheer numbers, the scaleskins seemed to have reverted to their normal brutishness. This allowed me to successfully retreat most of our forces from the city without major losses, and the few small parties of scaleskins that reached our streets before everybody had escaped, were disorganized and easily overcome."

He then proceeded to give a full account of how eight hundred of the city's one thousand defenders, were able to be successfully evacuated against the five thousand strong force that had breached their walls. It was an amazing feat, and other than the loss of two hundred soldiers who sold their lives dearly, the only major loss was the territory.

"And now to some even better news," he announced emphatically. "Very few people were aware of this including myself, but the high commander Darroch has been directing and constructing a stronger base west of Grantanmar for quite some time, while Charnel was letting the official headquarters slip into disrepair. It was this preparation that tipped the balance back in our favour, as all of the surrounding settlements were armed and ready for the scaleskins, who suffered enormous losses when they attempted to move beyond the city. The fortress of Sorrento is now the capital of the southern front and it is under far better command than the old headquarters.

"Darroch had kept his operations a secret for the most part, only sending confidential reports back to the emperor personally in Conorbatia, as any public knowledge of his plans would have caused a civil war between the battle-mages and the military when Charnel found out. However, in hindsight, we now know that the excursion would have been far safer if it had been held at Sorrento, and all field trips will be taken here in the future."

It *was* all good news and the outlook for The Plateau did look far better now. The fact that they knew Darroch was in complete command of the southern front moving forwards, made everyone feel safer, even those who didn't know him as well as Jaeger did. However, for some reason professor Worley still gave off the impression that The Plateau's problems would only increase from here, and he didn't seem overjoyed like everybody else at the series of good tidings.

Jaeger didn't hear any more of the war for the

next two weeks, as he was forced to forget the troubles of the world and bury himself into studying before exams. One by one his exams came and went and he felt better every time, surprising himself with how much he had learnt in one year and how far he had already come on the road to becoming a mage.

The practical exam at the end was nearly a formality by the time it came around and although he was nowhere near the most talented student at the college, the requirements fell well within what he was capable of. Within no time it was all over and he had completed all studies and testing for his first year, passing comfortably.

The graduation ceremony for Clouds College of Magic was held every year on the Monday evening of the week following everybody's final exam, and the moment Jaeger had stepped out of his last exam this became his new focus. The ceremony was ultimately for final-year graduates, but the entire College attended. It was also traditionally followed by a raucous night of celebration, which normally pushed well into the night and often involved the professors becoming just as merry and intoxicated as the students they drank with. Jaeger only had to wait a couple of days after exams for this night to come around and when it did, he was pleasantly surprised to be greeted by Kevlar and Korgan as he went to leave his room.

They had been sent by King Borgisliege to congratulate Jaeger on completing his first year at Clouds College of Magic. Both Emperor Hildebrante and Professor Worley had been aware of the surprise, inviting them to attend the ceremony.

"How did you find out what I was doing?"

Jaeger asked, astonished to see the brothers show up at his door. They had been standing there talking for a few minutes already and he had been too surprised to remember to invite them in.

"Old Borgis and your emperor have been keeping in touch on a regular basis, or did you forget the whole point of your mission to our mountains?" Kevlar said pointedly. Jaeger opened his mouth to protest but Kevlar spoke first again. "To answer your question, Borgis has been asking about you. He has tried to keep as updated as he can on you when he is not busy with more pressing business."

"You made quite an impression," Korgan added, noticing that Jaeger was still at a loss for words.

"I'm sorry, I don't know what to say," Jaeger finally managed. "It's great to see you both after so long, would you like to come in?"

Kevlar put his hand out to decline. "Sadly, our time is not ours on this trip, his royal highness gave us a big to-do list before we return. I will see you later tonight at the ceremony and we will get the chance to share a drink with you then."

"That we will do!" Jaeger promised, immediately energized by the rush of excitement building inside him.

All four year groups studying at the college, came together on the large oval in the centre of the campus that evening. The oval had been prepared days earlier and the rows of tables and seating now stretched out from a stage at the front across the field. As first years, Jaeger's year group was called up first to receive certificates, acknowledging the successful completion of all the year's outcomes at Clouds College of Magic. Only a handful of students had not passed, but none of these had been particularly committed and had given up before getting halfway through the year.

The majority of the year group had come with their families to accept their certificates at the front of the assembly on stage, and the parents of each student stood behind the stage as their children's names were called out. As a custom, these parents each stepped on stage to present the students with a small gift after they received their certificate from Harbold, while Worley called out their names with his booming voice. Jaeger felt guilty that he had not been able to see his own parents for a long time or invite them to come tonight, but he was not alone. Many students from outlying towns came to the stage to be greeted by Harbold alone, who was prepared for this and also presented them with small tokens provided by the school.

It was towards the end of the year group when Jaeger finally had his name called out. He had lost interest by now and like everybody else, he had stopped paying attention unless his own name or the name of a friend was called out. When he rose for his own certificate, Jaeger saw that Kevlar and Korgan had moved onto the stage to stand beside Harbold. A warm feeling of pride went through him as he realized for the first time, how far he had come since leaving West-Yield. He paused in front of Harbold, who shook his hand and gave him a neat piece of rolled parchment, then stepped aside to the stout brothers from Aridhold.

To everybody's surprise, Korgan then presented a magnificent looking sword and scabbard from behind his back. Jaeger stood staring at him in astonishment and the two brothers had to remind him to shake hands, before Korgan handed it to him and Jaeger had to move on quickly for the next student in the procession. Kevlar didn't say anything but was holding back his mirth at the look on Jaeger's face, as a rustle of chatter passed through the crowd. He hoped Kevlar and Korgan had not been offended that in his loss for words, he had said nothing as they presented him with the kingly gift.

When he returned to his seat, Aema gave him an inquisitive look and Jaeger shrugged back to indicate that he had had no idea he would be receiving the sword. There was a letter tied to the hilt of the weapon with a red seal on it and he looked around to see if it would be inappropriate to open it now. Everybody at his table was now looking at Jaeger eagerly, so he broke the seal to find that the letter was from King Borgisliege. It read:

To my brother Jaeger,

Congratulations on completing your first year at The Plateau's Clouds College of Magic. I have been preparing this gift for you throughout this year, while Emperor Hildebrante advised me that the most appropriate time to present it to you would be at the annual graduation ceremony.
The sword I have presented you with is forged from Hydrargyrum, and although it has not yet been imbued with any runes, it is still of far better make and quality than any of the swords forged in your nation. The weapon has been customized for you personally, on the advice of a master runesmith after seeing you wield a sword in battle.
Of all things, I believe this gift will serve you best in the times to

come. You are welcome in our kingdom whenever you are able to visit, where we will discuss the nature of the runes you would like on the blade, so that I can happily repay our debt to you by completing your sword then.

Yours gratefully,
King Borgisliege of Aridhold

Jaeger didn't even try explaining what he had just received and instead handed the letter mutely to Aema, who was also speechless when she read it and passed it around the table in turn. Jaeger remembered little more of the ceremony for the rest of the night and remained quietly seated where he was. Once the fourth years began to be called onto stage, everybody paid a little more attention despite their weariness. These students were receiving their graduation certificates from the College after four years of study, and were about to move out into the world to pursue their elected disciplines alone, without tuition or assistance.

This part of the night also signaled that the ceremony was not far from over, and everybody would soon be able to begin celebrating the end of their year of studies. Jaeger was now eager to see both Kevlar and Korgan, so that he could thank them for the gift properly and spend some time catching up before they went home.

Once the last of the fourth-years had moved across the stage, Worley spoke to the College about the year that had passed. For some reason, he refrained from giving the events of the field trip more than a footnote in his speech and instead most of his reflections from the year gone were on the fourth years, who he had taught from their first day at Clouds College of Magic. It made sense to Jaeger who listened keenly, and in what felt like no time, the ceremony was over and everybody was finally rising from their seats to begin the revelry.

Jaeger didn't have to look hard to find Kevlar and Korgan. The brothers knew where he was seated and found him before he moved off.

"Have you had a chance to admire the weapon yet Jaeger?" Kevlar asked him after he had received a rough embrace from them both.

"I didn't want to draw any more attention to myself by unsheathing the sword," Jaeger explained. "I cannot thank either of you, or Borgis, or the runesmith who forged this, or the people of the dwarf realm, enough for this gift. I will never be out of Borgis' debt now after everything he has done."

"That's not how he sees it," Kevlar disagreed. "It was the duty of his personal bodyguards to sacrifice their lives to protect him, they live for the chance to bring this honour to their clan. In our culture, *your* deeds were seen as those of a man willing to give his own life to protect a friend. When you see Borgis he will always be grateful for what you did, no matter how much he does to repay the favour."

"I understand the concept. Just like if I were to cause grievance in some way, the retaliation would be far more severe and even then, I would not be forgiven," Jaeger laughed.

"He learns fast!" Korgan chuckled. "Now take that sword out and stop making us wait."

Jaeger drew the sword for the first time and saw

that there was a smooth indent of slightly purer metal, stretched along the blade on either side.

"That's where your runes will be written in when you choose them," Kevlar explained to him, running his thumb along the shiny metal. "The runes are traditionally inscribed during the forging of the sword because it is easier, but there are ways to prepare this process so that it can be completed later if the work is done by a really good runesmith."

"I assume that Borgis must have gone to quite a skillful runesmith for my weapon then," Jaeger replied.

"The best, even now without runes you will be amazed at how much this weapon assists you in battle the next time you fight," Kevlar assured him confidently.

"It's no war-hammer, but it's still a pretty good-looking weapon for a sword," Korgan added.

"What runes do you have on your war-hammer?" Jaeger enquired.

"None, I don't need em. I can squash roaches easily enough without magic," Korgan boasted, and Jaeger didn't doubt this sizing up the enormous arms and build of the old miner.

They talked for a long time together, sharing news about what they had been doing since Jaeger parted ways with the brothers at the beginning of the year, and after a couple of drinks Jaeger decided he should put the sword away in his room, while he still had his wits about him. When he returned to the oval, he brought Aema and all his friends with him to join in the celebrations with Kevlar and Korgan.

The celebrations were now spread between the

local tavern and the grounds where the ceremony had taken place. Ample provisions of ale had been supplied to both, and soon all of Jaeger's friends were sitting and laughing with the brothers, like they had known them for years.

The two dwarves had a rough openness about them that endeared themselves to anyone they met, especially when there was drinking involved. Their persistent compliments to the girls around them were a little vulgar, but it was always meant well and Jaeger was surprised to see the girls were not offended.

Ellis and Kevlar seemed to hit it off especially and soon began challenging each other to drinking vast quantities of ale as fast as they could. This inevitably resulted in Kevlar winning soundly, while Ellis was reduced to sitting on the ground in a stupor, unable to raise himself properly when he tried.

Tonight, the weight of the world's problems had fallen from their shoulders, while they lost themselves in merriment and celebration. It was well past midnight by the time the celebrations started to settle down and by then the oval was littered with various small and large groups sitting around in circles on the ground, still drinking but much more slowly. Jaeger and Aema leant against a large log together snugly, while they all listened to Kevlar tell dwarven folk stories to the silent nodding of his brother. Nasgro and Odette had disappeared for a while, but were now sitting together holding each other's hands. Surprisingly Jaeger felt no desire to tease them about this tonight and continued to listen to Kevlar.

He was reciting an epic about a renowned

brewer from dwarf legend, when another rough looking dwarf spotted the group through the crowd, and approached the brothers with a handful of the emperor's soldiers at his back.

"Gerson! What are you doing here looking so sober at this hour?" Kevlar greeted him loudly, interrupting the quiet night air.

Gerson's demeanor did not change at all, and he began to address the group before he had even stopped walking up to them. "Kevlar, Korgan, I cannot dwell on small talk with you now." Even in his drunken state, Jaeger could see that Gerson was puffing and sweaty once he drew nearer, and was still covered with the underground dust that accumulated when riding the wind-up carts. "I have just arrived in Conorbatia from Aridhold hours ago, the eastern half of the city has been taken and only a few of us were able to reach the subway before the Roachkin cut us off."

"I'll kill em!" Korgan bellowed, standing up from his patch of ground. The entire field fell silent as every student within a hundred yards looked up at his outburst.

"I'm with you but we will need help, Borgis gave the order for as many miners as possible to seek help through the underground highway before we left him. The last I saw of the situation in Aridhold, was that he had fortified the western half of the city. We were still holding the subway platforms against the roachkin who were in between when I left."

"Then we have the advantage," Kevlar growled viciously. "Why haven't we exploited this on multiple fronts?"

"Just let me finish you two, it's not that simple,"

Gerson pressed. "The roachkin have attempted to break into the sub-way and platforms at many different points and we have our work cut out there. Emperor Hildebrante is sending every member of his guard that can be spared to build a large enough force on the platforms before we attempt this, I have come here to collect you two and a handful of the master mages at the college."

"I'll come!" Jaeger declared, jumping to his feet alongside the brothers. Korgan gave him a fierce nod of approval.

"No," Gerson interjected firmly, Jaeger was surprised. "Emperor Hildebrante has provided his aid on the strict condition that we do not involve any of the unqualified magical students in this."

"Then call me a soldier, I will fight with a sword," Jaeger protested, immediately realizing how disrespectful this proposal was after everything his emperor had invested in him this year.

"I won't take part in twisting the words of your emperor, he has been supportive beyond his means in this crisis," Gerson declined, which Jaeger was grateful for and he hoped his brash comments would not go further than here after tonight. "Come now with me," Gerson proceeded, turning to Kevlar and Korgan, "I believe there are mages waiting for us now so that we can return to the platforms as soon as we can."

The brothers shook hands with Jaeger and everyone else they had been drinking with, before promptly leaving the mass of revelers spread across the field in shock. Gerson had come and left with the brothers so quickly, that Jaeger could have sat back down and continued drinking without being sure that it had even happened. But it had happened, and nobody seemed to know what to do anymore. The merriment had disappeared and everybody now sat there discussing what this latest blow to their war meant. Although the dwarves were confident that they could retake the hold just like the humans had done in Grantanmar, it still felt like the mark of doom had finally fallen across their world.

The fortified holds of both men and dwarves had once been islands for civilized peoples, amongst a sea of hostile enemies. But now even these islands were beginning to falter and soon there wouldn't be anywhere else left to take shelter from death. This realization was thrown around the circle of friends a number of times before they were all too exhausted to continue talking.

Despite this exhaustion, Jaeger was unable to sleep when he reached his bed. His world now faced the unprecedented threat of total annihilation, and the dilemma made him feel completely powerless as just one person. The last thing he remembered before sleep took him, was pondering whether there *was* something that one person could do. Something that could possibly save the world from this fate.

24 THE HERO COMPLEX

When he woke the next morning, Jaeger was delirious from dehydration. He crawled across the room with his eyes still closed, to a large jug of water that he kept nearby for this very situation. He was relieved to find that it was at least half full, and began drinking eagerly. Jaeger had nearly finished it all in one breathe, when he was hit with a revelation, a dream he had had during the night had just come back to him. He froze in awe at what it would mean.

It had been an idea, a solution to his problems that his subconscious had shared with him in response to the desperate pleas of his conscious mind before he went to sleep. It had occurred to him before, but always seemed foolish when he tried to consider it. Now for some reason the dream had made everything clearer and simplified, as if all the mental barriers to believing it could work had just been tricks of the mind.

Throughout the many discussions about the war that Jaeger had heard or been involved in, there was always one key predicament that could not be solved; they were fighting a war they couldn't win with no more places left to find help. The humans and dwarves had already made contact with each other and were doing everything they could to work together. However, it all seemed too little too late. They had allowed themselves to become too vulnerable, before taking these actions.

Every civilized population on the continent capable of taking up the fight, already had, and none of these were able stand alone against the enemies opposite them anymore. The elves were clearly losing their ability to contain the evil pouring out from The DarkLand Portal, the dwarves were becoming overwhelmed by the roachkin in their strongholds, and the humans were no longer a match for the scaleskins pressing inwards from the surrounding lands. Every population capable of taking up the fight and providing aid to these failing civilizations already had. Everyone but the monks.

Whenever he had raised the idea, it had been dismissed as something that wasn't even an option, especially by professor Worley who seemed to know better than any when it came to the monks. Worley's argument though, had always been vague at best, and this time Jaeger felt an overwhelming sense of determination that wasn't there before. He realized that the hardest thing a person could ever do was take that first step, and he felt ready to take that step now.

Everything that Jaeger had to do was now laid

out in his mind clearly. The first thing he did, was go to find more water to help him recover from his dehydration, before visiting the washrooms to bathe and clean himself up. He then dressed himself smartly in his best clothes before heading off in search of Worley.

There were a lot of things that had been bothering him and he needed to inform himself as best he could, in order to decide what he was going to do next. It took him the better part of the morning to find Worley, who had been busy moving around on his own missions and was now sitting in his office poring over a number of documents and maps.

"Come in Jaeger, I am quite busy but something tells me you're here for something important," the old professor welcomed him insightfully.

"Thank you, sir. What are you doing?" Jaeger asked.

"I am trying to solve the world's problems my boy. Right here I have everything I need to know to plan our war. The problem is that these documents are not telling me what I want to hear."

"Can you share some of it with me?" Jaeger requested. "It is kind of why I am here and I think I will be able to help if I can find out everything that is going on."

Worley looked up, and after a few moments he seemed to have decided to take the request seriously. "Okay," he bobbed, "see here is a map showing the most accurate statistics we have of our population and how it is distributed across The Plateau. All told, there is approximately three hundred and thirty thousand people spread across our nation, a quarter of them living here in Conorbatia." Jaeger was astonished, West-Yield was one of the largest towns in his area and had no more than a thousand people living there.

"What you need to understand about this is that when you subtract the women, the children, and the elderly, you are only left with a fraction of this number who are able to bear arms, and of this number you also have to leave some behind."

"How many dwarves are there spread across their realm?" Jaeger asked, he seemed to be getting exactly what he needed.

"The dwarves have around the same population as we do, although theirs is densely packed within a few strongholds like Conorbatia. Then there are nearly fifty thousand halflings distributed evenly across The Plateau's northern province," Worley circled his finger around a thin border marked on the map. "So, knowing all these figures now, what is the next piece of the puzzle that we need to know?"

"How many scaleskins and roachkin there are out there?"

"Precisely and more! And it is this answer that has always been the problem. We estimate that the scaleskin population is in the millions, with over half of these in the jungles immediately to the south and west of The Plateau. The dwarves have no definitive idea of how many roachkin there are burrowed in and around their realm, but most estimations place the figure well over that number too. Dwarf miners find new colonies around their strongholds every week and now assume that any land that they do not hold themselves, is held against them."

Jaeger sat pondering the information Worley had shared with him. It was easier now to see the predicament they were all in. He then decided to ask Worley about something that had been bothering him since the professor had first returned from the south. Jaeger could probably have guessed the answer now, but saw it as a good opportunity to lead the discussion onto monks.

"When you told us that Darroch had been prepared for the fall of Grantanmar, you didn't seem to act like this news was as good as everyone else thought, why was that?"

"Don't get me wrong Jaeger, the appointment of Darroch as high commander of our southern province is one of the best decisions our emperor has made, however I fear that it is not enough. Eventually the southern province will still fall, entirely next time! Unless some change-of-the-tides could come from help unlooked for."

"Why can't we look for the help? Surely we have to do something!" Jaeger demanded working himself up.

"Because there is none left, the elves are already engulfed on their islands, we are doing everything we can with the dwarves already, and the halflings have no military force capable of any major influence."

"You didn't mention the monks, they could help."

"Ah, I wondered what you were trying to get at," Worley laughed, although it was without mirth.

"Jaeger, I know more about the monks than any other. If a man was to seek them with the intention of persuading them to join the war, then he would not survive the trip. There are, how should I say, 'enchantments' on their land, that are designed to guarantee this fate for those who are not welcome."

"So, they would kill anyone who came to them for help?" Jaeger challenged.

"The monks do not harm any living thing, but if you seek them to the point of death, then in essence you have killed yourself. They just refuse to intervene with this process at the expense of allowing outsiders into their land. Their beliefs are very unusual but surprisingly logical when you consider them without bias."

"Well, I refuse to accept that it can't be done, especially when we have almost completely run out of alternatives. Everybody said the same about Darroch's mission to the dwarves and that has helped us all immensely!"

"I agree with you Jaeger, most of the greatest achievements in history, were great because those who performed them were told they could not be done. But Darroch's mission was different to this, it was not considered impossible, the emperor just deemed it would be irresponsible to send troops on such a high-risk mission when he is already overcommitted. What you are proposing probably is closer to impossible."

"Well then you can mark it down in history if I make it back!" Jaeger declared adamantly.

Worley laughed, "I'd be happier than anybody to do that Jaeger."

Just like that Worley seemed to have given up on discouraging Jaeger, which seemed strange given his initial conviction. Whatever Worley's reasons, Jaeger now had the last piece of information he needed to make his decision. There was nothing else left that could save The Plateau, and if it was a suicide mission, then it was at least worth taking the chance.

Now that he had made up his mind, the next step he had laid out was to explain his decision to Aema. He hadn't really kept her informed that he was even considering the idea, so he knew that the announcement was going to come as quite a shock and therefore needed to be handled carefully. He found her easily enough in an out of the way area on campus where she went to relax. She was sitting with Dinara on an old collection of stone benches that had been arranged next to the small creek running through the campus.

The place was beyond all the classes and buildings, tucked behind and beneath a patch of tall trees that kept it relatively hidden. Jaeger knew the place well by now. Dinara waved to Jaeger and then left him and Aema alone without him even having to ask. Everybody seemed to be reading him very easily today and he wondered if his thoughts had become transparent.

"You look quite focused for someone who just started their holidays and should be feeling sick like I do," she said noting his neat clothes.

"Don't worry I'm feeling it," he promised holding his hand over his stomach.

"So then why so serious? and neat?" she cut to

the point. There was an edge of concern in her voice.

"I've been doing a lot of thinking I guess, and I went to see Worley earlier to talk about things."

"Go on," she prompted, Jaeger wasn't getting straight to the point and she seemed to know it.

"Okay, well I had to make a big decision and I don't know why, but I felt like it couldn't really wait, like it's urgent."

"This is about the bad news we got last night?" she guessed.

"Yes, I feel like I have to do something about it. I am going to the thin air peaks to convince the monks to join the war," Jaeger blurted, worried that if he didn't say it quickly, he wouldn't be able to get the words out.

The look on Aema's face was that of pure heartbreak. He could have spent another hour or so building up to telling her if he wanted to, but it would still have ended the same.

"You can't," she stammered, "I would never see you again," this time it was not a guess, she was certain.

Jaeger tried to block out the sick feeling that was rising in him at the thought of never seeing Aema again, and focused on what he needed her to understand.

"Aema, we need help if we are to stop The Plateau from falling, help that is not here. With the exception of the monks, there are no more people left out there who can help save this continent."

"Wandering off into the wild and beyond isn't help. It's not worth the risk. In fact, the word risk implies that there is a chance that you could make it, it's not worth anything!"

"Why is there no chance of making it? Just

because people don't believe it's possible, does not make this true," Jaeger disagreed passionately.

"What did Worley say about it? If anybody knows it's impossible, he does."

"He actually seemed to accept the idea quite suddenly after he told me not to," Jaeger said as encouragingly as he could.

Aema was a little surprised but didn't appear to be at all comforted by this. If anything, this only meant that the plan was gaining momentum. "Please don't start considering that you can do this, your no good to anyone dead."

"And I'm no good to anyone if I'm just another helplessly outnumbered mage fighting alongside everybody else in a losing battle. None of this is any good when you stand back and look at the big picture."

"I am looking at the big picture and I know things look bad, everybody knows this, but you don't throw your life away because of this. You may think we're doomed if we continue fighting the way we are, but at least death wouldn't be a certainty like it would if you took this path." Aema had tears in her eyes.

"Aema, I know that I must take this path, that has to say something about your certainty." His face was set and his words confirmed the strength of his resolve. Nothing Aema could say would stop him and she knew this now. She let out a cry and threw her arms around his neck, burying her sobbing face into his shoulder.

"I'm sorry. If there was anything that could keep me from leaving, it would be you. But some instinct I've never felt before is telling me that this is what I should do. I just wish I could do it without anybody else having to suffer."

"Every time you decide to play the hero, somebody has to suffer for it," she cried bitterly.

The harsh truth of Aema words hit harder than a sledgehammer. All Jaeger could do, was put his arms around her and stop talking.

This ends The Hero of Aridhold, book 1 of the DarkLand Portal series.
Aema's exploits return in book 2 The Monk's Apprentice

The DarkLand Portal Series

The DarkLand Portal Series is a fantasy epic that explores the desperate situation of mankind and the other estranged civilised races of Thylacine. Their survival exists among hostile territories dominated by scaleskins, roachkin and now demons too. To make matters worse, schemes and greed fester in Conorbatia - the largest and most sheltered city on The Plateau - where the need for unity is greatest.

The Hero of Aridhold

The DarkLand Portal Series Book I

"Every time you decide to play the hero, somebody has to suffer for it"

Jaeger hadn't hesitated to join Commander Darroch's mission when his small force passed through West-Yield. His decision however, was motivated by a multitude of reasons; Some were noble, while others simply stemmed from a desire to escape the direction his life was taking.

He never knew the far-reaching implications that his decision would have, or that it would one day land him at the legendary Clouds College of Magic.

The Monk's Apprentice

The DarkLand Portal Series Book II

"At some point we need to stop expecting our emperor to make everything fair and nice, and do something ourselves. The thing I liked about Jaeger is that he always seemed to get that."

Aema had been left picking up the pieces in Conorbatia after Jaeger's sudden departure. Amongst coming to terms with the sudden loss, she seemed to have a knack for thrusting herself right into the middle of the events and corruption that is slowly taking over the city.

Meanwhile, the emperor continues to prepare his people for war in the South, ignorant to the cancer gnawing at the centre of his empire back home.

The question of whether Jaeger is alive, what he is doing, and how he can possibly think that he is helping, seems to have eluded everyone. As the hero of Aridhold slowly becomes more of a memory than a person.

The Demon Prince

The DarkLand Portal Series Book III

The Demon Prince is the third and final installment in The DarkLand Portal fantasy epic that explores the desperate situation of mankind and the other estranged civilised races of Thylacine. Their survival exists among hostile territories dominated by scaleskins, roachkin and now demons too. To make matters worse, schemes and greed fester in Conorbatia - the largest and most sheltered city on The Plateau - where the need for unity is greatest.